He watched her watch the game...and couldn't look away

"I don't think I've seen a college basketball game since, well, since college," Max said, before a forkful of corn pudding disappeared into her mouth.

"Where did you go to college?" Trey asked, suddenly interested in everything about her.

She held up her fork and he waited until she swallowed. "Illinois, so I know a thing or two about college basketball."

Trey scoffed. "Big Ten basketball is fine, so long as you're in the Midwest." He turned on the accent he'd turned off for most of his adult life. "Y'all down South now, ya hear." When he turned to smile at her, she had an unabashed grin on her face. Her white teeth against her pale lips, her speckled skin, and the wild mass of orange hair were a shining counterpart to the flashes from the oversize television.

He wrenched his face back to watch the game. Right now he controlled her livelihood. Even if he wanted to know just how much of her body was covered in freckles, he was leaving in a week.

Dear Reader,

I grew up in southern Idaho with parents who gardened. And they didn't just have a small, "square foot" garden; our garden was about an eighth of an acre and included raspberries, strawberries, apples, apricots, pears and plums, along with vegetables. Between tilling in the manure, laying the drip lines, organic pest control, et cetera, this garden was a huge operation for one family. It provided all of our summer produce, along with produce to give away, and to preserve. No one ever had to tell me to "eat my vegetables" because fruits and vegetables made up the bulk of what I ate—although I did have to be told to eat my zucchini.

Now I live on a shaded plot of land and I am a terrible gardener.

Farmers' markets and community-supported agriculture saved me. While agriculture has always been an important part of North Carolina's economy, I have been blessed to live in Durham at a time when "eating local" really started to gain hold. One of the benefits of writing *Weekends in Carolina* is that I had an excuse—obligation—to get to know my farmers better. The amount of care, both for the land and for the vegetable, put into a single cucumber humbles me.

If this book inspires you to go to your local farmer's market and buy a pound of spring carrots, then I also suggest that you visit the bookstore for a copy of *World Vegetarian* by Madhur Jaffrey and make her stir-fried carrots with ginger and mustard seeds. You won't regret either purchase and you'll have the bonus of a delicious side dish.

Enjoy!

Jennifer Lohmann

JENNIFER LOHMANN

—

Weekends in Carolina

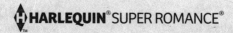

H HARLEQUIN® SUPER ROMANCE®

Recycling programs
for this product may
not exist in your area.

ISBN-13: 978-0-373-60853-9

WEEKENDS IN CAROLINA

Copyright © 2014 by Jennifer Lohmann

Printed in U.S.A.

www.Harlequin.com

ABOUT THE AUTHOR

Jennifer Lohmann is a Rocky Mountain girl at heart, having grown up in southern Idaho and Salt Lake City. When she's not writing or working as a public librarian, she wrangles two cats and five backyard chickens; the dog is better behaved. She lives in Durham, North Carolina, and has received a weekly box of vegetables from the same farm for eight years.

Books by Jennifer Lohmann

HARLEQUIN SUPERROMANCE

1834—RESERVATIONS FOR TWO
1844—THE FIRST MOVE
1898—A PROMISE FOR THE BABY

Other titles by this author available in ebook format.

To Elise from Elysian Fields Farm and all the small farmers selling week after week at farmers' markets across the country; thank you for growing delicious food for me to cook with and eat.

To all the people who helped me weather a rough year. This space is too small to thank each of you individually, but you know who you are. May life bless you as much as you have blessed me.

CHAPTER ONE

TREY WOULD HAVE bet substantial amounts of money that he would never have found a woman shooting tin cans with a .22 attractive. Or, for that matter, any woman standing behind his father's house. This woman was evidence that he would have lost both wagers.

He couldn't see her face, but she had a ferocity to her stance, legs set apart and knees slightly bent, elbows sharp and dangerous, and he could describe the pinch in her facial features without her having to turn around. Her mass of curly, carrot-colored hair was barely contained by the knot she'd tied it in, and the baseball cap it was shoved under was doing nothing to help lash the masses together. She must be keeping it out of her eyes by sheer force of will, as the wind blew wisps of curls everywhere but in front of her face.

Trey was surprised there was enough country left in him to find a woman in work boots attractive. Another bet he would have lost.

Whoever she was, her jeans skimmed over her tight butt before disappearing into her boots, and he was enjoying the way her shoulder blades poked through the white cotton of her T-shirt. And the way the surprisingly bright and unseasonably warm sun of a January day in North Carolina bounced off the freckles on her arms. Only a small amount of bare skin was visible, but what he could see was more freckle than not.

She pulled the trigger and the *P* in one of the Pepsi cans disappeared before the can toppled over. The woman herself barely flinched. Trey had just taken another breath and she shot the next can. Given the pile of fallen cans and the near-empty box of fresh targets, the woman had been out shooting for a while. He was loath to interrupt her to ask where Max was. Not only was he enjoying the view, but she was an angry woman holding a rifle. Trey knew nothing about Max and his competencies, but Trey's father had certainly been capable of making a woman angry enough to shoot any human with a Y-chromosome, even from beyond the grave. God knows Trey had spent much of his childhood escaping his house to punch trees while his mother had practiced her bland smile.

Clip spent, the woman put the rifle on the seat of a lawn chair and stalked to the line of dead cans.

"Hey," Trey called out as he walked to the chair. She didn't turn around or give any other indication that she'd heard him. His mother's lessons, always at odds with his father's example, had been to be polite and respectful to women, but he couldn't yell "pardon me, ma'am" with enough force to get the woman's attention, so he reconciled himself to a rude "Hey, you!"

The woman started, knocking over the pile of dead cans she had constructed. When she looked up at him, his spine tingled in response. Even through sunglasses, the force of her stare caught him off guard. As far as he knew, she wasn't supposed to be on his father's farm, much less here shooting cans. Or was it his farm now? Or maybe it was Max's farm. It didn't matter who owned the property at the moment. This woman wasn't supposed to be here.

She straightened, then reached up to her ears with both hands and pulled. Two small bits of orange foam bounced off her shirt, just above the rise of her breasts.

Of course she couldn't hear him. She'd been wearing earplugs. It had been so long since Trey had stood in his backyard and shot at cans that he'd forgotten some of the basic safety precautions.

She marched up to him, her stride as direct as her stare. After they were no longer in shouting distance, she lifted her sunglasses off her face, folded them into the neck of her T-shirt and said, "You must be Trey Harris."

The woman walked quickly. By the time she had finished speaking, she was directly in front of him. The part of Trey that had been admiring her backside also noticed the peaks of her nipples pressed against her shirt—even if it was a warm, sunny January day in North Carolina, it was still a January day. But Trey wasn't a complete caveman; he also noticed that she had clear, mint-green eyes.

"You have the advantage over me," he said, focusing his attention on her arresting eyes. For all that the rest of her was easy to look at, her eyes—and the straightforward way she looked at him—were mesmerizing. She was daring him to look away and he couldn't. "You know who I am, but I don't know who you are."

Or what you're doing here.

Her straight, pale eyebrows crossed in confusion. "I'm Max Backstrom," she said without offering her hand.

"You're Max?" A couple years ago, Trey had asked Kelly if his boyfriend had known he was spending so much time with Max. His brother had choked with laughter—and now Trey knew why.

Her confusion didn't last. She lifted one eyebrow, this time daring him to argue with her, and he didn't accept this challenge, either. This woman was his father's farmer.

THE ANGER THAT had been warming Max from the inside retreated enough for her to feel the cool breeze on her bare arms. After the one glance at her breasts, Trey had managed to keep his eyes on her face for the rest of the conversation, but she'd noticed that one glance. And his surprise at learning her name. She knew that father and son had barely spoken for years, but she had a hard time believing not one of those conversations had included the basic fact that Hank was leasing his land to a woman. Or at the very least, that Kelly hadn't told him. She had thought the brothers kept in touch through the occasional email.

The next puff of wind brought a strand of hair across her face and goose bumps to her arms. She debated continuing to stand there in her T-shirt just to see how long he could keep his eyes off her erect nipples, but good sense won out. The ownership of the farm was in flux and she needed Trey's support. Plus she was cold. She pulled her sweatshirt off the back of the chair and shoved her arms into the sleeves before zipping it up all the way.

Finally buffeted against the chill and Trey's shock, she said, "Max is short for Maxine." Which was short for Maxine Patch, but she only used the full ridiculousness of her name when signing contracts, and they weren't at that stage in their relationship yet. "Let me clean this up and then we can have a cup of tea and talk."

Having known Trey's father and seeing the shine on the son's loafers, Max hadn't expected him to follow her up the small hill to collect cans. Today was sunny, but the past few days had been nothing but rain. Some of the ground was soil. Some of it was red clay. All of it was mud. Cans clinked against one another as they tossed them into the box. Her supply of targets was going to be much smaller now that Hank Harris was dead.

"Where to?" Trey's arms were wrapped around the box of cans and he was looking around. Through his eyes, the farm in winter probably didn't seem like much to look at. The only greens were the loblolly pines at the edges of the fields and the hardiest bits of grasses. Everything else was brown either because it was dirt or because it was dead. Even the winter cover crops were fading.

She bit her lip before the urge to defend the bareness of the land in winter escaped her mouth. This man didn't care about the land. Hank had said neither of his sons had cared about the land. Of course, Hank had only cared that the land was still in his possession—"got a responsibility," he used to say, though Max had never been certain who the responsibility had been to. Surely the ancestors who'd first settled this plot of land would have wanted to see it farmed more than they would have wanted to see Hank stand on the dirt with his thumbs tucked into his belt loops.

Max didn't know where Trey stood on the responsibility line, and she hoped he saw that the land was only useful if it was being *used*. And she could use it. "Put them in the back of my truck," she instructed. "They need to go to recycling."

He nodded then walked off in the direction of her ancient blue pickup truck. If he was concerned about the mud on his fancy shoes, he didn't show it. Max sighed. Trey wasn't the only one who'd apparently made judgments based on little information. Neither was he the only one who'd made those judgments poorly. All she had known of Trey was that he rarely talked to his father or brother and wore suits to work. Hank had emphasized the last fact every time he talked about his older son, saying, "I can't believe I let Noreen raise that boy up to wear suits to work," with his tone somewhere between disgust and pride. Since Max had occasionally heard Hank brag to his mechanic about Trey, she gave Hank the benefit of the doubt and credited his disgust as a cover for his true feelings.

Max had seen the crisp white collar of Trey's shirt poking up from the navy blue of his striped sweater and forgotten that he'd spent his childhood on this farm. His full, nearly black hair, cut in a conservative style, thick, black eyebrows and clean-shaven face fit her image of preppy Capitol Hill policy wonk better than son of a Southern good ole boy. But add some stubble to his square jaw and change the intelligent curiosity in Trey's dark brown eyes to Hank's amused condescension and the resemblance was clear. Replace his flat stomach with a beer belly, add a ratty #3 Earnhardt cap and twenty-five years, plus a stint in Vietnam, and Trey would be the spitting image of his father.

Her uncharitable thoughts were unfair to Hank. The man had been a jerk, but he'd also leased her land to farm for cheap and helped fix up one of the tobacco barns for housing. Hank may not have understood the changing face of farming in central North Carolina, but he wasn't going to stand in its way. Besides, the mess she was in now was her fault, as much as Hank's. She should have pressed him harder on the specifics of the ownership of the farm once he passed away, but she hadn't wanted to risk pissing him off and losing the farm while he was alive.

No, that wasn't fair to Hank, either. She'd been afraid to learn he had changed his mind about writing the lease into the will and that she would have to make another plan. Now she was stuck with her three-year plan, and no idea if she would need another by December. She wished she had her mother's ability to leap into the unknown and reinvent herself every couple years, but—like her father—Max was a farmer, plodding along through life.

She grabbed the rifle and the chair and followed Trey to her truck. She didn't know how he'd managed it, but there was not a single speck of red clay on his sweater from carrying the box.

"Where are you staying?" she asked.

He looked uncertain. "I'd planned to stay at the house, but…"

"But that was when you thought I was a man."

"You're a farmer named Max. Can you blame me?"

"No." Trey hadn't been the first person to be surprised at her lack of penis and he wouldn't be the last. Despite many small organic farms being run by women, people still expected a burly man with a piece of straw sticking out of his mouth and a John Deere hat when they met a farmer. "I'm just surprised the subject never came up."

A noise somewhere between a laugh and a scoff escaped Trey's lips. "I'm sure my father meant to be alive and present when I finally met you. Like a big practical joke."

She laughed at the irritated resignation on his face, especially because she could sympathize. "Hank always did find it funny that he had a 'lady farmer' leasing his land. You can still stay at the house. I live in one of the barns. Though Kelly didn't think you'd be coming today, so the heat's been turned off and I doubt there's much edible in the kitchen."

"Is the offer of tea still on the table?"

"Sure." She looked at the watch face strapped on to her belt loop. "I'll even throw in lunch."

"Great. Let me put my stuff in the house and turn the heat on. Then I'll be over. By the time we've finished eating, perhaps the heat will have pushed the damp out of the walls."

"Deal," she said, with more cheer than she felt. Then she watched him for a moment as he walked to his fancy car for his luggage. Whether it was the long line of his legs or his power over her future that interested her so much, she wasn't sure. Both made her nervous.

CHAPTER TWO

TREY WAS STANDING on Max's front porch, about to knock, when his phone buzzed. While in the house he'd texted Kelly, asking why his brother hadn't told him their dad's farmer was a woman. Kelly's response was simple.

Hah! I thought Dad had finally told you. Be over after work.

He shoved his phone in his pocket, along with the feeling that his entire family was playing a joke on him. Only his father, the originator of the joke, was dead and Kelly hadn't ever been interested in traditional gender roles, so this wasn't a joke he would have played on purpose. Which made this nothing more than a painful reminder of how little connection he'd had to this place after his mother died. In the hereafter, his father was likely cackling that Trey's discomfort at being surprised was just punishment for only calling his dad on occasional birthdays and Christmas.

A dog barked when he knocked on the door, and

from somewhere inside Max called out, "Sit." When she opened the door a mottled black, white and tan dog was at her feet, looking at Trey with a mix of curiosity and annoyance. It was much the same way Trey had felt looking at Max, when he had wrongfully thought she didn't belong on his father's property shooting cans, before he knew she was Max.

"This is Ashes. Don't mind him. Cattle dogs are a protective breed." As if to prove her point, the dog growled. Trey thought about growling back—*this is my land*—but pissing contests only rewarded the fool who drank too much. Better to be smart than a bloated idiot. Plus, for all he cared, the dog could claim the land by peeing on every blade of grass; Trey sure didn't want ownership of the useless hunk of clay.

With this inauspicious start, Trey stepped through the doorway into Max's barn. "I figured the barn would have fallen down by now."

The last time he'd been here, for his mother's funeral, the barn door had been missing and some of the beams had been rotted through. Now it was downright cozy with stairs leading up to a loft, a large woven rug on the floor and a woodstove along one wall. Trey blinked and took a second look.

The walls and floor were bare wood and the kitchen at the back had a small fridge and an even smaller stove, giving the place the look of someone's hunting cabin instead of a renovated barn where people lived. So maybe not cozy, but livable, which was still a damn sight better than it had been five years ago.

"The first winter I lived in the farmhouse with your father while we renovated the barn to make it livable." She blinked and opened her pink, cracking lips like she was going to say something else. Her lips opened and shut one more time before she'd made up her mind about continuing. "I'd planned to move into the farmhouse and use the barn for housing when I finally bought the place but..."

He realized that whatever leasing agreements she had with his father carried over with the property, but that didn't mean Trey couldn't toss them all out the window and eat the breach of contract cost just to wash his hands clean of the place once and for all. That was *if* he even owned the farm. They could both hope that his father had left the property to Max in his will. Because truthfully, Trey didn't care if his father had left it to the Earnhardt Foundation, so long as he didn't have to come down here again.

"Anyway, no matter what you decide to do, it seemed crass to move into the house right now."

"Better to wait until after the funeral?"

"That wasn't..." she said, but he waved off her apology.

"I know that wasn't what you meant. I don't want the farm, though I probably now own it. I'm sure whatever agreement you had with my father will be fine with me. We'll sort this out. You can move into the farmhouse and I can go back to D.C. Hell, you could move in now, for all I care."

Trey supposed sadness was the proper emotion to feel after his father's death, but the only emotions coursing through him were relief that the man had only killed himself and nobody else in the car accident, and irritation that he hadn't sold the land before dying. The man had been a drunk and a bastard—why did he also have to be irresponsible?

The kettle on the stove whistled and the dog cocked his head to the sound, but didn't bark. Max pointed at a dog bed in front of the woodstove before heading to the kitchen, and the dog obediently went to lie down.

"Sorry about the mess on the table," she called over her shoulder. "If you could dump the papers and laptop in the box by the table, we'll have space for our food."

As Trey shoveled everything into the box, the receipts and invoices for seeds, straw and ladybugs didn't surprise him, but the resumes did. What did he know about farming anyway? He'd worked on his uncle's tobacco farm only because he had to, but when college brochure time had come around, he'd tossed into the trash any pamphlet with *Ag* or *Tech* or *State* on the front. He'd wanted to toss all the applications for North Carolina colleges in the trash, too, but money had been short. In the end, a degree from Carolina and the connections of a fraternity brother had gotten him to D.C. and a congressman's office and that was enough. He realized he was staring at an invoice for strawberry plants—probably had been doing so for a while. He shook his head, tossed the invoice into the box and then placed the laptop in last, weighing down the pile of papers.

The table cleared, he went to the kitchen to help Max with the plates.

"I hope egg salad is okay," she said, as she handed him a plate and a mug of tea.

"Egg salad is great." The plate was brimming with food. The egg salad and some lettuce was on wheat bread, cut diagonally, he noticed with a smile. Also on the plate were apple slices, a pickle and a pile of potato chips. Despite the oddness of drinking hot tea with his lunch, Trey was grateful for it. Max's cabin wasn't cold, but it was cool. And it was one of those odd North Carolina days when the inside was colder than the outside.

Their plates each made different clinks when they touched her small table and Trey noticed they were mismatched. So were the mugs. Max got back up to get them some water and returned with mason jars, rather than regular water glasses. He took another look around the barn. There was not a doodad or tchotchke in sight. Judging by her residence, Max had no patience for pretense and no interest in owning things that didn't have a use. Everything was well cared for, but nothing was fussy. Even the dog, who had been fixin' to get up from his bed before a look from Max settled him back down, probably had a job.

"Thank you for the reassurance about the house," Max said before taking a bite of her sandwich. "Clearly, I had expected to live in the barn this summer, but having it to offer for housing will make finding seasonal help easier."

"I have no interest in ever living back on the farm and I'm sure Kelly doesn't, either. And the house does us no good standing empty. Kelly and I will take a week to pack up and store anything personal, then you can move in."

He took a bite of his sandwich. The egg salad was rich with mayonnaise and the yolks were the bright orange of the eggs he remembered eating as a child, when his mother had raised hens. "Do you have chickens?" he asked, a little embarrassed that he didn't know what Max grew, other than vegetables.

"They were Hank's. After we finished renovating the barn, he had some leftover wood. There's a little chicken coop on the other side of the house, built to look like a tobacco barn." Her smile must be at the thought of the chickens; it couldn't be at the memory of his father. "It's cute."

Trey tried to imagine his father designing a *cute* chicken coop and got a headache. He also couldn't imagine his father wanting chickens. Trey, Kelly and his mother had built the original chicken coop after his father's response to his mother wanting hens had been, "You want 'em, you gotta work for 'em." Kelly and Trey had gone with their mother to pick up the chicks from a nearby farm, and though Trey had pretended to be too old and too manly at thirteen for anything *cute,* he still remembered having to repress a giggle at the sight of the cheeping biddies. His father, however, had never once referred to the chickens without the adjectives "smelly" or "dirty." He'd also never once turned down fried eggs or a slice from one of his mother's delicious sour-cream pound cakes.

"I'm sorry about your father," Max said. Her tone held the same sharp honesty of her stare and Trey wondered if she meant it or was the best liar on the planet. He decided to give her credit for honesty.

"I'm only sorry he didn't sell you the land before he killed himself. Seems like that's the only thing you should be sorry about, too."

It was eerie, watching those short, pale lashes lower over her light eyes. Trey almost felt like he'd said something he shouldn't have. Almost.

They finished the rest of their meal in silence.

MAX APPRECIATED BOTH Trey's help carrying the dishes to the sink and his quick exit. She didn't know how to respond to the anger simmering under the surface of his skin. Hank hadn't been a paragon of anything, but he at least deserved for his children to be sad at his death.

She scrubbed the plates and stacked them in the small dish drainer. The winter season was slow on the farm, but she had to finish plotting out her fields before the spring vegetables went into the ground. And she must make sure she had enough wax boxes in stock for when the Community Supported Agriculture, or CSA, began. *And* arrange for the intern candidates to visit. She'd been about to send those email invitations when Hank had died, then she'd wanted to wait until she'd met Trey.

Of course, she thought as she folded the kitchen towel and hung it off the oven, she could still lose the farm for the summer. She didn't think Trey's promises could to be trusted. She would have to go on with her work as though everything was normal and be prepared to stand tall when everything came crashing down about her feet.

But starting the broccoli in the greenhouse would have to wait until tomorrow, since she'd wasted the morning in useless, irritated shooting and would need to spend some of the precious daylight picking up shell casings. Her irritation with herself for wasted hours would last until she turned the week in her calendar and didn't have to look at "shot Pepsi cans" as her record for daily farm duties. Maybe if she added "made lunch for new landlord" to it, the day wouldn't look so wasted on paper.

When she'd asked Hank what happened to the will and he'd said, "I've taken care of it, sugar," she should've pressed him for more details. Her morning spent in target practice had been as much a reaction to her own stupidity as to not knowing what Hank had meant by *taken care of it*.

She whistled and Ashes eased his old bones out of his bed, stretched, then finally wagged his tail. The old dog wasn't ready to retire from farmwork yet, but this might be his last season. The geese were starting to get the best of the old dog. She wished he could live out the rest of his days in a farmhouse with central heat rather than the often too-cold barn. She opened the door and together they set out for their respective jobs in the fields.

"So you met Max, huh?" Kelly had let himself into the house without bothering to knock. Which was fair, Trey supposed, since their father should have left the house and all the land to both of them, though Trey would bet the farm that the old man hadn't. The old man's prejudices coming in strong, even in the end.

Kelly set bags of Bullock's barbecue on the counter and the smell of vinegar, smoke and pork filled the kitchen. Trey was happy to see the food, even though he had no idea what they were going to do with all the leftover barbecue, especially with whatever food would be brought by the house tomorrow. "She's pretty neat."

When Trey opened the containers, it was the first moment since arriving that he was happy to be in North Carolina. Kelly had brought over barbecue, slaw, Brunswick stew, collards, butterbeans and a greasy bag of hush puppies. As Trey loaded his plate until his wrist nearly collapsed from the weight, he couldn't remember the last time he'd eaten so well.

"She—" Trey put the emphasis on the pronoun "—is not what I expected. I mean, Dad couldn't find a man to lease the land to?"

"What, you leave the big city and all of a sudden women have their proper place and it ain't anywhere outside the kitchen?"

"No, but Dad…"

"Calm down, Trey. I'm mostly just funnin' you. Everyone but Dad was surprised when Max the farmer turned out to be Maxine the farmer. Max was Mom's choice."

That Mom would pick a woman to lease the farm to made sense. However… "I didn't know they had been planning this since before Mom died."

"What you don't know about the farm could fill the Dean Dome. Mom has always been on Dad's case to do something useful with the land. He finally said he'd agree to whatever her plan was if she did the legwork." He'd probably capitulated so his wife would shut up and just bring him another beer—much the same way he'd agreed to the first chicken coop. "When she was diagnosed, she sped up her plans a little. The lease with Max was signed two weeks before Mom died.

"That's gross, you know."

"What?" Trey asked as Kelly pointed to his plate, where he'd mixed his slaw and barbecue into one sloppy, hot-sauce–topped mess. "I've been eating my barbecue this way since we were kids."

"It was gross then and it's gross now." There might as well be force fields separating the food on Kelly's plate. Even the pot likker from the collards didn't dare seep across the expanse of white into the slaw.

"I guess I'm surprised Max is still here." Even though Kelly was in the room, Trey said the words more to himself than to anyone else.

"You mean that Dad kept his promise to Mom or that he didn't drive Max away by calling her his 'lady farmer'?"

Trey winced. How had their father been able to withstand Max's frank, cutting gaze and still say the words *lady farmer* aloud? "Both, I guess."

Kelly's look was somewhere between pity and disgust. "I'm sorry it took Dad's passing to get you to come back to the farm."

CHAPTER THREE

TREY WAS ASLEEP when the first knock came on the front door. He pulled on some pants and a sweater then stumbled down the stairs to see who was there. Whoever it was hadn't stopped knocking for even a second. His aunt Lois stood on the front porch, a dish balanced on her left arm as she knocked with her right fist. He didn't even have a chance to wish her a good morning before she sailed past him into the house and wove her way to the kitchen.

He thought about stopping her, but no man had stopped Lois Harris since the day she was born a Mangum over fifty years ago, and he was unlikely to be the first. When he caught up to her, she was standing in front of the open fridge, shuffling take-out containers of barbecue around.

"I expected it of you," she said into the fridge, "though your brother should've known better. Noreen raised y'all both to know better."

Trey wasn't entirely certain what he and Kelly had done—or failed to do.

The brine-only pickle jars Aunt Lois pulled out of the fridge clinked on the metal edge of the old, laminate counter. "Honestly, did Hank think he would break a nail throwin' out empty bottles?" She pulled other empty jars and bottles out of the fridge, shuffled more stuff around before declaring the fridge as good as it was gonna get and slamming the door. She must have left the beer cans in the fridge because all that was on the counter were empty mustard bottles with a heavy layer of crust around the lip.

"Aunt Lois, what are you doing?"

The counter was now covered in trash from the fridge and his aunt was opening random drawers and pawing around.

"What does it look like I'm doing?" She didn't even look up when she said it.

Digging through Dad's stuff, he thought, though he had the smarts not to say that. When she found a trash bag and the jars crashed into the bag with one big sweep of her arm, Trey had a partial answer. His aunt Lois was going to clean the farmhouse. But why?

"Go out to my car and get the tea I've ready-made. People will be coming by for visitation in four hours. If you and Kelly had the sense God gave a mule, you would've cleaned this house yesterday."

No wonder his brother had smirked when he'd said it was Trey's responsibility to get ready for the visitation, that he had a project to work on and couldn't take the entire day off.

"Lord in Heaven! Henry William Harris the Third, don't just stand there. Get!" She made a shooing motion with her entire body. "And get my cleaning supplies while you're at it."

Taking a detour up the stairs to put on shoes felt devious after Aunt Lois's clear instructions, but he needed to take a piss and get something on his feet before going outside. When he returned to the kitchen with a box full of jugs of tea and buckets of cleaning supplies, the hands on his aunt's hips made it clear he'd dawdled.

"I found your daddy's supplies, though Lord only knows how old some of this stuff is. Take a bucket and broom and start with the upstairs bedrooms. I'll work down here."

"Aunt Lois, I doubt we will have many people show up." If Trey had been looking for excuses not to come to his father's funeral, surely everyone else in the county was, too. "And even if we do, no one is going to see the upstairs."

"We may not have time to give this house the scrubbing it needs, but we can dust shelves, sweep floors and make beds before everyone gets here." As far as his aunt was concerned, if she didn't want to hear the words, they hadn't been said. When he didn't move, she shoved a broom into his one hand and a bucket into the other. "I'm not your mama or your wife and I won't do this alone. You either re-

spect Noreen's memory by making her house tidy
for company, or I go home."

Still feeling as if he were putting lipstick on a pig
for a fair no one would come to, Trey plodded upstairs and began cleaning. Out the window of Kelly's room—which was dusty and full of crap his
brother should have thrown away or taken to his
own home years ago—he saw Max load something
into her truck and drive off into the fields. Dark
clouds bullied away the nice weather of yesterday,
but that didn't seem to be stopping the farmer. He
wondered what she was doing and why? More important, he wished he could watch her work and admire the swift, purposeful movements he had seen
yesterday translated from shooting Pepsi cans to
growing food.

"Trey, hon, are you dawdlin'?" his aunt shouted
up a few minutes later. "I'm not cleaning Hank's
bathroom on my own. Get down here."

He couldn't blame her. His father's bathroom had
offended his bachelor sensibilities—skirting mighty
close to the memories of the bathrooms in his frat
house. Knowing what was in store for him didn't
speed up his steps down the stairs.

Aunt Lois obviously had more practice cleaning a house before a funeral than Trey did, a fact
evident in the way the wood of the banisters sparkled. He peeked into his dad's bedroom. Photos of
his father and mother with different relatives were

nicely displayed on the dressers. His mother's sick
room across the hall looked like any other guest
bedroom in an old Piedmont farmhouse. As soon
as his mother had gotten too sick to sleep through
the night, she'd moved across the hall rather than
disturb her husband's sleep, a gesture Trey would
have found touching if there was a possibility his
father had ever said, "Don't worry about me."

Aunt Lois was attacking the stove when he
walked into the kitchen. "Bathroom." She didn't
even look up.

"Aunt Lois, nobody liked my father and there's
no wife to console. I seriously doubt anyone besides
you will be dropping by with casseroles."

"Trey—" she still didn't look up from her scrubbing "—I don't care if you're five or thirty-five, if
you don't get in that bathroom and start cleaning in
thirty seconds, I will take a switch to your behind."

His aunt had always made good on her threats.

Bathroom.

THE FIRST RELATIVE knocked on the door thirty minutes before Aunt Lois had predicted. "That Gwen
Harris," his aunt muttered, "has had no respect for
keeping decent time since she moved to the city."

Durham, a city of two hundred and fifty thousand souls, was the city Aunt Lois referred to, and
downtown Durham was a bare thirteen miles from
"downtown" Bahama, despite Aunt Lois's sniff im-

plying the other side of the world. But Aunt Lois and Uncle Garner had taken their share of Harris farmland and withstood mechanization, buyouts and the bald fact that tobacco causes cancer to keep and expand on a successful tobacco farm. She had no patience with the farmers who gave up their land for pennies to the dollar—even though she and Uncle Garner had profited from their sales—to move into the city. And she also had no respect for a man like Trey's father, who had clung to his farmland like a virgin to her panties, but had been unwilling or unable to make the land useful.

But, as Cousin Gwen dropping off her rolls being the first of many in a parade of relatives evidenced, blood is thicker than respect. And Aunt Lois had made the house presentable because Hank Harris had been a Harris, even if he'd been a distasteful one.

Kelly slipped in through the kitchen door just after Gwen had said her condolences and left. "I saw her on Roxboro Road driving up here and took my time, just so I'd miss her," his brother whispered to him. "I'll see her at the viewing and that will be plenty enough of Cousin Gwen for me."

Unlike his aunt, Trey didn't care that Cousin Gwen and her husband had left their farmhouse for a split-level in the city. Hell, having escaped to D.C. as soon as the ink on his college diploma had dried, he wasn't one to judge. However, Gwen had been a crushing cheek pincher all of his childhood, and hadn't even stopped when he'd hit puberty. Her kids had been just as awful, though in different ways. The eldest always made sure to include the mention of major life purchases in his Christmas letters. Every year between his accomplishments at work and the achievements of his kids was a description of the new boat/car/RV/lawn mower that the family had just purchased. It had bothered Trey a lot more when he'd been a poor country cousin. Now Trey just thought it was in poor taste and felt for all the pinched country cousins getting that letter every Christmas.

During her short visit, Cousin Gwen had apologized for her children, who had to work and couldn't make it over. Lucky for him and Kelly, they would be at the viewing. And the funeral. And back here after the funeral to eat all this food.

His whining buzzed about in his head, but he couldn't seem to swat it away. With each relative, family friend, acquaintance and Southern busybody who walked through the front door of his father's home bearing casseroles and condolences, the house got smaller and smaller until it pressed in on his temples and made his eyes bulge. Out of respect for his mother, Trey smiled and said thank-you to each salad that had been "Hank's favorite," but by the time all the people left, the farmhouse felt small enough he could call it skinny jeans and hang out with the hipsters at the new downtown bars.

"I owe you," he said to Kelly before walking out the door and leaving him with all the food to put away. "I'll be back in time to leave for the viewing." The scolding Aunt Lois would subject him to for leaving was nothing compared to his need to escape the confines of the farmhouse.

Storm clouds that had been threatening all day broke the moment Trey left the cover of the porch. Their punishment for the beautiful weather of yesterday was an icy January rain, but he popped up his collar to protect his neck and trudged on, desperate to be anywhere else. As soon as he reached one of the fields, he knew this was his destination.

It looked like Max had spent the day repairing fences. At the edge of the fields was an eight-foot metal and chicken-wire fence with metal wires running along the top, tied with pink flags. Like Trey, the pink flags were hanging their heads to avoid the pounding rain. He could see where she had been making repairs. Some of the flags were brighter and less downtrodden than their brethren. Some of the wires were more taut, still eager to impress with their ability to stand sentry, and some of the wood less worn. It was a deer fence. He wondered if she ever electrified the top wire. Probably, he decided. Max and her electric-green gaze had a definite look-but-don't-touch luminescence.

Like some Irish sprite who knew she was on his mind, Max suddenly appeared in the distance with Ashes fast on her heels. While he was soaked through, she had on a complete set of rain gear and was probably dry and cozy underneath it all. It was impossible to tell the drips pouring off Ashes from the raindrops, but Trey was fairly certain he saw a big, sloppy grin on the dog's face, his tongue lolling out the side of his mouth.

"How was the visitation?" she asked.

"Is the fence electrified?"

She slowly lowered her pale lashes over her eyes, but didn't comment on his change of subject. "I had hoped to avoid it, but deer have already tested the fence and I don't want them to think they can do it again." When she moved, rain slid off her head in sheets, though she seemed not to notice. His father's lady farmer was tough. "Would you like a tour while you're out here?"

He looked out over the field that in just a few months would be awash in green. "No, but maybe you could email me a picture."

"Sure." Her slicker rustled with her shrug and more water poured off. "But there are also pictures on my website." The farmer had a website. Of course. Every business had a website, and Max's Vegetable Patch was as much a business as any other. She probably even had a Twitter account.

"You could come down and see it in the summer, if you'd like. You could stay with Kelly, or at the farmhouse—it has plenty of bedrooms." She paused and he let his silence continue through the tattoo of the rain. He didn't really want a conversation, hadn't even wanted company until she'd come upon him. He didn't want her to leave, but he didn't want to talk, either.

"I'll send you pictures throughout the growing season," she finally said, filling the vast, dead emptiness of the fields. "Your father loved how the land changed during the growing season."

"I probably won't come down and visit."

"Well, I won't take it personally." Her voice carried a smile he couldn't see in her face. "The land might, though. After all these years, she's finally producing and you won't even come and admire her beauty."

"*She*—" he rolled the female pronoun Max used around in his mouth, enjoying the feel "—shouldn't take it personally, either."

Even though his father was dead, Trey still didn't want to be near anything the old man had touched. Henry William Harris Jr.'s touch was poisonous and the toxins lingered on the farm like gases too heavy for the wind to blow away. The miasma would outlast the stinky grime of cigarette smoke on the walls and the farmhouse would never really be clean. Not to him.

Max was talking again and Trey only caught

the tail end of what she was saying, but he got the gist; Max would tell the land not to take it personally, either. "I have to clean up before the viewing," she continued. "And you probably have to change clothes now."

She didn't wait for a response, just left him in the fields and the rain, without even granting him the protection of Ashes to bark at his bad memories and keep them at bay.

THIS WASN'T MAX'S first Southern funeral—she'd been to the funeral of her maternal grandfather over in High Point—so she knew the viewing meant Hank would be cleaned up from his heart attack and subsequent car accident and on display. As much as funerals played a role in the North Carolina gossip chain and anyone with a claim of kin or friendship on the deceased or the survivors' side was expected to go, this couldn't be Trey's first funeral, either. But every time he looked over at the open casket, his eyes closed in a barely concealed grimace. No one should look so attractive while looking for an escape hatch.

Each person who expressed their condolences to Trey and Kelly probably didn't notice Trey's discomfort. But they probably weren't pretending to talk farming with neighbors while really watching the grieving family like Max was.

"Maxine!" The voice of Lois Harris jolted Max

out of her thoughts. "Did that mechanic Garner rec-ommended work out for you?"

Max had given up asking Miss Lois to stop call-ing her Maxine. It wasn't worth the wasted breath, plus Lois and Garner had been invaluable in provid-ing local farming contacts. So Miss Lois could call Max whatever she wanted and Max would call her by the not-quite-formal-but-still-respectful name of Miss Lois, and they would both be happy.

"Yes, he's been quite helpful." The used trac-tor had seemed like such a deal when she'd bought it, but it turned out to be a piece of junk. Luckily, the Harris's mechanic got it working at the end of last season and it appeared to be making it through the winter. Still, saving for a new tractor seemed smarter than trusting in the magic of the Harris's mechanic, even if she now had three pots of sav-ings money and keeping track of them strained her Excel spreadsheet. Asking to borrow a tractor last summer had been professionally embarrassing—and she had no desire to repeat the exercise.

"Now, don't let him…"

Max stopped listening to Miss Lois warn her about the mechanic's propensity to predict doom. Not only had she heard it before, but she was curious about the attractive brunette grabbing on to Trey's hand with both hands and pressing it to her heart.

"That's my second cousin." Miss Lois leaned in to whisper to Max. "Never been to a funeral or wedding she didn't cry at, bless her heart." Sure enough, the young woman had both moved on to Kelly and been moved to tears. "The Roxboro Mangums always have a pool going on when she'll burst into tears. She's no blood relation to Trey, but she's not your real competition."

Miss Lois was a wily woman and it was a fool who turned a back to her. She "y'all'ed" and "blessed hearts" and "sugared" like a Southern cliché, but she wasn't a fragile flower of womanhood. Max hadn't been in North Carolina long when she realized that Lois's politeness was a bit like a rattlesnake's rattle—the more polite Lois was, the greater the warning about the coming bite. The ruse didn't only work on Yankees like Max; Southern men were equally gullible. Garner might be the farmer on that side of the Harris family, but Miss Lois was the businessman.

"I'm not worried about competition." There was always the chance this was the *one time* Miss Lois could have the wool pulled over her eyes.

"Oh, Maxine, you've been staring at my nephew the entire time we've been in the funeral home."

Max hauled her gaze from Trey to Miss Lois. "He's my new landlord. Of course I'm curious about him. And he seems troubled."

"You're welcome to try that on a fool, honey, but don't try it on me." Miss Lois's words carried a reprimand, but her voice was kind. "He hasn't wanted anything to do with the farm since he was five years old. Hank and Noreen are lucky he didn't run away and join a circus. Unless you give up farming and move to D.C., there is no future in that man. You can hear it in his voice."

Lois's words highlighted something about Trey that had bothered Max from the moment he'd spoken to her. Trey had no Southern accent. Kelly didn't have much of one, but Trey's was nonexistent. His voice was completely flat—as if the drawl had been purged from his soul. And he must have grown up with one, as Max had yet to meet a Harris other than Trey without a *y'all* lingering somewhere on the lips.

And if he'd eradicated the accent, why hadn't he started going by some name other than Trey, which was a constant reminder that he was the third Henry William Harris? Max tried to look at Trey in his charcoal-gray suit out of the corner of her eye, but the side view gave her a headache. Miss Lois was watching her with raised brows when Max pulled her eyes away. "I'm not watching him for any future, Miss Lois—or any future beyond him being my new landlord, but...he doesn't seem all that upset." That wasn't right; something was clearly wrong with Trey. "Or at least not upset about the death of his father."

"Trey and his daddy never did rub along, and Hank didn't care until it was too late."

Was Trey thinking about his lost relationship with his father as he stared at the cold body lying on satin? Or was he irritated that he was saddled with a farm he didn't want left to him from a father he had no affection for?

Reading any emotion beyond stress into the tightness of Trey's eyes was nearly impossible.

"So long as he doesn't try to sell the farm out from under me, his relationship with Hank doesn't affect me." But even as she said those words, she couldn't take her eyes off the tension evident in Trey's neck as he ducked out the door. Max told herself that Miss Lois wouldn't notice and slipped out the door behind him.

TREY TURNED AROUND at the sound of someone stumbling and swearing under their breath behind him. The voice was soft, so he'd figured it was a woman, but he had expected his cousin Nicole to offer up another slippery round of tears, not solid, stable Max. She hesitated a little, then put her hand on his shoulder, her palm warm even through his suit jacket. He shivered. He should have grabbed his coat.

"I'm sorry," she said.

"You already said that." He struggled to keep the anger in his voice in check. He wasn't angry with her. In truth, he wasn't even angry at his father right now, but the pressures of pretending to be sad were wearing on him. And then there were the pokes from stories people had about his father. When he'd made a face at one such tale, Aunt Lois had given him *a look* and told him not to speak ill of the dead.

Max's fingers curled around his shoulder, their strength pressing into his collarbone. Somehow, the simple gesture was more reassuring than any enveloping hug he'd received from his relatives. "And I'm *still* sorry—for Hank's death and for whatever drove you outside."

"My cousins were beginning to tell stories of going to the Orange County Speedway and what a grand time they all had, especially after my dad got really drunk and his insults got both creative and unintelligible." Trey could picture the scene, including his father throwing beer cans until he was tossed out.

"I imagine what seems like a funny story among cousins is less funny to his children." She hadn't moved her hand from his shoulder, so he could feel her step closer to him in the movement of the joints in her fingers. Even in the dark, through his shirt, her fingers felt sturdy. Solid. Stable. He wanted her to press up against him so he could feel her strong, purposeful body up against his. To be able to go home with her and draw patterns in her freckles as he forgot himself in her body.

But she was his tenant and he was at his father's funeral, so his thoughts would remain thoughts only.

"You say that like there could be something funny about the belligerent drunk." Unexpected sexual frustration made the words come out with more anger than he'd meant.

"When I knew him, he was only belligerent."

The bald honesty of her statement forced a laugh out of him. "And yet you still have some affection in your voice."

Her fingers tensed on his shoulder. "I won't force it on you."

"Why?"

"Why won't I force it on you?"

He turned to face her and her fingers slipped off his jacket. He wished she had kept them there. "Why the affection?"

She shrugged. "For five years we shared the farm, and worked together some. He wasn't a very good farmer, but Hank liked to have a cup of coffee with me in the mornings and hear what I was doing to the land. He even came to the farmers' market occasionally. It's hard not feel some measure of affection."

"I lived with him for eighteen years and I managed." Even in the dark, he could tell he'd startled her again. And again, he had the inkling that he'd said something he shouldn't have, yet knowing the words that would come out of his mouth next would make him sound like a petulant child didn't stop him. "Despite what you and every person in that room want to think, my father should have been tossed into an unmarked grave with a bucket full of lime and forgotten about." Max's mouth fell open, but Trey wasn't going to back down. "And if I was in control of this funeral instead of Aunt Lois and Kelly, that's exactly what would happen."

Trey turned on the hard heels of his dress shoes and stomped back to the viewing, away from one person who had pleasant memories of his father and toward a crowd of them. He would shake hands, accept hugs and look sad as was required, but there would at least be one person who would know the truth of how he felt. And somehow, it was important that the one person was Max.

CHAPTER FOUR

THE FUNERAL WAS just as awful as Trey had imagined it would be, although in ways he didn't have the creativity to have foreseen. First, there was the knowledge that he'd had a near temper tantrum at the viewing and the bland look Max gave him wasn't enough to pretend it hadn't happened. Second, the church was packed, and not just with family members. The mayors of Oxford and Roxboro were both there, along with one Durham County commissioner, proving that you could be a drunk and an asshole and still have dignitaries at your funeral so long as you were from an established family. The mayor of Roxboro was perfectly polite, but the mayor of Oxford was determined to talk with Trey about upcoming legislation and its effects on small towns. Trey had been prepared to talk with family members he had no interest in and express sorrow he didn't feel to people whose names he couldn't remember, but feigning interest in a rider on a farm bill had not been on his agenda.

The preacher droned on and on about our reward in heaven—though Trey wondered how many people were picturing his father someplace more *tropical*—until finally a cell phone ringing in one of his great-aunt's enormous purses and the subsequent digging through said purse derailed the preacher's lack of train of thought. "God bless both the phone and the purse that ate Atlanta," Aunt Lois muttered to Uncle Garner, then gave Kelly a dirty look when he snickered.

A slight black man with glasses and a trim beard was waiting by his car with what appeared to be a pie in his hands when Trey made it past the crowds of mourners. "Jerome, buddy, I didn't expect to see you here. Thank you for coming." He meant the words and the welcoming handshake more sincerely than he had for any other guest at the funeral. "I haven't seen you in ages, and you didn't have the beard then. How does Alea feel about it?"

"She likes it fine. And the last time I saw you was at your mother's funeral." Jerome Harris gave a shrug and a slight smile. "I try to attend all my kin's funerals. It's the only time I get to see certain people."

Trey smiled at the small joke—and the truth behind it. "You're one of the many people here *not* here for my father, but for some other reason. Gossip seems to be the main reason. Respect for my mother is another."

"Oh, I'm hoping my presence has your father rolling around and knocking in his grave, but my parents said he'd gotten less overtly racist in his old age."

Jerome wasn't the first person at the funeral to mention that the prejudices that had strangled Trey's father most of his life had loosened their grip in his old age, though he was the first person to put it so baldly.

"Alea's home watching the kids and I can't stay, but she baked a pie for you. I felt certain your father would like a bean pie in his honor."

Trey laughed. Most Southern food was Southern food with little racial distinction, but not only was bean pie black food, it was Nation of Islam food. It was also delicious, so Trey had no trouble taking it out of Jerome's hands. "I'm sure everyone will appreciate the pie. And Kelly will appreciate the gesture."

"You're in the big house now." Jerome had always had a wry sense of humor. "I hope you won't be a stranger to Durham."

"I used education to get out. I'm not sure why I would voluntarily come back."

Jerome harrumphed. "I have basketball tickets. Maybe I'll invite you to the Duke game."

"Of course I'd come down for the game." Agreeing was easy since it wasn't likely he'd actually receive an invitation. Jerome had better friends to share those tickets with, plus a wife who might want to go. "I've got my priorities straight."

"I mean it, now."

"Get home to your wife. Thank her for the pie."

After they said their goodbyes and Jerome was walking to his car, Trey wondered if his friend knew the pivotal role he'd played in Trey's escape from the farm. They'd met in seventh grade, when they'd been assigned to work together on a science project. Trey had been certain he would end up a lazy, good-for-nothing drunk like his father. He'd been angry at his future and pissed at his father for the inheritance. Another option was to turn into his uncle Garner, but Trey hadn't wanted to be a tobacco farmer. Option three was join the military, but he was pretty sure Vietnam had turned his father in the direction of alcohol. But those were his only choices as he saw it back then.

When Jerome had insisted Trey actually do some work for the project, Trey had scornfully asked Jerome why he studied so hard. The look Jerome had given Trey through his thick glasses hadn't been the look of a cross teenager; it had been the look of a thoughtful, mature man. A look Trey only recognized because of his uncle Garner. "My grandparents used education to climb out of poverty," Jerome had said. "I'm not going to be the first person in my family to leap back in."

By asking around, Trey had learned that Jerome's grandfather was a preacher and his father was a vice president at Mechanics and Farmers Bank. Jerome's great-grandfather had been a sharecropper and his family before that had been slaves on some Harris's farm. Jerome Harris, a professor of history specializing in the history of the South at the University of North Carolina at Chapel Hill, probably knew which, but Trey didn't.

Jerome had opened Trey's eyes to new possibilities. He'd started looking around at the family he met at weddings, funerals and reunions. Most were working class—farmers, mechanics, retired mill workers and the like. But there were also a number of teachers, and every once in a while a doctor or a lawyer popped up. There was even an army colonel. And the one thing all these escapees from the farm had in common was that they had studied hard enough in high school to get into a good college.

Since that moment, Trey and Jerome had leveled into a relationship somewhere between acquaintances and friends. They had nodded to each other in the hall all through middle and high school and kept in touch through college. No matter where their lives had drifted, occasional emails were exchanged and major life changes kept track of through Facebook, if nothing else. Like distant but friendly cousins, Trey supposed.

Jerome had always regarded Trey's desire to escape Durham with a bit of amusement, saying, "If I can get along as a black man in the South, you can survive as a white one." But Trey had watched his father drink and grow nothing but anger, dirt and kudzu while his mother worked long hours at a job she hated. If he didn't pull up his roots and flee, he wouldn't do any better. His destiny had been sown in the clay.

Even now, as he climbed into his car to parade to the graveyard for the burial, the familiar rolling hills of the Piedmont were more oppressive than picturesque. Trey wasn't even able to feel relief that his father's overbearing spirit was gone from the earth. The only positives about the day had been talking with Jerome and seeing Max's muscular legs sticking out beneath her black skirt.

THE FIRST DAY of packing had been surprisingly easy, Trey thought as he watched his brother leave. His father had an absurd amount of clothes for an old man who never went anywhere, but it hadn't been hard to sort them into donation and trash piles. Some of the clothes weren't worth wearing to muck out a pigsty—apparently the man never threw anything away. And their father's pack-rat tendencies would make the rest of the week harder, especially since the man hadn't cleaned out their mother's stuff in the five years since her death, either.

It was a two-for-the-price-of-one deal at the Harris family farm. Or Max's Vegetable Patch, which was what the sign on the refrigerator van said. The name was cutesier than Trey associated with the woman who'd shot Pepsi can after Pepsi can without flinching.

Though he'd tried, he hadn't been able to convince Kelly to stay for supper. His brother had taken some of the leftover food with him but had muttered on about his own life, leaving Trey alone in the house surrounded by his parents' stuff. At least there was a Carolina game on and conference play had started.

His plate filled with a variety of casseroles, he looked out the kitchen window to see the light on in Max's barn. Maybe he didn't have to be alone in the house watching a basketball game. Trey stuck his plate in the microwave, set the timer and headed out the back. Ashes barked when he knocked on Max's door.

She opened the door wearing an oversize turquoise sweater that looked surprisingly nice with her red hair, though a bit ridiculous with the pink-bunny pajama bottoms and fuzzy, purple slippers. As Trey had come to expect, Ashes was sitting at Max's feet, though the dog looked less annoyed with his presence this time. Max was the suspicious-looking one now.

"I'm sorry for the way I acted at the viewing." Which was true; he wished he'd had the sense to keep his anger to himself much like he'd managed to control his attraction to her.

"Losing a parent would be hard. Losing a parent

and not being able to feel sad about it must be harder, I think."

Is that what she thought? That it wasn't that he *shouldn't* feel sad, but that he *couldn't* feel sad? He took a deep breath before he got distracted from his purpose. "Anyway, I was heating up some leftovers and wondered if you wanted any, though it looks like you've already eaten." He gestured to her pajamas.

"No." She smiled, and the rigid air that usually surrounded her relaxed. "I'm just too lazy to put on another set of clothes after I clean up for the day."

"*Lazy* is not a word I would associate with you." Every time he'd looked out a window today, Max had been busy *doing*. Trey wasn't always sure what—when she wasn't disappearing into the fields of the greenhouse, she was lifting things out of the back of her truck or walking around making notes—but she and the dog were always *doing*. At least he could tell what the dog had been up to. Ashes's job seemed to be to keep the Canada geese out of the fields.

"You've not seen how tall I let the pile of dirty clothes get before going to the Laundromat." She stepped back from the door and let him in.

"Dad didn't let you use the washer in the house?"

"Sure, if I did his laundry, too." That sounded more like his father than any nonsense about a cute chicken coop. "Hank and I got along better if he never saw me do anything that he might construe as 'woman's work.' Though I think sometimes he said that phrase just to get a rise out of me."

"I'm sure he meant the words."

"Maybe at one time, but after your mother's death, there was plenty of woman's work to be done and no woman to do it. Hank got to be quite good at making biscuits in the morning. He would even share them. Though I'm not even sure he attempted to clean." She seemed to be smiling at the memory of his father, which Trey still had a hard time believing. "What's left for dinner?"

"A little bit of everything. And I was going to watch the Carolina game, if you're interested."

She appeared to give his invitation more consideration than he'd given it when the idea had hit him. Finally, she said, "Sure. Let me put some shoes on. Can Ashes come?"

"Of course. Did Dad not let Ashes in the house?"

"He did. Hank liked the dog quite a bit, but Ashes is always a little dirty. Just a warning."

"Whatever mess he makes, I'll leave for you to clean up when the farmhouse is yours."

"Deal."

He waited for her while she exchanged her slippers for shoes, wrapped a purple scarf around her neck and shoved a bright green *toboggan*—the local word for a knit ski cap—over her hair. From the hat on her head to the red shoes on her feet, she was a mass of bright colors. Since Trey had only seen her in either her work or funeral clothes he hadn't expected the rest of her wardrobe to be so vibrant. He found himself wondering if she wore utilitarian, white underwear—as he would have guessed if asked—or if her panties were as vivid as the rest of her. Betting either way seemed dangerous. She had messed with his odds from the first moment he'd laid eyes on her.

And he'd never get to find out the answer anyhow.

His father hadn't bothered to upgrade the electric baseboard heat in the house or add air-conditioning, but he had gotten a satellite dish so that even out in the country he could have ESPN. The man had had priorities, and Trey only disagreed with most of them. By the time Dick Vitalle's annoying voice had started in with, "It's Syracuse's first time playing Carolina as an ACC team, baby," Max's food was hot and they were settled into Trey's father's recliners.

"I don't think I've seen a college basketball game since, well, since college," Max said, before a forkful of corn pudding disappeared into her mouth.

"Where did you go to college?"

She held up her fork and he waited until she swallowed. "Illinois, so I know a thing or two about college basketball."

Trey scoffed. "Big Ten basketball is fine, so long as you're in the Midwest." He mimicked the accent he'd abandoned for most of his adult life. "Y'all down South now, ya' hear." When he turned to smile at her, she had an unabashed grin on her face. Her white teeth against her pale lips, her speckled skin and the wild mass of orange hair were a shining counterpart to the flashes from the oversize television.

He wrenched his face back to watch the game. The fact was, right now he controlled her livelihood. Even if he wanted to know just how much of her body was covered in freckles, he was leaving in a week. And he controlled her livelihood, he reminded himself again. The surge in his blood pressure would have to be attributed to the 10-0 run Carolina had just gone on. "So what does an organic vegetable farmer study in college?"

"Farm management, though I didn't go to college planning on farming a small plot of land," she said with a hitch in her voice. Had she felt the attraction between them, as well? "What does a— Oh, I don't even know what it is you do besides wear a suit to work and do something with the government."

Max was saying the words, but Trey could hear his father's voice. *Only crooks and politicians wear suits. Makes it easier for the crooks to blend in.* Nothing in his father's life had worked out the way he wanted it to and everyone but his father— the government, the immigrants, the blacks, the feminists—had been responsible for his troubles.

North Carolina was full of the new South and the new Southerners to go along with it, but his father hadn't been one of them. The only way Trey could figure Max had ended up leasing the land for an organic vegetable farm was that his father had been really drunk when the contract was signed and too lazy to find a way out of it afterward.

"I'm a lobbyist, though I used to work on Capitol Hill. I studied public policy in college."

"Sounds important."

Trey couldn't judge the tone in her voice, so he risked another look at her between bites before replying, "I think so. I got into it because I can make a real difference in my government, and I make a good living at it. I'm not sure many others can say the same about their jobs." Why he felt the need to defend himself in front of his dad's *farmer,* of all people, he didn't know and didn't want to examine too closely.

"I wasn't being sarcastic," she said, her hands up in a show of honesty. "It really does sound important. I should pay more attention to legislation and my elected officials and such, but I only really know about what comes into my email from the farming associations I belong to."

Unused to being complimented in this room, much less in this house, Trey turned the conversation back to Max. "What kind of legislative issues come into a farmer's email?" At the suspicious face she made, it was his turn to hold up his hands and say, "No, really, I'm curious."

There was just enough light in the room for him to see Max raise her eyebrows at him. "But not curious enough to take a tour of what I've done to your ancestral landholdings."

The ridiculousness of that statement forced a laugh out of him. "Ancestral landholdings?"

"Sure. Your family has lived on these lands since time began, haven't they?"

"Well, yes, but I've never considered this forty acres to be anything but a mud pit that money and time fall into."

"Yeah," Max said with a mixture of sympathy and amusement on her face. "Hank doesn't seem to have been a very good farmer."

"And you?"

"Am I a good farmer?" She shrugged. "What's your metric? I sell out of my vegetables most weekends at the farmers' market. My CSA subscriptions fill up every year, providing me with the money to buy seeds and plants without having to borrow. I'm not going to get rich, but I have a small savings account and some money for retirement. Plus, I grow nutritious vegetables people want to eat and my job allows me to spend most days outside, hands in the soil and the sun on my back."

"And the rain."

Max's laugh was full and hearty. "You really are

determined to spotlight the negatives of the farm. Yes, and the rain, which gets me wet, but also makes the plants grow."

Her accusation stung a bit. He hadn't meant for his hatred of the farm to bleed into his relationship with Max because, no matter how he felt about the farm, he *was* interested in the farmer. "You tell me about the legislation emails that interest you so much and I'll let you give me a tour of the farm tomorrow."

"More of that rain you're so afraid of is supposed to hit tomorrow. Buckets of it."

Her voice was warm, like the rays of sun she described hitting her back, even as she talked about the rain, and he wanted to see the land as she saw it. To understand what had attracted her to this life and had kept her willing to put up with his father when he called her a *lady farmer*. "Tell me what worries you, and I'll agree to a tour, even if it's in the rain."

"Okay." She took a deep breath before the words poured out of her. "Despite looking at the maps and hearing the reassurances, I worry what fracking will do to my water quality and thus to my plants. I worry about regulations designed for a large corn grower like my father's farm but which don't take into account the scale of farms like mine or the different safety issues we face. I worry about changing labeling requirements and how that could weaken the value of my product and the work I put into it.

And those are just the legislative and policy worries." This time Max's laugh had a self-deprecating edge. "Do you want to hear about the nonlegislative worries, too? I mean, while I'm spilling my fears into the dark."

"How about we save the nonpolicy worries for Friday," he responded, surprised to find he meant it. "We can watch another basketball game together and I'll have had my tour, so what you tell me will mean more."

The television erupted in cheers, jolting both their heads up to see a replay of a Carolina fast break and dunk. "Tar," Trey called and Max's lack of response reverberated around the room. "You're supposed to respond with 'heel.'"

"Even if I live in North Carolina, I'm still a Fighting Illini."

"Tar," Trey called again.

"Oh, fine." She laughed. "Heel."

"Now with more feeling. Tar!"

"Heel!" She had a powerfully booming voice that shook the farmhouse and made Ashes raise his head.

"Good. Now I wouldn't be embarrassed to take you to the Dean Dome."

Trey was pleased when she laughed again. "Is that what this is about?"

He didn't entirely know what this was about, only that he had forgotten how much this house weighed on him while Max, with her intense eyes and serious manner, laughed.

MAX WAS TOUCHED when Trey walked her back to the barn, insisting despite her contention that she walked the farm alone most of the time and had done so for years. Plus, she had Ashes to protect her from raccoons and coyotes. "I'm not doing this for you," Trey had said, "but for my mom, who would be appalled if I didn't walk a girl to her front door. I recognize that it's a mostly empty gesture, but—"

"So long as we both know it's a bit silly, I'll let you do it for Noreen's memory."

The walk across the grass had been silent and awkward. An evening spent watching a college basketball game and eating the leftovers from a funeral wasn't a date, but at some point it hadn't felt like two friends hanging out, either. Flashes of light from the big-screen TV had emphasized the attraction in Trey's eyes and she had been grateful for the oversize woolen sweater hiding the way her nipples had answered. She could have pretended it was the cold, but she would've been lying. Trey was attractive and she liked the way his silliness escaped despite heavy, black eyebrows and a serious career.

He was here for the rest of the week—right next door and very convenient. And then he would leave and she wouldn't have to worry *what next?* Responsibility-free sex would be nice. Could she do it, though? And shouldn't she pick a better candidate for such an indulgence than the man who owned her land? Only she couldn't socialize while at work and the men at the farmers' market saw a farmer rather than a woman. She went out with friends only occasionally, and even on those rare nights out she wondered if money spent at a bar would have been better put aside for buying land.

That last sad statement was reason enough to give this a try.

Her hand had wanted to reach for his on the walk over—like they were in middle school or something—and she'd had to yank it back. Her pajama bottoms didn't have pockets to give her hands somewhere to go, so the one closest to Trey still twitched. At least her nipples hardening had been a sexual response. She was an adult and he was good-looking, so that was easy enough to explain away. But hand-holding implied a desire for a relationship and, while she now knew what job required Trey to wear a suit, he was still a stranger and he still lived in D.C. Sex, rather than hand-holding, was what should be on the agenda.

They stopped on her front porch, the wind blowing the storm in, mussing up her hair as surely as his short hair stood on end with no escape. Ashes sat at the door and stared at the wood. "Thank you for dinner and the game. This is the latest I've stayed up in ages." That statement was true, even if she didn't have her watch on her. "Farmers up with the chickens and all," she finished awkwardly.

God, this was weird. His eyes were warm and steady on her lips, despite the wind buffeting about everything else in the vicinity. Like some out-of-body experience, she could feel her lips part and her chin lift a little. Her heart fluttered. Warmth flooded her body and she wanted to take off her sweater to cool down. She shifted slightly forward. Trey's hand was coming out. She wanted him to slip it under her big sweater, to feel his grip tight on her waist.

Ashes barked. Trey's hand brushed her breasts, more accidental than not, on its way up to the back of his neck. "So, my tour. What time tomorrow?"

She blinked. The spell was over. "I have to start seeding broccoli tomorrow in the greenhouse. Come find me whenever you're ready."

"Okay."

They stood at her front door. Trey was probably waiting for her to go in. She didn't know what she was waiting for, so she reached behind her and turned the knob. Ashes rushed inside to his bed by the fireplace. "Thanks again."

"My pleasure." He leaned back onto his heels, but didn't leave her porch. "Do you need help getting the fire started?"

Bone-warming, dry air from the woodstove drifted across her back through the open doorway. "No. I left a pretty good fire going. I'll just need to add some logs and it should keep me through the night."

"Tomorrow, then." He wasn't going to leave. Max didn't really want him to. She either had to go inside and shut the door on him or invite him in.

She nodded, stepped back until she was inside and closed the door. Only when she heard his feet bounce off her steps did she take off her shoes and head up the stairs to her bed. When she asked Ashes what the hell that had been about, her otherwise reliable dog had no answer.

CHAPTER FIVE

WHEN TREY FOUND Max in the greenhouse about ten o'clock the next morning, she had already planted the first table of broccoli and was ready for a break and a chance to stretch her legs. The monotony of the task plus the patter of the rain against the thick, plastic roof had lulled her into a trance. The only way she knew she hadn't planted two seeds into one cell was because she was out of cells and seeds at the same time.

Since all she'd seen Trey wear so far had been jeans that were nice enough for any place in Durham; dress pants, complete with dress shirt and sport coat; and a funeral suit, she hadn't known what to expect him to don for his tour in the rain. His boots looked a little too big, the rain slicker a little too small, and his jeans would get soaked, but they would do. Especially when she gave him something to cover his pants. He called out to her, but she couldn't hear what he said over the drumming of the rain.

She walked across the greenhouse to where he stood petting Ashes. "There are rain bibs on the peg behind you."

"Won't you need…" he said before looking up and noticing the rain bibs she was wearing. "Will they fit?"

"Better than any of the clothes you have on."

"Dad's clothes are packed. These are my grandfather's. Apparently, he had big feet and tiny shoulders. I found them in the closet off the back porch."

Max thought it would have been simpler to have unpacked Hank's clothes, especially as he and Trey were of a size—minus the beer gut. Perhaps it was easier to step into his grandfather's shoes than his father's.

Trey sat on the bench and tugged off his boots before stepping into the bibs. He was wearing dress socks. Max was about to comment that for a man who grew up on a farm, he didn't know how to pack to visit one, when she realized that was probably the point. He hadn't planned to step out of the farmhouse long enough to need woolen socks. After he and Kelly had packed up all their parents' things, would Trey ever come back to the farm?

"Ready," he said. The bibs covered the flannel shirt he'd also apparently found in a closet somewhere and he fastened the slicker over them. Max put on her own raincoat and, in unison, they flipped their hoods up over their heads and stepped out into the cold rain. Ashes had to be cajoled out of the greenhouse into the damp.

"I thought a farm dog wouldn't be so averse to rain," Trey said.

"Ashes is now an old farm dog. He likes to pick and choose his farm duties, but he wouldn't want to be shut in the greenhouse, either."

Trey kept up with Max easily as she strode past the packing shed and the second tobacco barn to the fields, Ashes bounding alongside. Now that being out of the rain wasn't an option, the dog was determined to enjoy himself. Plus, rain wouldn't scare away the geese and Ashes still had his farm chores to attend to.

Max walked more quickly than normal, but couldn't seem to slow herself down. She didn't want there to be any strangeness between them. Here she was, a grown woman in a man's job, upset because Trey didn't seem to have any leftover feelings from their near kiss last night!

Or had that near kiss been a figment of her imagination and he hadn't been reaching for her when Ashes barked? Just because she couldn't escape her thoughts by walking faster didn't mean she wasn't going to try.

When they stopped at the first field, Ashes dashed off after some geese cheeky enough to encroach on his territory. "I have four fields, each divided into two sections, and we rotate the crops. This field will have peanuts for a season, which will add nitrogen back into the soil. In the past, I've planted cowpeas or clover for the same purpose, but I had a request from one of the downtown restaurants for peanuts, so I'm giving it a try." The peanuts were part of the joy and the fear of farming. She'd never grown them before and she didn't come from a part of the country where they were grown, so she lacked a gauge to measure her progress. But there was also exhilaration in trying something new: reading the literature, testing the soil, shoving something in the ground and then looking to Mother Nature for the rest. Knowing that only some of your success or failure was under your control and that the forces of nature held tight to their power. She scanned the field, trying to read her future in the soil, then shrugged at her own silliness. If the peanuts didn't work out, there was always next year. And regardless of whether she got a cash crop out of them, they would add nitrogen to her soil.

"Crop rotation, like during the Middle Ages?"

"Well, yes." When she nodded, the rain dripped off her hood, obscuring her view of the field. "I have a tractor instead of oxen, a pickup instead of a wagon and I can buy ladybugs over the internet, but the basic principles are the same. Rotating your plants keeps insects from gaining a foothold and your soil from being depleted. Cover crops and tilling in add nutrients. That plus elbow grease, sun and rain and you will grow good food."

She didn't know why she was so intent on having

him understand, having him be impressed with her land management. Probably because of his dismissive attitude toward the land that was his by birth, but she didn't want to accept that. She'd never let one person's opinion, especially one man's opinion, of her business affect how she felt about her life choices before.

Mud squished and squawked under their feet as they walked up the small rise to the next field. Ashes let out a woof when he finally noticed they were gone, and vaulted some rocks up to them. The gray, wet weather obscured the breath of her fields, but land was alive. Max could walk it, plant it and make it grow.

She wished Trey could see the land's value, as useful as wishing she could plant infertile seeds plucked from hybrid plants. Max continued her tour, which had turned into a treatise on crop rotation. She talked about how she would schedule carrots in fields that had previously had potatoes because the potatoes cut down on weeds and how she planted clover between all her crop rows. If Trey was bored, he hid it well.

By the third field, Trey was talking about his life on the farm as a boy. He pointed out places where he'd hidden from his father and where he had surprised Kelly with an angry and aggressive water snake, telling him it was a water moccasin. He also pointed out where he'd been bitten by a cottonmouth, which he'd deserved for poking it with a stick, and where his brother had broken his arm jumping out of a tree into the pond during a drought.

As they rounded the dirt road from the fields back to the greenhouse, Max asked the question that had been burning inside her since Trey had actually expressed feelings other than disgust for the land. "You talk about your memories fondly, even though they involved physical pain. Why don't you enjoy coming back here?"

"Do you want me to decide to become a gentleman farmer and kick you out?"

The hard tone in his voice pushed her into a defensive position. "Well, no, but…"

"Why don't you return to Illinois and farm there?"

"I didn't come to North Carolina to escape my father. I came to North Carolina because the growing season is good, the local produce market is strong without being saturated and my mom lives in Asheville. I was *attracted* to North Carolina, not repulsed by Illinois or my family."

Though everything she'd told Trey was true, it wasn't the whole truth. She'd grown up thinking she would farm her father's land with her brother, but one summer spent interning at an organic vegetable farm outside of Chicago had changed her mind. Her brother and father grew the food that fed the world, no mistaking that, but she wanted to feel the sun directly on her back, not through the glass of a harvester window. Despite her father's claim to her childhood, she was her mother's daughter after all.

He harrumphed, the same noise Ashes made when scolded. "Maybe that's the difference, then. I decided at an early age that whatever my parents were, I didn't want to be that. Farm included."

His use of the plural *parents* was interesting. "I know you didn't like your father, but no one ever has a bad word to say about your mother. Surely she holds some tie for you."

"My mother was an uneducated woman who worked a job she hated with people who made fun of her. She was afraid if she quit that she'd never get another job. And we needed the money because my dad was a failure at life." Max turned her head to look at him. He raised an eyebrow at her, though the disgusted look on his face softened before he spoke again. "She was a lovely, kind person who spent her entire life being trampled on by people who never noticed she was there."

Trey said the words with the hesitation of someone who didn't know whether to be disgusted or sad. Max saw what he described but she credited Noreen with being a woman of untapped strength. She had to be, to put up with what Trey had described so that her children would have one stable parent and food on their table. Noreen may not have been a role model for her children, but she'd provided them with enough stubbornness to grow up and get out of a trap. Max supposed Noreen would think Trey's success was worth the antipathy he felt toward the farm.

The wind started again, and Trey's slicker wasn't as weather-hardy as Max's; the wind and rain were starting to break through. "Let's go inside the greenhouse. It's not much warmer in there, but we'll be out of the weather and we can share my thermos of hot tea."

TREY DIDN'T SAY anything as Max took a sip from the thermos cup before handing it to him. She'd stripped off her slicker as soon as they had stepped under cover, so now she was wearing her rain bibs, a neon green thermal undershirt and a navy blue flannel shirt. With her masses of hair, she looked ridiculous and underdressed. And also like the loveliest thing he'd ever seen. A fire burned inside her that warmed her from the inside out. It made her glow. Trey gripped the tiny plastic cup with a fear that he would never be warm again. He tried to step closer to Max, but she moved away, busy in her greenhouse on her farm.

Despite the official ownership, this was more her farm than his—or than it had ever been his father's. She'd taken a ratty, falling-down piece of property and was turning it into something productive and wonderful. He wanted to pack up his clothes and drive back to D.C. Sell the dirt under his feet to the highest bidder and forget he'd ever lived here. Instead, he poured another cup of tea.

Max was laying out flats on one of the long tables. When her hands stopped moving, he handed her the cup and she took a big gulp. "Thank you."

"What are you planting?" Besides the flat, she had seeds and soil.

"The last of the broccoli for today." She was already looking down at her task. Tour was over and tea was shared; he'd been dismissed for work. "Broccoli gets started early then transplanted into the fields. In another two weeks, I'll seed more broccoli. I should have three weeks of broccoli for the CSA and six weeks of broccoli for the market."

"Can I help?" He couldn't say where the impulse behind the question had come from. A lack of desire to go outside into the rain made more sense than wanting to spend more time with Max.

Her head jerked up and her pale eyes were questioning. "Sure, I guess. Planting's not that hard." She demonstrated, filling the flat with soil, adding a seed to each cell and topping it with a little more soil. "It's basically your same seed-starting process as in a garden, only on a larger scale." She gestured to the table of flats. "I'll need 2600 feet of broccoli in the field. Makes for a lot of little transplants."

"You don't have help?" Trey didn't know what

he'd pictured winter on a vegetable farm to be like, but he'd expected more people.

"No." She stopped, putting her hands down on top of the flat. "I have three interns March through September, otherwise I'm the only one. It's a lot of work, but not more than I can handle."

"I didn't mean to imply…"

"The winter's slow, spent mostly planning the coming summer. I've thought of starting a winter CSA. Or maybe selling at the market in the winter. I already grow a winter garden for myself. But selling means I'd need another person and I've never been willing to risk the cost, especially since I wouldn't be able to provide housing. If I'm living in the farmhouse, the second person can live in the barn and a winter CSA might be feasible."

As she was talking, he realized he'd opened his hand out in offering to her. All of her dreams depended on him and his willingness to keep leasing her the land. But she didn't appear to notice that the land wasn't resting like a gift on his proffered palm. Once she had stopped talking, she had started planting again. Trey followed her movements until he'd gotten the hang of them enough to find his own rhythm. Ignorance of the farm and Max had been preferable to this…whatever their relationship was now. He'd rather think of the farm as his personal trap than as soil for dreams. But he still couldn't help asking, "What other plans do you have for the farm?"

She glanced up from her planting and her uncertainty looked tinged with fear. But that was ridiculous. A woman with her forthright gaze couldn't be afraid of anything. Yet it was written on her face.

When she didn't answer, he clarified his question. "If money was no object, what would Max's Vegetable Patch look like?"

"I've toyed with the idea of raising animals, but—" she stalled and he could see the objections to her grand plans piling up in her brain "—they're expensive and unless you've got the staff you can't ever go on vacation."

He raised a brow at her. "Money is no object."

"What about time?" she retorted.

"If you have money, you can hire extra people to cover the time."

"Right." She went back to planting and Trey gave her some space to organize her thoughts. What he'd meant to be a simple question asked out of curiosity clearly was not.

"Right now I'd like to own the land I farm. Renovate the second tobacco barn so I can offer housing to two interns. Past that, I have no plans."

When she stepped away from her finished tray of broccoli to begin another, he thought their conversation was over. Max didn't hum to herself. She didn't whistle or mutter. The only noise she made was the brushing of her clothing against itself as her hands busily planted seeds and the occasional shuffling of a seeding tray against the wooden tables. Outside the greenhouse the rain pounded—on the ground, on the sides of the greenhouse, on the trees. But even with all the noise Mother Nature could muster in the storm, Max was so centered in her thoughts and her work that the greenhouse *felt* silent. Trey knew it wasn't. When he stopped working to listen, the rain buffeted about outside and Ashes panted at Max's feet. So long as he didn't resist, Max and the work pulled him into a meditative state.

It wasn't until Max checked her watch that Trey noticed how the light had faded. He'd spent several hours in contemplative, comfortable peace with a woman on his dad's farm. No anger, no frustration, no resentment, just the repetitive movements of planting seeds.

"Finish up your tray and then we're done. I got far more finished today than I'd hoped. Thank you for your help."

Trey stretched his hands out in front of him and rolled the stiffness out of his neck. "You're welcome. Thank you for the tour and conversation." Now that he was moving, anger poured back into the empty space left from his meditation. The tightness that had been in his shoulders from stillness morphed into the restrictive straitjacket he was familiar with.

He tilted his head from the left to the right, hoping to add ease back into his muscles.

Max directed him through cleaning up and they walked out of the greenhouse into the drizzle together. Only the noise of the rain, the shuffling of their steps and the rustle of their clothing accompanied them, leaving Trey to concentrate on Max walking next to him. Even Ashes seemed contemplative. As they were passing the chicken coop, Max spoke again. "I thought a lot about your question."

"My question?" After the absorbing quiet of the greenhouse, his question now felt intrusive. His idea of bigger, better and flashier was out of sync with the peace of the farm.

"There are so many things I could do with this farm that would make a splash in the organic farming world. There's this guy in upstate New York with a complete CSA. People pay him a yearly fee and once a week they pick up all their food, meat, cheese, bread, preserves, vegetables, everything. His wife wrote a book about it. Closer to home, there's a farm in Orange County with a complete rotation of their animals and vegetables. They do things with organic farming I could only dream about."

"But?" Just because he felt like he was intruding, didn't mean he was going to stop.

"I'm pretty simple. My dreams for the farm are

modest: a winter CSA, a renovated tobacco barn and land I can count as mine."

"What's wrong with saying that?"

"What are your dreams, Trey?"

Trey stopped and stared at the farmhouse. His mouth opened to speak but drizzle dripped off his nose into the emptiness of what he couldn't say and he had to shut his mouth before he drowned. He either said what he didn't even want to admit to himself or never speak again. "All I ever wanted was to get away from my father and this farm."

"And after you moved away, how did you decide what to do next if you didn't have dreams?"

Max's eyes were clear and bright, even through the fading light and the spit coming down from the heavens. Trey started walking again, to the farmhouse. He'd never imagined wanting to enter those doors, but the house was dry. And warm.

When Max and Ashes caught up with him on the enclosed porch, he could feel the cowardly way he hadn't answered her question in the prickle in his spine. The drips off the metal roof were louder now than the sound of the rain, but neither noise was loud enough to drown out the truth he didn't want to admit to himself.

"Since I packed up my car and left North Carolina, I haven't had a single dream for my life. I've taken logical and practical steps to further my career and the agendas of my employers, but *nothing* I've done has been my dream."

Ashes's wet tail made a squishing noise as it swept back and forth on the concrete floor. Max was silent.

"Kelly's coming over soon so we can do more packing. I should go inside." Trey hadn't looked at her during his confession. He didn't want to see pity in her eyes.

The irony of the situation wasn't lost on him as he watched Max and Ashes shuffle down the steps and around the back of the house. Max had one very simple dream, and he owned it. He had had one simple dream, too, and owning Max's dream meant he hadn't fully realized his.

CHAPTER SIX

"ARE YOU SURE you don't want to drive?" Max asked with a smile in her voice as Trey opened the passenger door to the truck late the next morning.

"No, I'm comfortable enough in my masculinity to let you drive."

Trey had looked in the cab while they were filling the bed with his dad's crap. The rust around the gearshift hadn't given him much hope that the transmission actually worked, though he'd seen Max drive the beast around the farm. This would be the first time he'd seen her drive the truck—instead of her small sedan—off the property. When Max hopped up into the seat and caught him eyeing the stick shift with suspicion, he knew his answer hadn't fooled her.

"Your car is a standard, so I know you can drive one."

"My car also doesn't have rust." Or a thick layer of dirt and torn seats, but he didn't say any of that. This was a working farm truck and it wasn't meant to be beautiful.

"Well, make sure you have your cell phone," she

said as the engine cranked, "in case we need to be rescued." She seemed to be using all of her arm strength to shift the truck into Reverse, though the mischief in her voice made him wonder if this, including her asking if he wanted to drive, was all an act. Another side to his farmer?

"You're not helping. One of your dreams for the farm should be a new truck." He was guessing this hunk of metal was from the eighties.

"Bertha is from one of Ford's greatest ever truck years." Her struggle with the gearshift had clearly been an act. She had easily shifted into first gear, too busy defending her truck to fake difficulty this time. "She's a collector's item."

"Does that include the price archeologists would pay to carbon date the dirt they scrape from the floor?" He said the words lightly, so she would know he was teasing. And she laughed.

Everyone's mood was lighter today, it seemed. The clouds from the day before had evaporated, though the water it had left behind still gave everything a sparkle in the bright winter sun. The birds seemed to chirp a little louder this morning, as if they knew that this load of junk would mean the farmhouse was almost completely cleared out.

Important-looking papers had been sorted and shoved into boxes that went up into the attic, along with the family pictures Kelly hadn't wanted. Anything that Kelly had felt a sentimental twinge for also went in a box and into the attic. They'd already made several trips to the Goodwill with anything that still had a use, and this should be the only trip they had to make to the dump.

Trey rolled down the window enough to let a little breeze in then settled into the torn seats and the dust for the novelty of being driven into town.

Max was apparently an experienced dump-goer, because she knew where to pull in to unload their hazardous materials, where to unload the boxes of broken electronics and where to dump the trash bags. Trey was just along for the ride because it was his father's crap—and because spending his time with Max yesterday had been surprisingly relaxing. He wanted to see what she could do with a trip to the dump.

Lightened of its load, the truck seemed to drive better and Trey was settling in for the drive back when Max pulled into the small parking lot of a corner grocery store. "Do you mind?" she asked, though not until turning off the engine and engaging the parking brake.

The trip to the dump meant he was one chore closer to being back in D.C., so Trey said, "Of course not." Given how old the store looked, complete with handwritten signs in the windows advertising the week's specials, he must have passed this store a thousand times in his life as he drove up and down Roxboro Road. "What are we getting?"

"King's has good local bread and milk, plus dried peaches for my oatmeal in the mornings," Max said as she exited the truck and walked into the store, with Trey right behind her.

"Hey, sug," the clerk called as Max grabbed a shopping basket. "How's the farm?"

"Slow right now, but it'll pick up soon."

Trey trailed after Max through the aisles of the small store, content to play tourist and look around. The store had some items he expected, like bags of frozen chitterlings and other things that he didn't know existed, like molasses in what had to be a ten-gallon bucket, and some things he'd never expected to see at a small grocery store in Durham, like bags of organic and fair-trade coffee.

Trey stopped in front of a packaged-meat case and stared at the small tubs of pimento cheese. He couldn't remember the last time he'd had a pimento cheese sandwich, though they had been a staple of his childhood. Max came up behind him. "You should buy some. They make it fresh in the store."

Her breath was soft and intimate in his ear, and suddenly the entire stop had a casually familiar feel. Stopping in for a few groceries was something couples did together. "Are you a regular here?" he asked, reaching forward to grab a tub, more to put some distance between them than because he actually wanted it.

"Anyone who comes here more than once is a

regular." She reached past him to grab her own tub, the movement defeating his desire for space. "Plus, they support local farms and businesses, so it's hard not to return the favor.

"Do you sell here?"

Max waved at the butcher behind the counter before answering. "No, but I know the baker for some of the bread they sell here and the brewer of some of the Durham beer. If I gave up on the diversity of my farm and specialized in one product, maybe I would. Right now I don't produce enough of any one thing to sell at a store." She looked back over her shoulder at him. "I'm not sure I would want to."

Here in the store, Max wasn't just the farmer on his dad's land, but a real person—related to the farm and his past but not *of* the farm and his past. It was like realizing your parents had a life before you were born. The thought made him laugh and realize how self-centered he'd been this entire week.

Trey followed Max to the front of the store, put his tub of pimento cheese on the conveyor belt and pulled his wallet out of his back pocket. He no more knew what to do with his tub of pimento cheese than his newfound realization.

THOUGH TREY AND Kelly had packed up enough of their dad's stuff that he could've driven back to D.C. Friday morning, Trey kept to his original plan of leaving Saturday. He had made a tentative date with

Max for another basketball game and he wanted to keep it. He drove to Chapel Hill for a late lunch with Jerome, took a side trip through Orange County for Maple View Farms ice cream and stopped for more barbecue takeout for dinner with Max. He didn't plan on returning to North Carolina until Kelly got married—which probably depended more on politics than Kelly—so the memory of this barbecue would have to last him a while.

When he opened the door to Max's knock, he was surprised to see her in jeans. "Does access to your own washing machine starting tomorrow mean no bunny-print pajama bottoms?"

When she turned from hanging her coat up, a flush rose up her neck, turning the pale parts of her skin bright red and her freckles a deep oak.

"The pajamas were cute, but the jeans look nice, too," he offered as a lame apology for whatever he had said to make her blush. *Nice* was a weak description of how Max looked.

The long sleeves of her dark purple T-shirt covered her arms, but his eyes followed the trail of freckles down into the deep V of the fitted shirt's neck, and his hands wanted to accompany them. Her hair was pulled back into a long, tangled braid that looked like a fraying piece of rope with strands and ringlets sticking out every which way, giving her otherwise tidy look a wild quality. Max hadn't lost the unsullied glow he'd discovered in her yesterday, even back on this contaminated soil. A pleasant, but uncomfortable realization.

"Mama would say I know how to treat a girl right," Trey said as they walked into the living room with their plates of barbecue. "TV trays." He gestured to the room he'd set up for their evening. "No low-class eating with the plate on your lap tonight." She laughed, as he had known she would. "I think these were my grandmother's and I didn't know they were still around until I found them in the attic. Mama always insisted we eat at the table. Dad would use these trays sometimes, but after Mama died, I guess he didn't feel the need to put his beer anywhere other than his mouth."

"I don't remember Hank drinking."

"Maybe he learned to hide it better. Anyway, let's leave my parents to their resting places and talk basketball." Talking about his father left a sour, hungover taste in his mouth that the vinegar in the barbecue couldn't overpower.

"I can't talk basketball, so you talk basketball and I'll eat my dinner."

"That 'I'm still a Fighting Illini' wasn't a sign you could debate the finer points of fast-break ACC-style basketball versus *slooow* Big Ten style?"

"No." He looked over to see her smile dancing over her raised fork piled high with barbecue. "It was just a sign that I didn't want to yell out 'heel.'"

"Well, I'll be crushed and deceived. You owe me something, then."

"I owe you something?" A chuckle came out on the tail end of her words.

"Sure. I'm feeding you barbecue as payment for having someone to talk basketball with. If you can't talk basketball, what am I feeding you for?"

"Company? Enlightened conversation? A thank-you for the tour?"

Trey pretended to think over her response. "Nope. None of those are good enough."

In the dim light of the lamps and the television, he could barely tell the difference between her pale raised eyebrow and her pale skin, so he didn't back down. He was certain Max was the kind of person who enjoyed being pushed, and who liked pushing back.

"Okay," she said finally. "I'll give you something, but if you tell a soul I will wallpaper your apartment in D.C. with pictures of the farmhouse."

He'd been right about the pushing back part. Max knew how to make a good threat. "Deal."

"My mother's family is from the Winston-Salem area. My grandparents used to come to Illinois for visits, but I didn't visit North Carolina until I was ten or so, when my parents divorced and my brother and I were shipped out of town for the process." She grimaced at the memory. "My grandfather took us to Stamey's in Greensboro for my first taste of barbecue. I didn't know any better so I asked the waitress, 'What kind of meat is this?'"

Trey smiled, knowing where this was going.

"'It's barbecue,' the waitress replied. I pressed her to tell me what kind of meat it was and she kept telling me it was barbecue, like I was dumb or something."

"A reasonable assumption on the part of the waitress," Trey said. "The rest of the South can smoke what it likes, but barbecue in North Carolina is *always* pork."

"I should've made not teasing me part of the deal." Max wrinkled her nose at him, but she was smiling. "This back-and-forth went on *forever*. Now that I'm older I can see that my grandfather's grimace was him trying not to bust a gut laughing, but at the time I was just frustrated. The waitress wouldn't answer my question and Grandpa finally told me it was pork about the time I was ready to walk out. Or when the waitress was going to kick me out. One or the other."

"On behalf of mah state—" Trey put on his fine Southern gentleman accent "—may ah say how delighted we are that you gave us a second chance."

"Now you're just being ridiculous." She made an exaggerated motion of wiping her hands on her paper napkin. "Is there dessert?"

"There's banana pudding. If you can wait just a minute for me to finish my last cold hush puppy."

Trey popped the fried ball of cornmeal into his mouth, then stood. "Let's go into the kitchen."

Trey blinked several times when he passed the muted TV. The game was nearly at halftime and he hadn't looked away from Max once to see the score.

THIS TIME, WHEN Trey offered to walk her and Ashes across the yard to the barn, Max didn't object. She'd planned on him walking her to her door, actually. Worn a low-cut T-shirt, donned her most flattering pair of jeans and put on lip gloss in the hopes that he would notice. His eyes had warmed when she'd taken off her coat, so she was pretty sure he'd taken a peek. He was leaving tomorrow morning and that was all the more reason for her to take a chance on him tonight. When they reached her door she let Ashes in then stood on her porch with Trey.

"I imagine you'll be working when I leave tomorrow." He was looking at her lips when he said the words.

Taking a step closer to him seemed like a good first move. Give him a chance to make a second move without the risk of two different sets of expectations bumping into one another. "I work a little on Saturdays, but I'll be around. You should come find me."

Their two evenings spent watching basketball and eating dinner together had been fun. When he let go of his anger, Trey managed to walk the line between serious and goofy without falling into the abyss on either side. She didn't want him to come find her tomorrow morning; she wanted him to be next to her when she woke up. Just this once.

He shrugged, not taking his eyes off her lips—and he didn't take a step back when she took another step closer. "It will be a pleasure being your landlord."

She cocked her head. The cold air between them warmed with their shared breath and there didn't seem to be enough oxygen for them both. Would he be okay with kissing his tenant? Would communication between them be awkward if they spent the night together? God, what if he thought she wanted something else out of this night besides good sex?

What if I do want something else out of Trey? That last thought was stupid. He was *leaving* in the morning and wouldn't come back to North Carolina unless forced.

"Well, good night, Max." When she pulled herself out of her thoughts, she could see he'd stuck his hand out for her to shake. "I hope to see you tomorrow before I leave."

She blinked, wondering when her expectations and her reality had gotten so far out of whack. She was supposed to have reached up to kiss him, not stuck out her hand for a solid shake. She took his hand in hers, because really, what else was there to do? "I'll try to stay near the farmhouse to say goodbye."

"All right, then." He nodded.

Would that goodbye be as awkward as this one, or would the sunlight enable her to see how silly her expectations had been? More likely, she would go over every detail of the night and wonder if she could have been more forward in what she wanted. Or maybe he just wasn't interested—wasn't that a lowering thought?

Trey cleared his throat. She'd been standing there holding his hand for who knows how long. Long enough for their hands to get warm together. "Thanks for dinner," she said, reaching up to press a kiss to his cheek. What she'd intended to be a light kiss turned deeper when he pressed his cheek against her lips before pulling away.

"Good night." Without even a backward glance, Trey marched down the stairs and back to the farmhouse. She must have imagined him leaning into her lips.

Max stood at the door for several seconds, cursing herself. She'd dolled herself up and all but puckered her lips for a kiss. But she had to go and think too much until she'd darn near talked herself out of making a move, and she'd sure as hell communicated "go away" before kissing him on the cheek, passing the mixed messages she was getting from her head onto his face.

"Ashes," she said as she shut the door, "why do I have to think so damn much?"

I<small>N THE END</small>, it didn't matter if Max stayed close to the farmhouse to say goodbye. She may have been up with the chickens to get started on farm chores, but he'd been awake with the owls. Whatever time he'd packed up his stuff and driven off, she'd been fast asleep.

CHAPTER SEVEN

TREY WAS SITTING at his desk in his office, trying to down enough coffee to transition from low-key farm life to the rush of Washington politics when his phone dinged. His personal email account had received a new message, subject heading "Max's Vegetable Patch, in full bloom." He put down his pimento cheese sandwich to read it.

Trey,

I'm sorry I didn't get a chance to say goodbye and to thank you for the two dinners. I'd thank you for the basketball, but I didn't really pay attention to it. So thank you for the blinking lights and buzzer noises. I'm sure Hank's TV will be lonely without him, but I will try to give it some company after I move into the farmhouse. Maybe I can leave it on to keep Ashes company, especially once he retires.

I sense you will be more of an absentee landlord than Hank was, but I don't want you to miss out on the beauty of the farm. Kelly took this picture last summer. Know that the land will be productive and make people happy.

Sincerely,
Max

Trey stared at the link to the attachment, grateful Max hadn't called him a coward for scurrying out of the farmhouse in the middle of the night like a rat with the raccoons laughing and pointing at him. He had called himself a coward.

Standing there on her front porch, with the light from her cabin igniting her hair from behind, Max had been tempting. She'd stepped closer to him several times, even lifted her chin to look at him. The cool green of her eyes had looked dark—hot—in the dim light of the porch. Her lips against his cheek had been chapped from her work spent outside. He had wanted to press his entire self into the solid wildness she represented. He could have kissed her. He could have kissed her, wrapped his hands around her waist and stepped forward. She would have stepped back into the barn and he would have woken up the next morning knowing how it felt to be next to her soft, warm body in bed.

On the drive home, he'd thought about each and every step he could have made into her barn and up her stairs. Lived every moment that hadn't happened. Counted the freckles he had never seen at the soft indentation just under her hip bone, which he'd also never seen.

His mouse hovered over the link to the attachment, switching from hand to arrow to hand to arrow in concert with his indecision. Sex with Max would have been easy. Life after would have been hard. Nearly impossible. For all that Max had been offering herself freely, the land would demand. Unlike the tub of pimento cheese, neither Max nor the land could be packed up and brought back to his apartment in D.C.

Bravery was easier while in his office. Here the land's claims on him were paper shackles. He clicked the link. At the edge of the picture that popped up on his screen, Max had just finished putting something into the bed of her truck. Her arms were still reaching down but her face was up and laughing at the camera. A floppy straw hat covered her eyes and purple zinc covered her nose, but her white teeth were shining against her sun-darkened freckles. Behind her was the whole of the farm, in all of its summer glory. The camera wasn't close enough for him to see what all was growing, but everything was a lush, bountiful green. And it looked nothing like the wasteland his father had overseen. But he could see the farmhouse in the background with its peeling paint.

He looked back to Max smiling at the side of the photo. Neither her ponytail nor her hat could fully contain the wild curls that framed her face in a mass of orange. Snow was beginning to fall outside his office window and traffic in D.C. would be a nightmare in an hour or so, but Max and her smile and her hair was like coming across a persimmon tree with its tomato-looking fruit shining through the bare winter branches.

Trey closed the photo and the email, then went back to his work, ignoring his sandwich for more coffee.

"MAX," TINA, HER stepmom, said into the phone, "your dad just walked in the door. Do you want to talk to him?"

Tina didn't wait for an answer, just hollered "Nick," into the house somewhere.

"Hi, Patches," her dad said into the phone, using the name only he called her. "How's the farm?"

"Big money for easy work," she said. Her dad had responded to questions about the farm with those words for as long as Max could remember and, somewhere along the way, she'd picked up the habit when on the phone with him. All their conversations, phone or otherwise, started off this way.

"You met the new owner yet?"

"Yes, Trey was down for the funeral and to pack up his dad's things. He'll be an absentee landlord." She didn't know if that was a good or bad thing.

"Farming is hard work. It'd be nicer if you were

nearby, Patches." In his voice she heard the wistful-
ness he'd never express in words.

Max's decision to set out on her own for a vegetable farm in North Carolina had hit her father hard.
He had been certain Max and her brother Harmon
would take over the farm together—right up until
she'd packed her bags, Max had been certain the Illinois farm was in her future. Like her father, she'd
thought the summers spent interning at vegetable
farms were a small rebellion, that she'd tire of it and
move back home.

Then her brother had graduated from college and
her mom had announced she wasn't living in the
Midwest any longer, but was moving back to Asheville, North Carolina. Her dad seemed to think Max
had chosen her mother over him. Sometimes Max
wondered if he was right.

"I know. The Triangle is a good location to be a
small farmer, though—much better than near you.
Lots of support down here. Lots of interest in local
ingredients. Another few years and I'll even feel
good about buying the farm."

"Farming isn't always about feeling good. Sometimes you just have to go to the bank with your hat
in hand and hope for the best."

Max couldn't imagine her father ever following
the advice he'd just given her. The problem was he
just didn't understand the choices she'd made. He
couldn't imagine why someone would roll back one

hundred years of farming technology for a tomato too ugly to sell to a supermarket. It wasn't her work ethic he questioned but her sense.

One Christmas she'd teased her father that she was the natural hybrid of a Midwestern farmer cross-pollinated with an Appalachian hippie. Her father had responded with a grunt. When she'd told her mother the joke, her mother had laughed until she'd cried.

"Don't worry, Dad. I've got my goals all planned out."

When her father didn't know what else to say, he grunted. Max interpreted this grunt as "Of course I'll worry. I'm your father," but she didn't press him. A quick conversation with her brother and she was off the phone to make her dinner. Max had only been cooking in her real farmhouse kitchen for a couple nights and she still got a kick out of using as many pots as possible, if only because she had counter space to put them on. She thought about having a beer while she cooked but, in deference to Hank's memory, got out a can of pop instead.

TREY WATCHED THE senator's golf ball sail into the trees. "That was a powerful swing, sir." Some men in power wanted to hear about the world as it was. Some about the world as it could be. This particular senator wanted to hear about his successes and never his failures. He also claimed to be undecided on the bill Trey was lobbying for, so Trey would compliment the man's golf swing if his ball landed in China.

Even if the words left an oily taste in his mouth.

A Sunday spent golfing with senators and congressmen was work. As were the drinks he'd had with staffers from another senator's office who were writing a bill that Trey wanted a hand in. And the lunch he had planned for tomorrow. He shouldn't have to remind himself that he was helping to make legislation for his country. He'd come to D.C. after college to shape policy decisions and was more influential as a lobbyist than he'd been as a Capitol Hill staffer. The work he did was important.

Trey walked up to the tee, arranged his shoulders and aimed the ball to the trees, coming just short of the tree line. He had *some* pride after all. "Must be the wind, Senator. Ball's just not going where it should."

There was not enough Scotch in Scotland to make the ass kissing feel good, education bill or no education bill. The snow from the previous week had melted and the groundskeepers must have a top-secret chemical in their arsenal because the grass was green, even in February. Mother Nature's seasons had no place on the golf course.

Together they climbed into their cart and rode off to the trees. The senator liked to drive. Trey was playing caddy—all part of the sycophant role he was starring in today.

"I heard your father died," the senator said. "A shame. You have my sympathies."

Trey had received flowers from the senator's wife after the death of his father. She must have told him. "Thank you."

"I hear he was a good man."

Even though the senator had heard no such thing, another day Trey might have agreed with the senator because he wanted his vote. "He was the reason I got into politics." A dodge was the best he could muster today.

The sun was bright and shining overhead, though the cold was crisp. They couldn't ask for a better February day to be outside playing golf. The senator was in a good mood. Trey could get a commitment on the vote today if he played his cards right.

"My dad owned a small farm. I inherited it."

"What are you going to do with the farm now?"

A vision of hair blowing wildly in the wind flashed through his mind. Max was probably also working today. She'd be outside, but instead of tromping on grass made green through fertilizer and water, she was probably tilling—or something. Trey was fuzzy on the details of what she did in the fields, but whatever it was, she had turned his father's wasted land into a productive thing of beauty.

"I don't know," Trey said, wanting to go back and despising himself for the weakness.

"Sell it," the senator said. "Durham County, North Carolina. Is that right?"

"Yes. It was once a tobacco farm." He didn't want to say what it was now. Didn't want to sully the image of Max's lushness by letting the senator know she existed.

The senator's club banged against the others as he pulled it out of the bag. He was good at show but failed at substance. His wife was the political brains in the family and if they'd been of a different generation, she would be the senator.

"A friend of mine is doing developments all around that area of North Carolina. Luxury houses on large plots of land. He's always in the market for good acreage."

Visions of Max competed with memories of piles of crushed beer cans and the smell of his father after a bender. The lines in his mother's worn face growing deeper and deeper when she came home from work every day. The rot in the wood of the front porch that spread through the family living in the house. The fights and the taunts and the stench of country poverty made worse by a man who couldn't get out of his own family's way.

Selling the land would make wanting to go back meaningless. Impossible. Max wouldn't come out of the front door to welcome him. She wouldn't offer him a bed or breakfast. The farm and all of its memories could finally be erased from his mind.

"Have him call and make me an offer."

Trey barely managed to lose the golf game. His heart wasn't in it, and the senator was a poor enough player Trey had to work at each and every stroke that went awry. But between losing the golf game and selling Max's love out from under her, he had the senator's vote.

When Trey got back to his apartment, he stood under his showerhead until evolution granted him gills.

CHAPTER EIGHT

MAX HEARD ASHES barking as she walked from the greenhouse to the farmhouse for lunch. He'd always barked at a ringing phone, and the ring seemed to escape his increasing deafness.

"Hello?"

"Max, it's Trey."

"Oh. Hi. How are you?"

"Fine." Even over the phone she could hear the tightness in his voice, the kind of tone people used when they delivered bad news. She couldn't imagine what bad news he could be the messenger for, but she sat down anyway.

"Look," he said. "I've gotten an offer on the farm."

"An offer of what?" She wasn't so dumb not to know what he was talking about, but she wanted him to say it.

"A developer wants to buy the land and I have no interest in being a landlord. Your lease is up at the end of the year."

"You can't sell it. Hank's will states you have to offer me another three-year lease."

There was silence on the other end of the line.

The farm was hers in everything but name. Another three years to save up some money and she could be the one to buy it from him, and then he wouldn't have to be a landlord anymore. She just needed those three years.

"No," he enunciated both letters. "The will says no such thing. It leaves the farm entirely to me, with no conditions."

"Hank promised. He said he changed the will." Ashes must have enough hearing left to catch the anxiety in her voice because he came over and put his chin on her knee. She rested her hand on his warm head, but didn't have the energy to scratch his ears. If she moved too much, the actuality of what Trey was telling her might fall into her brain. And if she fell apart, she wouldn't be able to fight him.

"If my father excelled at keeping promises as much as he excelled at making them, I would be a different person right now. And you wouldn't have gotten to lease the farm in the first place."

"I know how Hank was, but he never broke a promise to me. He loved that the farm was finally being productive. He wouldn't have forgotten to change the will."

"Max, I'm not suggesting he forgot. I'm suggesting he never intended to keep that promise." Max could hear some unidentifiable noise in the background. Paper shuffling. "Maybe there's another farm nearby you can lease."

Like packing up all the work she'd put into re-forming the soil was as easy as boxing up dishes. "If there are so many plots of land around for sale, maybe your buyer can buy one of those."

"You don't have a say in this. I'm selling the land and it will be out of Harris hands."

Max didn't bother to say goodbye before slamming the phone into the receiver. She might not have a say, but there was another Harris who did.

TREY WAS WRITING talking points for a bill soon to be debated in subcommittee when his cell phone rang. The screen said "Kelly," which was odd because his brother never called him. They had an email/text-only relationship. "Harris."

"Don't make any promises to any developers you can't keep. I'm contesting the will."

"You can't contest the will. You don't want the farm, either."

Kelly didn't disagree with him. "But Dad told me he had written a new will. And I talked with his lawyer. There was a new will drafted."

"The lawyer didn't mention any of this."

"Dad took it home to review and never brought it back to the office. If it's still with Dad's stuff somewhere, then it's the official will."

"We didn't find it when we packed his stuff."

"We weren't looking for it. And you didn't want to go through his papers, so those are all still in a box."

"What the hell do you expect to get out of this?"

Trey could hear Kelly's shrug through the phone. "Maybe he left me half the farm."

"Bullshit." His brother claimed his relationship with their father had improved over the past five years, but there was no way their father would leave the family property to Kelly. Their father's homophobia was marrow-deep. The old man had always said he couldn't understand why Kelly would have any interest in owning property, since he'd have no kids or wife to pass it down to. "This is all a ruse to get me to change my mind about selling."

"It's not a lie that he said he was changing the will and the lawyer said he did it, Trey."

"Did the lawyer say you were getting half the farm in the new will?"

"No." The word came out in a drawl. "But I want to see the new will, just to make sure."

Trey opened his mouth to argue more, but he wasn't a two-year-old being denied a cookie. Kelly was within his rights to contest the will. The new will wouldn't leave his brother half the property—Trey was certain on that point—and if a new will did have a contingent that Max be offered a second lease, well, the cost of breach of contract would be the price of freedom.

"I'll come down this weekend to search with you.

If we can't find the will, does this limbo go on forever?" Trey asked.

"No." Disappointment was evident in Kelly's voice. "We get a reasonable time to search. If it's not with important papers or we don't find a safe deposit box with the will in it, then I have to assume it's been destroyed."

What a pointless waste of time away from work. And another weekend spent on the farm.

And seeing Max again.

THE PORCH LIGHT above her head gave Max an angelic glow, though her face wished him to the devil. She didn't greet him. Gravel crunching under his shoes was the only sound the cold night emitted. Ashes wasn't even barking.

"Hello," he said, the word failing to fill up the empty space between them.

She raised an eyebrow at him, keeping her arms folded against her chest and making her sweater bulge up at her ears. As always, when not clad in work clothes, she was wearing a rainbow of bright colors most redheads would have the sense to run from. Since he existed mostly in a world of dark suits, her polychromatic clothing choices hurt his eyes, even in the dim light. And she looked fantastic.

"Where's Kelly?" Trey asked.

He took a step forward onto the porch, and she

didn't budge from blocking the door. Not that he was expecting an invitation to stay at the farmhouse again—he'd booked a hotel room downtown—but he and his brother were supposed to start searching for the will.

"Home." Irritation clipped her words. He tried to let her anger roll off his back, but it bit and clawed to stay there, his conscience its lifeline. Finally, her shoulders relaxed. "He's coming tomorrow at seven so you can get an early start."

Trey was turning back to his car when the question hit him. "How did you get him to contest the will? Kelly has less reason to want the farm than I do."

"Kelly doesn't confuse the land for your father. He wants it to be in the best hands."

"Those hands being yours, of course."

"At least they're not some land developer's. Have you seen how the landscape is changing? If central Carolina isn't careful, all the natural spaces not either flood planes or state parks will be developed. If it's not a Bojangles or a Walmart, it will be housing developments. The local produce and farming history that attract people here will be gone."

He wasn't going to back away from the developer deal, but Trey wanted to go back to when they were working side by side in the greenhouse and she was telling him her dreams. Stupid, because he was razing those dreams to build luxury homes. But the desire to be here with Max and the desire to be anywhere else except standing on this farmland waltzed together in his soul.

Trey wanted to go back to the night they were standing on the porch of her barn, when she was cocking her head up at him and he'd decided to be honorable and walk away. Sex wouldn't have changed his mind about selling the land and would have only made this current situation worse, none of which meant he didn't still want it. He wanted to hear her talk about her tractor, but he wanted to hear it when they were lying in bed, warm and satisfied, and with her hair tickling his nose. He wanted her to explain crop rotation when they were lying naked in the sun with only her vegetables to spy on them.

"I won't be here, so I won't care" was all he said.

It wasn't her farm, it was his, and it was his to do with what he wanted. What he wanted was to not be in North Carolina ever again, even if Max was here.

The skin under her freckles flushed a dark red, and her freckles were nearly a coffee color at his words. He wanted to apologize, which was stupid, because he'd said those words exactly to hurt her, so she would never ask him to stay.

"I gave Kelly a key so you can start your search immediately, without coming to find me." She was in the house and turning the bolt in the lock before he could reply.

Trey collapsed into the driver's seat of his car and slammed the door. Since when did he need a key to enter his childhood home?

CHAPTER NINE

WATCHING TREY STEP out of his car, his dark jeans crisp and green sweater fresh as spring grasses, was physically painful. Max tried to scoff at the idea of him sitting in the dusty attic in his clothes. She tried to laugh at the cobwebs that would be clinging to him when he came down the attic stairs, but both efforts were halfhearted at best. She should be attracted to someone who wore Carhartt and liked to dig in the mud, but the eye was attracted to what it was attracted to and, in her case, that was the crisp, clean lines of Trey's clothes, his thick hair, which she wanted to run her fingers through and his heavy eyebrows that were made more expressive by an unexpected sense of whimsy.

She was dressed for a farm interview, which meant jeans, work boots and a University of Illinois hoodie. Foolish of her to be lusting after a man who wore a suit every day. Just because she was interested didn't mean he was interested. He was trying to sell her livelihood out from under her, which made her interest self-defeating anyway.

"Who's the guy?" Trey nodded at the car leaving her, no, *his* property.

"Someone I was interviewing for one of the summer intern positions." The interview had been yesterday and he'd slept over in the barn.

"How'd he do in the interview?"

She shrugged. "Strong back. Seems genuinely interested in farmwork. He needs more hustle."

The eyebrows she admired so much were crossed when he turned to look at her. "Hustle? I would think strength would be more important and he looks like the kind of man who has a *strong back.*"

"It's all well and good to be able to lift up a full crate of potatoes into the bed of the truck over and over and over, but I can do that. I need someone who can get all the lettuce harvested before the summer heat kicks in and kills the lettuce, the worker or both." She shrugged. "Whoever works the farm with me this summer will get strong if they're not already. Hustle is related to the drive to work in the sun during a North Carolina summer. No hustle, no drive."

"It sounds like experience has set you straight."

"Experience and your father. I was stomping around complaining about how long it took to harvest the tomatoes my first summer when Hank pointed out that one of my interns had no hustle."

"My father would know. The only thing he ever hustled for was a beer."

Max didn't know what to say, so she relied on her father's old standby and grunted.

"Did you just grunt at me?" She must have surprised laughter out of him because it came out more as a cough.

"Hank wasn't much of a dad to you or Kelly, but I never saw him take a drink of anything stronger than Cheerwine." She had no taste for the sweet, cherry-flavored pop that was native to North Carolina.

"He just got better at hiding it."

"I guess it's possible," she said, but didn't put any conviction into her words. She knew alcoholics could hide their drinking, and she hadn't spent much time with Hank, despite living on the same property. However, arguing with a wounded son wasn't on her to-do list for today, so she let it pass.

Trey looked down the driveway to the road, where there wasn't even a cloud of dust to show someone else had been here. The pity she thought she saw in his eyes was confirmed when he shook his head. "Poor fella."

"Don't worry about him. I might still offer him the job. He applied through a program I'm participating in that teaches veterans to farm."

"And overlook the hustle?" He looked disappointed. "Pity hires are no good."

"It wouldn't be a pity hire. As you say, he's strong. And he has a vision for his future that might provide the drive he needs. I may not be able to teach hustle, but I can light a fire under his toes if he provides the kindling."

"How many interns do you hire?"

"Three. I'm now able to provide housing, though only for one of them, so it's nice if I can find some locals."

"Our hustler over there?"

"Would need housing. But I've got some other good candidates who wouldn't."

"I assume they don't know anything about the farm's future."

"I assume the farm's future is with me." The words were easier to say than to believe, but if she wasn't able to say them, she wouldn't be able to believe them. "Hank said he made provisions for the farm, and I choose to trust him on that."

Trey opened his mouth to respond, but she turned her back to him and walked down the hill to her fields. She had carrots to plant.

Silly though it may be, Max believed the plants took in the energy of the person tending them, and her anger was likely to turn the carrots from sweet to bitter. She would have to put herself in mind for sweet.

The metal of the seeder was heavy when she lifted it out of the bed of the truck, and the seeds sounded like rain as they tumbled against each other from the bag into the hopper. She found it hard not to think, *This is the last time.*

She pushed the seeder in front of her, down the row of drip line, her legs splayed as she lumbered behind. The seeder was an easier and faster method of planting than doing it by hand like she had when she'd gardened with her mother, but there were times Max missed the feeling of dirt under her nails. Carrots were planted early, which meant the soil would still be cold.

Next year... Well, next year might not bear thinking about. Next year she might be back gardening with her mother. Better to enjoy the experience of seeding *her farm* while she had it.

She didn't understand why Trey was so intent on selling the farm. He could continue to lease it to her and never have to think about it. She'd take care of everything and, if he could be patient, eventually she'd be ready to buy it. He'd seemed so interested in the life of a small farmer—in her troubles and her dreams.

Maybe that was what hurt so much about his sudden betrayal. They'd developed a bit of a friendship. She'd shared her work on the farm with him, walked around the fields with him and updated him about farm developments.

When she had the seeder positioned at the next row, Max had her answer. Trey was being entirely truthful about his reasons for selling the farm. He hated his father and anything his father had touched. Maybe her determination to share the glory of the land with him had only made him more determined to sever any connection. She'd chased after him like he was a reclusive housecat and, like a cat, his reaction was to hide.

And if she could go back in time to change her own behavior, she'd start by demanding to see the will Hank had promised her instead of just taking his word for it.

Even though she knew she wouldn't be able to see over the rise to the farmhouse, Max stopped and looked.

She had wanted to help with the search for the will, but both Kelly and the lawyer thought it was a bad idea. Kelly would keep Trey honest and, as she had the most to gain from the new will, it was better she remain on the sidelines. Kelly knew as well as she did that any new will wouldn't include him. He was contesting the will for her, and for the transformation she had wrought on the land of his childhood.

Even though Max was pretty sure Trey's determination to sell wasn't about her, she still felt like a fool being attracted to him.

Ashes bounded up to her, the bright winter sun and squawking geese giving her old dog new life. He sat, near her but never next to the drip line, and smiled with his tongue hanging out of his mouth, dripping with pond water. All of him was dripping. Ashes had pursued the geese into the pond, their usual refuge from him.

She patted his damp head, enjoying the way he cocked his head toward her when she started scratching his ears. Without geese to chase, how would Ashes find his inner puppy for his last years? Without a purpose, her dog would more quickly grow old before her eyes. Into an early grave.

Tears slipped down her face and her nose ran. She sniffed, wiping her cheeks with her sleeve. Crying would do her no good, but she couldn't help herself. If they didn't find the new will, five years of turning dirt into soil would be sold off to someone who would pour concrete where her potatoes had been and she'd be a farmer without a farm.

No need to worry if her sadness made the carrots salty; she wouldn't likely need to worry about repeat customers.

TREY KEPT EXPECTING—hoping, really—to hear Max's footsteps in the house. He knew he was hurting her, knew he was tearing her livelihood from her and by rights she should want to castrate him with a garden hoe, but that knowledge didn't dampen his desire to be near her. Hell, not only was he going to rip the land away from her, but he was also tossing their fledgling relationship out the window. No more watching basketball games. No more emails with pictures of the changing landscape. No more lunches in her kitchen.

Kelly handed him the box cutter and Trey ripped open the tape. They should've labeled the boxes. Aunt Lois would have made them label everything they'd packed, but two men weren't smart enough to think ahead. So instead of opening only the boxes with papers in them, they had to open each and every box. This search would take all weekend. His clients would be pissed that he'd spent another two days in North Carolina instead of working. At least he was at a hotel and had reliable internet.

Maybe he'd get to eat dinner with Max tonight. And tomorrow was Sunday. Even she wouldn't feel the need to work on Sunday just to stay away from him.

The box Kelly had opened was full of papers. Judging from the coffee stains on the old electric bill his brother handed him, this was the pile from the kitchen counter that Aunt Lois had dumped into a box with one great sweep of her arm. The next sheet Kelly handed him was a bank statement. Their father had remained land rich and money poor until the day he'd died, though the income from Max's rent seemed to have helped.

"I don't know why you want to sell the farm so badly." Kelly's words accompanied another bill, this one for satellite TV.

"We've been over this. I don't want any part of something Dad had, even the farm."

"Why not make the move to sell right after the funeral? Why wait until now?"

"I needed the right buyer." To avoid looking his brother in the eye, Trey looked down at the paper in his hand, some piece of junk mail about alarm systems. He could lie to the house majority leader while laughing and looking the man straight in the eye, but he couldn't lie to his brother.

Avoiding Kelly's gaze didn't help. Trey could feel the lie hanging in the dust of the attic and knew his brother felt it, too.

"Max isn't Dad. Max's Vegetable Patch isn't Dad's dead tobacco farm."

No. Even though much of the furniture in the farmhouse was the same, the colors on the walls were the same, hell, even the dishes in the cabinets were the same, the entire piece of land and every building on it felt renewed. Like someone had opened all the windows at the edge of the property and a storm had blown his father's funk into the great beyond. It was fresh and light and he wanted to stay here.

Trey shook his head at the thought. He'd escaped rural poverty and obscurity. He had an interesting and important job that made him a lot of money. Red clay dust no longer clung to his shoes. Wanting to stay here with Max, enjoying the fertile world Max had created, converged into regression.

"I have a life in D.C. and I don't want the bother of a farm in North Carolina." Trey set the piece of junk mail on top of all the other bits of mail he'd looked over from the box. They should throw the entire box out when they were done. Or better yet, bring the box outside and put a match to it. If not for Max, Trey would put a match to the whole house. His brother's silence made him look up. Kelly was holding a piece of paper to his chest, regarding his brother. There was pity in his eyes.

"Is that the new will?" Part of him hoped it was. Maybe he could pretend he didn't have the money to break the lease, take the pages out to Max and promise never to sell her land out from under her. It wouldn't be like last night when she'd barred him access to the house and her heart with her hands crossed over her chest. She would open herself up to him. Welcome him, and this time, when she looked up at him, he'd bend his head down and kiss her.

He was a fool.

Kelly stretched his arm out and Trey took the paper. He could tell by the length of the page that it wasn't the new will, but he looked at it anyway. Another bill, this time for services rendered to produce a will. The bill was dated December of last year. His dad had promised Max a new will and gotten Max a new will.

Trey sat back on his heels. "Don't you ever wonder why Dad couldn't keep a promise to us but kept his promise to a stranger living on his land?"

"You've been gone a long time. Dad changed. Max being here is the result of his change, not the cause of it."

Conflicting thoughts banged against each other in Trey's head. He respected what Max had done with the land. And was attracted to her. But he resented the hell out of her right now for getting their father to keep a promise where flesh and blood family had failed.

"This—" he wadded up the bill and threw it onto the pile of other trash "—isn't proof of anything other than that Dad got a new will made."

"We know the new will has a contingent for Max's lease. Why would he lie about that?"

"You said it yourself—if the new will isn't findable, we can assume the old man destroyed it. It was never in him to let something beautiful survive."

"D.C. turned you into a real asshole, you know that?"

"Don't give me credit I don't deserve. I was always an asshole. D.C. gave that part of me voice."

"What's worse about this is that I think you like Max and you're going to sell anyway."

"She seems nice. Attractive. That hair's pretty crazy. But I'm suspicious of anyone who would choose to be a farmer."

"Well, how about that." The awe in Kelly's voice made Trey look up. "You're jealous."

"Of who?"

"Of Max. You're jealous that Dad kept his promises to her. You're jealous that she had the guts to take on the farm and make something of it. You think you succeeded, but Max has won where you lost and she did it wearing work boots covered in mud."

The accusation pierced through his gut, leaving a weeping wound. Trey glanced down to make certain he wasn't bleeding. "You're nuts."

"Maybe, but I'm dead-on."

"We're never going to get out of this filthy attic if you don't shut your mouth and look through those papers. This is the most promising box we've seen. If it's not here, he destroyed it."

"*All* the boxes have to be looked through. You can't throw Max's life away based on a half-assed search."

No. Trey was going to throw Max's life away even if they found the will; it would just cost him more. But he was pretending not to be a slimeball, so he stuck his hand out for the next piece of junk from his father's box.

MAX CLEANED HERSELF up enough to meet with another intern candidate. This one was a college student from North Carolina State University over in Raleigh. Much like Max, the girl had grown up on a large farm and was interested in spending a summer learning about small-scale farming. She had a place to stay locally and she seemed chipper over the phone.

She met Sidney at the end of the drive. "Welcome to Max's Vegetable Patch," she said to the girl as she stuck out her hand. Despite looking like she was barely a teenager, the girl had a firm grip and thick calluses on her hand. Max sneaked a peek at the girl's fingers. Her nails were cut short and her hands were clean, but also well used.

Sidney's smile was infectious. "Thank you. I'm glad to have a chance to see your farm. My second cousin gets your CSA and loves it." The girl was both cheerful and confident.

"It's always nice to hear when my members enjoy the food they get. Let's start with a tour and then we'll sit in the pack house and talk." Max walked away from the house, making her stride purposefully long to see if the girl could keep up.

She pointed out field four and the compost pile, answering the girl's various questions about what they used in their compost, Max's record keeping and the inspection process. By the time they arrived at the next field, Max realized that she probably shouldn't call the woman a girl. Sidney may look younger than she appeared, but she asked smart questions and had clearly done her homework. She knew what varieties Max grew and what new vegetables she had advertised growing next year. All this information was available online, though Max was surprised how few of her intern candidates thought to look around her website. Or check out her Facebook page for farm pictures and updates. Running Max's Vegetable Patch may be a philosophical statement, but it was also a business and had to make money like any other.

Max pointed out where she'd seeded carrots earlier that day. Sidney talked excitedly about different carrot varieties and which ones her mom grew in their garden and how she'd been trying to talk her mom into planting some heirloom varieties. And there were also some varieties of eggplant she wanted to try. All in all, Sidney had many bright ideas about the future of the farm—her farm, Max's farm, any farm. But Max didn't know if her farm had a future. And interviewing both Sidney and Sean with Trey's plans hanging over her head felt like offering false promises.

But she couldn't *not* interview interns, just like she couldn't *not* plant carrots. The farm had to move along like always, in case the best happened.

Together they moved up to the pond, and Max talked about their irrigation, laying drip lines and the water pump. Sidney brought up the many droughts they'd had in the previous years and how hard that must have been for the farmers. She wanted to know if the pond had ever run dry and did they have a contingency plan.

Max listened with half an ear on the intern candidate and most of her mind on the search process in the house. What was the best that could happen out of all of this?

Ashes barked and chased after some geese that were getting a little too comfortable walking around the fields. Leaving Ashes to his business, they moved on. Max answered all of Sidney's questions, leaving her own flashing in her mind.

Her goal had always been to buy the farm. She had a plan laid out for when she would be able to afford the property and, according to the plan, she was right on target. Trey's goal was to get rid of the farm as soon as possible, which meant selling it now. And she couldn't buy it, not yet.... Suddenly her dad's words about going to the bank, hat in hand and hoping for the best popped into her mind.

They walked past the packing shed so Max could show Sidney the greenhouse. As they talked about what Max had seeded and when it would go into the fields, the idea that Max could offer to buy the farm from Trey now grew in her head. Could she work her arrangement with Hank into a contract and make her obligated to buy the farm at the end of her next lease or lose everything completely? Then Trey would have what he wanted. The farm would be sold in everything but actuality.

Ashes bounded up to them as they backtracked to the table and chairs set up in the packing shed. Now the interview would actually start and Max had to focus on what Sidney said. In truth, what Sidney said wasn't as important as whether or not they could get along. Max could teach farming principles—or reteach what the girl had learned at State—but you couldn't teach the ability to get along. Long, hot days spent working outside with only the four of them meant there couldn't be petty disagreements and short tempers. Max needed hustle and likeability. If someone wanted to be crotchety and bad tempered, they could do it on their own farm.

Max got some water out of the cooler for them to share and they each took a seat. Ashes lay down on the concrete floor.

Sidney seemed friendly enough. Once the girl stopped trying to impress Max with all her farming knowledge, she came across as intelligent and curious and very chatty. Max could see working long hours with her. They'd never be at a loss for conversation, making a contrast with Sean, who had been silent unless directly answering or asking a question. Sidney's passion for the land was in her words; Sean's was in his face.

On the walk back to Sidney's car, Max's thoughts returned to her idea of writing buying the farm into her lease. Tying herself to a future without actually owning the land made her heart flutter, though Max couldn't decide if it was fear or excitement. Probably both. If, in three years, she didn't have her money together to buy the farm, then she'd be out of a future and have lost everything.

If she didn't get another chance at a lease, she'd lose everything anyway. She balanced the options in her head. When she talked to Sidney about how much she loved the farmwork and the farm, what a pleasure it was to get her hands dirty, she was talking about her true self, the self she'd discovered years ago in college.

What was the worry, then? She'd be committing herself in a contract to something she'd committed herself to in her mind years ago. The difference was negligible—a signature was all. She'd still be on the same path she'd promised Noreen she would take.

She shook hands with Sidney one more time and promised the girl that she'd have an answer about the position in a week or so. Then Max headed to the greenhouse to do a little more seeding and prepare her sales pitch to Trey. She could do this. It wasn't much different than shooting cans—find your target, aim and fire. The rest was in fate's hands.

MAX INTERRUPTED TREY when he was walking to his car. "Did you find it?"

She was shifting her weight from one foot to another and worrying the edge of her flannel shirt.

Trey wasn't surprised she was worried—he knew what he was doing to her future—but he was surprised to see her showing it. This was the woman who hadn't needed to be holding a rifle in her hand to stop him in his tracks—her eyes had done it for her.

"No, we didn't find it." He stepped up to his car and put his hand on the driver's-side handle. The car beeped to unlock. He blinked when she slipped in to the passenger's seat, her clothes covered in dust. Ashes sat outside, barking at the backseat. "That dog isn't coming in the car."

"I'm not inviting him. Drive up to the top of the hill. Ashes can meet us there."

Trey didn't want to. He wanted to get the hell out of here. But he wasn't going to physically pull her out of the seat, and he'd be gone tomorrow, whether or not they found the will. She could have this. He started the car and slowly headed up the hill.

When they got to the top, Max hopped out to the excitement of her dog. Trey debated driving away, but whatever she had to say to him wouldn't change his mind—he was going to sell the land and she would have to find a new farm. To show he wasn't a total jerk, he'd even help her find one. There had to be thousands of dead tobacco farms in the Piedmont. He didn't care if Max stayed a farmer; he just didn't want her farming this land.

Ashes sat next to her, his tail kicking up dust as

Trey approached. The fields looked much as he'd seen them a couple weeks ago, only one field had been completely tilled.

"Do you know what I did today?"

"Farmed." If his brother's earlier words over the box of papers hadn't killed him, the look Max gave him might. He ran his hand through his hair, giving the ends a short tug before putting his hand back in his pocket. "I'm sorry. That was rude. My mother would've made me eat soap for that as surely as I had to eat soap for swearing."

She acknowledged his apology with a nod, which was probably as good as he was going to get. "I planted carrots. I've already planted radishes, and both garlic and strawberries went into the ground in the fall."

Trey looked a second time at the brown earth, trying to imagine the plants growing under the surface. He failed. "I hope they all turn out okay."

"What did Hank do to you that could possibly justify destroying that?"

There was the problem. His father hadn't beaten him. There was always food on the table, even if it was cheap shit-on-a-shingle for five nights in a row or grits and greens for a month. They also had health insurance because his mother had a decent job.

Trey stopped to pick up some of the gravel from the road. "He drank. When Kelly fell and broke his leg, my dad was too drunk to drive us to the emergency room. I drove. I was twelve." He hurled a rock into the falling dusk. "When I was eight, my mom got some award at church. My dad hooted and hollered for her—not because he was proud of her, but because he was drunk." Another rock, this one thrown with enough force to hurt his shoulder. "Every time he lost a job because he showed up to work smelling of moonshine one too many times, he blamed my mom. Or his 'gay-ass son,' Kelly. Or me. Or the Jews. Or the blacks. For all I know he blamed Jesus. Never once did he put down the bottle and blame himself."

Fuck it. Trey didn't need to half-ass throw rock after rock. He transferred the handful of gravel from his right to his left hand and chucked the whole lot of it into the sunset.

"Why blame the land? Your dad wasn't growing anything. It had no part in your childhood."

Trey reached down to pick up another handful of rocks, but Max's hand on his arm stilled him. "Don't. I don't want to have to make you pick rocks out of my fields tomorrow. I'd rather you spend your time looking for that will." The strength of her grip through his sweater emphasized her words. Her energy ricocheted through his body. Longing screamed through him, nearly stretching him to the breaking point before he was able to rein it in and focus.

"Once, my mom found a buyer for the farm. Not a farmer, like you, or a developer. Just some rich guy who liked the idea of being a gentleman farmer and had the money to back up his desires. It would have been enough to buy a nice house in town, with some left over. We could've even paid for the help Dad needed to stop drinking. He said no. Because as much as he hated this land, he couldn't let go of it. 'Heritage,' he said. Like that meant anything more than shit."

With nothing to throw, Trey put his hand on top of hers and squeezed, crushing her hand and her arm and not caring. "But you know what? I'm not my father. This land has no hold on me. I freed myself and I'm not letting it pull me back."

Before she could respond to his confession, Trey released his grip on her arm and walked to his car. Driving her back to the farmhouse was the polite, Southern-gentleman thing to do. Instead, Trey left her there to walk to the farmhouse in the dark.

CHAPTER TEN

AFTER THE FUSS Trey had made about walking her from the farmhouse to the barn those two nights—nights that felt like they'd happened a lifetime ago—Max was surprised to be left alone in the dust and the falling night. Fear wasn't the emotion making her eyes go wide—shock was. She whistled for Ashes and walked down the road to the farmhouse.

With the last of the sun disappearing into the horizon, winter chill fell fast. Humidity in the air meant it didn't much matter how warm the day had been because the damp sank through Max's shirt into her bones, spreading through her body like the dark was spreading across the sky.

Gravel crunched as she took steps in her heavy boots. Ashes's darting about made the little rocks skitter. None of the noises drowned out the irritation that had welled up over her fear. Why couldn't Trey think of his mother and what *her* dream for the farm had been instead of concentrating on Hank and his drunkenness? Or at the very least Trey could have come down to the farm *once* and seen his father sober. Hank had still been an asshole, but he'd been trying to make amends for the mistakes of his life.

Kelly was still at the farmhouse when she returned, waiting in the kitchen for her with a cup of tea. "Despite me fancying boys and Trey fancying girls, my brother was always the dramatic one."

Ashes sank down next to the heater, the bouts of youth he'd displayed outside gone for the night. Max took Kelly's unsaid apology along with the cup of tea. The mug was warm, burning the cold skin on her hands through the crockery. She welcomed the pain because tingles were a sign her hands would defrost and her fingers would soon not be numb. She shouldn't have gotten into Trey's car without gloves and a coat, but she hadn't expected to have to walk back to the farmhouse. Tonight's temperatures would be bitter and there'd be frost in the morning.

Kelly waited while she sipped her tea. The burn slid down her throat until it lit a fire in her belly and she was pissed. Pissed at Hank for squirreling away the will, pissed at Trey for his hatred of the land and pissed at herself for not taking better care of her future.

She doubted Trey would accept an offer to buy the land tomorrow, even if she could make one. There were too many strikes against her. He wanted the memory of the Harris farm blasted from the earth and buried under housing.

But she wasn't going down without a fight. Asking Kelly to contest the will and trying to show Trey what the land really meant were only the first shots fired. Trey had control of the land, but she was the one standing on it, and that had to count for something. Possession was nine-tenths of the law, as the saying went.

When the tea and the heat had warmed her, she asked Kelly the question she'd wondered as she'd walked home. "Why don't you share the same level of hate for the land as your brother?"

He shrugged. "Once puberty hit, the secret of my gayness wasn't so secret anymore. My dad caught me with a *Sports Illustrated* swimsuit edition—but it wasn't the actual swimsuit edition, and I was… Well, I was only *interested* in the pictures of male swimmers and divers." His voice got nostalgic and Max smiled. "Anyway, after that moment Dad made it clear I wasn't going to get any piece of the farm."

Kelly paused to pour more hot water into his cup and held out the kettle for Max. She shook her head, more interested in understanding the Harris family than in more tea.

"So I never got the chance to care or hope for something better out of this piece of land. Dad would always be disappointed in my choices. He would always find failure with me. I was always going to be the gay son. High school was hard, but home life was relatively easy because Dad ignored me. I knew I would never hear praise from his mouth, so the scorn hurt less." Kelly took a long slurp of his tea and Max was wondering if he was done with his story when he continued.

"It was different for Trey. Dad promised Trey things. Like if Trey spent a summer learning farming from Uncle Garner, Dad would quit drinking. If Trey made the football team, Dad would quit drinking. If Trey went to State for college instead of Carolina, Dad would quit drinking. The promise of approval was always there, but the actuality of it was further away for Trey than it probably was even for me."

"Different expectations of Hank." Kelly and Trey's father had been a different person during Max's years on the farm, but not a *completely* different person. He could be mean, spiteful and judgmental. He'd even tried to withhold his approval of her farming methods until it became clear to both of them that he was an ignorant fool about farming anything but tobacco. And unless they went back in time to farm tobacco in the 1960s, he probably didn't know anything about that, either.

But those bad qualities had always been tempered by a work ethic, a pleasure in seeing the land rise from the dead and a curiosity about the new breed of small farmer.

Alcohol would certainly kill all of Hank's good qualities, leaving him only the bad with which to torture his sons.

"We had different expectations of our father and he had different expectations of us." Kelly's eyes were sad as he said the words, mourning a lost childhood that could never be recovered.

Max digested what Kelly had said, especially in light of the relationship Kelly had had with his father before Hank's death and Trey's complete absence. "Knowing what I know about Hank sober, it's hard for me to believe life for you in this house was easier than it was for Trey."

"Being ignored left its own scars. I spent my college years pretending I was an escaped stereotype from San Francisco in the 1970s." Kelly shrugged. "Later, the novelty of hearing from Dad meant I was more willing to take his phone call. I guess we fit perfectly into the roles assigned us. The ignored kid runs back at the slightest hint of attention from the father figure, while the kid on whom all attention was paid turns a deaf ear to the ringing phone."

Max considered her mostly happy childhood. Her parents had divorced when she was in middle school. She'd stayed with her dad and she liked her stepmother okay, but her mom had also been around and taken an active part in her childhood. Her father was disappointed that she hadn't taken the path he'd chosen for her, but he wasn't angry. No one was an alcoholic and she wasn't in competition with her brother for attention. She should call them and thank them for being *normal*. And despite her anger at Trey, learning about his childhood gave her more respect and understanding for the man he was now.

"Do you think Trey would sell me the land if I asked?" The man Kelly described didn't give her much hope.

Kelly shook his head. "I don't know, honestly. There's more going on under his fancy clothes than just his anger at our father. He's jealous of you."

His words surprised Max enough that she had to catch her cup before it fell after setting it too close to the edge of the counter. By the time "Why would he be jealous?" left her mouth, she had her answer. "He's mad because Hank made promises to me, and at least made the attempt at keeping them." If he'd really kept his promise, the Harris brothers wouldn't be looking for the will, but Hank had probably come closer to keeping a promise to her than he'd ever come to keeping his word to Trey.

"Yes. I doubt you can offer him enough money to make up for Dad being a better father to you than he was to his own kids."

The truth of the words pushed Max against the counter, the edge digging into her back.

"I don't mean to discourage you," Kelly said, "and I'm happy to help convince him, but I don't know if it's possible. Trey and I were always jealous of what the other got from our father and we were never really able to be friends. My words might not have much effect."

She nodded, because really, what else could she do? "Do you want to stay for dinner?"

"No. I have a date tonight." Kelly gave her a wry smile. "Always on the hunt for love."

"I hope you find it."

Despite the seeming hopelessness of the situation, Max skipped dinner in favor of opening her laptop and making calculations about her finances. She had to believe that Trey could make the right decision.

MAX WAS WAITING for Trey when he drove up, Ashes at her side. Her dog could always read her mood, and he didn't greet Trey with a wag of his tail, but neither did he growl. They were both nervous and didn't want to piss off an already angry man.

"I'm sorry for driving off in anger," he said, by way of greeting, his hand out in offering.

"Um, good morning." She didn't tell him it wasn't a big deal, even though she was perfectly capable of walking around the farm in the dark. Trey had talked enough about his mother's views on how a gentleman treated a lady that she knew driving off had been a big deal to him. She slipped her hand in his. He had nice hands. With few calluses, they were the hands of a banker or a lawyer, but he had a firm grip that tingled her toes. "Apology accepted."

She pulled her hand away before his touch overwhelmed her senses.

"I'm glad you're out waiting for me, though I didn't expect you to be."

"After last night? I'm not a sulker." He blinked, but otherwise didn't respond. "Besides, I have a question for you." After she'd gone over her finances and decided it would be possible, she'd debated how to approach Trey with her proposal. Eventually, she'd decided it would be better to ask early in the morning, before she lost her courage. "Do you want to come in for a cup of coffee?"

"Sure." His manner was open and curious, so Max upped the odds of her success a bit.

Once in the kitchen, she poured him a cup. He turned down milk and sugar. As he sat, his dark eyes scanned the financial calculations on the table. He didn't say a word, just watched her with a steady gaze as she sat down.

"If you want to sell the farm, let me be the one to buy it from you."

"Do you have the money?"

This was the sticking point. "No. In three years I will. That's why Hank was going to add in the condition of the lease to his will, because I've always planned to buy the farm. I just need that extra time."

Mentioning Hank and his promises was a strategic error on her part. His face darkened to match his eyes and the curiosity was gone. "Your offer today is no different from what you said last night. I don't want to sell the farm in three years. I want to sell it now."

"We can write the lease so that I either buy the farm in three years or lose it to someone else. It will be sold in all but actuality."

"No." The word was frosty, like the tips of the grasses outside her kitchen window.

"If you're worried I won't be able to afford the land in three years, I have the figures here on the table."

Max watched the muscles of Trey's throat move as he drained the entire cup of coffee then looked at her with a sour face. "I'm not sure I can make this clearer. I want the land out of my hands. If you can make me the same offer as the developer, I'll take it. Otherwise, I'm selling. Even if we find the will, I'll pay whatever it costs to break the lease. I didn't want this land yesterday. I'm not going to want this land tomorrow and I sure as hell don't still want to be holding on to it in three years."

"Even if we…" Trey's words hung in midair for several seconds before crashing, like Wile E. Coyote dropping off a cliff, only not funny. The farm was gone. All her work washed away in the torrent of his anger.

Five years ago, she'd agreed to move across the country to farm land sight unseen, and her worst-case scenario was now her reality.

Max took a drink of coffee, but the acid burned down her stomach until she was afraid she would vomit. She looked across the table at Trey, part of her thinking it would serve him right if she ralphed her breakfast on his shiny shoes, part of her worried about showing weakness in front of him.

He sat there looking at her as if he hadn't just jerked the rug out from under her after backing her up to the edge of a cliff. The slight scruff of his beard she'd found attractive over Hank's funeral now looked like the dark smoke of the devil, but calling him the devil gave him more power than he had. Max gritted her teeth at the truth. Under his collared shirt and sweater vest was an angry little boy who'd never forgive Hank for being a terrible father.

It took Kelly opening the door and walking into the kitchen for Max to realize the pounding hadn't been in her head but footsteps on the back porch. "Oh, good, coffee's made. I'd like a cup before we continue looking for the will."

She only had the energy to nod at Kelly before tossing her mug into the sink and calling for Ashes. Working the ground would be the only solace she'd find right now, even if the land wouldn't be hers after December.

TREY WATCHED MAX storm out of the kitchen, her shoulder blades sharp against the thin cotton of her

T-shirt as she rolled her shoulders against the truth. Better to be honest with her. Promising to care about what the new, probably nonexistent, will said would only make the truth hurt more later. Much like "I'll quit drinking," saying "I'll think about selling you the farm" would be offering a promise he never intended to keep.

The cabinet door banged shut and Trey turned to see Kelly pour himself a cup of coffee. His brother hadn't bothered to knock on the back door but had walked in like he owned the place. Trey thought back to yesterday, when Kelly had also been comfortable in the house. Maybe not like an owner, but like an old family friend. Which was odd, because he'd never been comfortable in the house when they were kids. Neither of them had, but while Trey escaped to the fields to avoid tirades, Kelly had lurked around the rooms in corners, like a dog expecting to be kicked. Trey didn't know what was more tragic—that Kelly would have taken a strike from their father if it meant he got attention or that their father couldn't even find his son worthy of abuse.

Steam rose from Kelly's coffee cup, swirling around his brother's face before disappearing into the cold kitchen air. "What's up with you and Max?" Trey knew it was stupid to ask, stupid to be jealous of Kelly, especially as Trey would never mean more to Max than the man who ripped her land away from her. But he asked anyway.

"Gay men can't have female friends?"

Trey ran his hand over the back of his neck before saying "That's not what I meant." Which was true. But if Kelly had asked him what he meant, Trey wouldn't have had an answer. All he knew was that for the rest of the year, Kelly would get to spend time with Max while Trey was busy selling her hard work to a developer from two hundred and fifty miles away.

"Never mind."

Kelly made a face as he took a sip. "It's a wonder Max has any taste buds left. She makes terrible coffee." When he drained the last of his coffee, he shook his head as if he needed the extra help to get the beverage down. "Are you ready to go find the will?"

No, but he didn't say that. Trey would rather be with Max, even if she contemplated his death the entire time they spent together. But they needed to either find the will or determine to Kelly's satisfaction that it no longer existed. And Trey wanted to do that as quickly as possible.

"Sure."

BY FOUR O'CLOCK they'd been through every box in the attic and had not found a will. His father had apparently boxed up and saved all his *Playboy* magazines and they'd found letters from long-dead relatives his mother must have kept, but the single document they sought was nowhere to be found.

Trey sat back on his heels and rubbed his face, wishing he'd shaved this morning. All this crap belonged to him and he wouldn't be able to sell the land until he cleaned it out. The developer wasn't Max; he couldn't leave the stuff in boxes in the attic for the magical time in the future when he was ready to deal with it.

"Do you want any of this stuff before I finalize the sale?" he asked Kelly.

"You're still going through with it?"

"You can only contest the will so long as it's reasonable to think a new one might be stashed somewhere." Trey gestured to the boxes, some still open, scattered around the attic. "I'll even grant you that Dad made a new will, but he didn't stash it anywhere. He probably tore it up during some drunken rage."

"Dad had quit drinking."

"That's what he claims, but hitting a tree in daylight on a road he'd driven at least twice a day since he was tall enough to reach the pedals? You can't tell me he was sober."

Kelly looked at Trey like *he* was the confused one, not Kelly. "He wasn't drunk. Dad had a heart attack."

Aunt Lois had said the same thing when she'd called Trey to tell him his father was dead. "Not you, too. The man's dead. We don't have to tiptoe around his pride anymore." Trey's laugh was hollow.

"Dad stopped drinking when Mom got sick."

Trey laughed harder, the air coming out of his throat in painful gasps. During their mom's illness, he'd also believed their father when he said he was sober. The constant smog of stale booze that had surrounded his old man for as long as Trey could remember was gone and his father's face had lost some of its fleshy redness. But…

Trey had to wait until he'd gotten control over his guffaws before he could speak again. "He was drunk at Mom's funeral." He took a deep breath. "It's nice that Dad died in a car accident so we don't have to pretend it wasn't liver failure, but he broke that promise *again*. And had so little respect for Mom that he broke it at her funeral."

The second round of the laughter wedged in his throat at the pity on Kelly's face.

"Maybe it's easier to cleave yourself from this land if you hold on to lies, but do you think I could stand coming around the farm if Dad was still a drunk? It took him thirty years, but he kept this one promise."

The stale air of the attic bore down on his shoulders. Before he suffocated, Trey stood and went downstairs. Back in the woods, nature having almost taken over, were the falling-down shacks laborers had used before he was born. Trey had hidden from his father's lies in those houses all through his childhood. Feeling like he was nine years old again when he still believed in miracles, he left the farmhouse for the shacks and whatever black widows lurked inside them.

CHAPTER ELEVEN

MAX ADDED HORSE manure from a nearby stable into one of her compost windrows, even though this windrow wouldn't be ready for use before she had to leave the farm. She backed her tractor up and added another scoop of manure, noting on her clipboard which pile she was adding it to and how much of it she was adding. Habit more than anything else kept her noting how many turns she gave each pile and checking the number of turns against the National Organic Program stipulations and her recipe. No one would be on this farm to use the tended compost. The developer wouldn't care that she'd managed the compost heaps with the same amount of attention a vintner gives his wine; he'd see piles of rotting shit and do away with it.

Could she take the compost with her? Assuming, of course, that she had somewhere to go, which she didn't.

Her father's farm was always available to her, but she wasn't interested in conventional farming. It was a science and she preferred the art. She also preferred working a farm where birds felt safe to nest amongst her trellises. Her mom was a closer refuge. Her mom would tell her that embracing the experience would make her a stronger person, but Max didn't have the patience for that right now.

She had plenty of farmer friends who could take her compost, if she could get it to them and figure out the regulations that applied to moving compost from one farm to another—because there were sure to be regulations. And come the end of summer, what else would she have to do but haul truckloads of compost off to her friends?

Had she already given up? Max stopped her tractor midturn. Did she continue with the meticulous record keeping and work of farming or did she call it quits?

The wind shifted directions. She could tell by the scent the breeze carried on its back that the compost was maturing well. When she finished turning all the piles, she'd stick thermometers into them and record their temperatures into her little book. At night, it would just be her and Ashes and she'd transfer all that information to her Excel spreadsheet, where she had five years' worth of composting data. If she didn't do it for the future of the land, she'd be doing it for her own satisfaction.

Mother Nature had originally drawn her to organic farming, and she wasn't about to shirk the woman because some man threatened to take the dream away. With the finality of that thought, Max shifted the tractor back into gear and turned the pile again.

TREY WAS WAITING for her when she got back to the packing shed to park the tractor. For the first time since she'd met him, he looked dirty. Trey had packed up Hank's filthy house and not gotten a spot of dust on his nose but now—Max blinked—he had red clay on the knees of his jeans and the ball of a sweet gum tree stuck in his hair. He was leaning up against the wall of the shed, his knee bent and foot flat against the wood. Stick a piece of straw in his mouth and cowboy hat on his head and he'd look like an escapee from some cowboy movie. He already walked like he'd been on a horse for too long.

She ignored him and her negative thoughts as she walked around to unhook the front-end loader attachment from her tractor. Trey didn't really walk like he'd been sitting on a horse for too long. Just because she wanted to shove a stick up his ass right now didn't mean she didn't like the way he walked. And just because she liked the way he walked didn't mean she couldn't dream of dropping the front-end loader on his head.

"I was watching you," he said as he pushed off the wall, "as you did whatever it was you were doing with the dirt."

"Compost. I was turning the compost."

"You stopped for a long time, then started again. Why?"

She didn't trust him. "Thirsty."

"You didn't drink anything."

"Hungry."

"You didn't eat anything."

"I had to pee." She enunciated each word, in case he missed the irritation on her face.

"Did you have a thunder jug in the tractor and I missed you using it? Because while I'm not into that sort of thing, I'm really curious about the physics of it."

Max felt her face go hot and knew she was fifteen colors of red, seventeen if she included her freckles. "What I really mean to say is that it's none of your business."

"Do you believe in God?"

Honestly, if he wasn't the most calculating person she'd ever met, she'd say he was nuts. "I'm sure that's *not* any of your business, either."

"What's important to you? What will you swear on?"

She opened her mouth to tell him to piss off then noticed the intensity of his eyes. "Those compost piles are important to me. The garlic I've got in the ground and am waiting to sprout. The plants slowly unfurling in the greenhouse." This time her face was hot from anger rather than embarrassment and her blood boiled and rolled through her body to match. "This whole damn farm is important to me, which you know and you're selling it anyway."

He shook his head and Max couldn't tell if the rise of his mouth was irritation, amusement or both. "If piles of rotting shit are what you want to swear on, you can swear on them. Did my father drink?"

"If he did, he hid it well. I never saw him."

"He'd never hidden it well before. I don't know why he would start."

"I know Hank was an alcoholic. He never made a secret out of it and he warned me no alcohol would be allowed on the property if I wanted to farm it. As far as I know, neither of us ever broke that rule."

Trey turned from her and walked away. She went back to her tasks in the packing shed, certain he was leaving, when she heard his voice again. "I'll sell you the farm."

"In three years?"

"No. Kelly said Dad quit drinking and I believe him and you, but I still don't want to own this farm any longer than I have to. When your lease is up, I'll give you right of first refusal."

Max thought about her compost piles and the investment they were to the future of the land. And she wished they were the kind of investment that she could cash out. "Even if I do get a mortgage, I won't be able to afford to pay you what the developer can offer."

"I'm not asking for you to match their offer. We can figure out what a fair market value is."

She put her hand on her chest and leaned against the wall, decisions pounding in her ears. Her heart alternated between racing for some unknown starting gate and slowing down to a crawl as she debated whether this was good or bad news. Planning and working for the farm only to have it not happen might be worse than planning to pick up and move in December. Not just a dream deferred, but a dream ripped out of her grasp because she didn't have the strength to hold on.

He walked toward her with the slow, purposeful stride she had admired. The clay mud patches on his jeans had dried and they cracked with each step. Her eyes traveled up his body, noting each imperfection in his clothing that hadn't been there this morning.

She didn't know how someone should react to the news that their father had stopped drinking. Trey had apparently reacted to it by falling to his knees in prayer. Or sliding down a hill.

After pausing to wonder how he was going to get the pine needles out of his sweater, she met his gaze. Like this morning, his eyes were dark and steady.

"I'll think about it," she finally said.

"Think about it?" Now his face showed a reaction and it was easy to read. He was angry, though he had the same tight control over his voice that he'd had over his eyes. "This morning you were begging me to sell you the farm, and now you'll think about it?"

"If you had looked at the spreadsheets this morning, you'd have seen I have a plan and it doesn't have me buying the farm for another three years. I'm not sure if I can afford it by December or if I'll even get close enough to qualify for a mortgage. Before I promise either of us this solution, I want to run the numbers."

Her words washed the anger off his face and he nodded. "I'll help you."

"Run the numbers?"

"Find a mortgage. Manage your money. Whatever it takes so that you can afford the farm by December."

She knew how to manage her own money, but the help would be nice. When harvesting started, she would barely be awake long enough at the end of each day to record everything in her spreadsheets, much less spend the time looking for a mortgage. Passing on that burden would be a relief.

"Why? Why did you change your mind?"

Trey looked away and Max didn't think he would answer. When he began to talk, the crack in his voice was the only indication that he felt anything. "When I was kid, all I ever wanted was for my daddy to quit drinking. I made regular deals with God about what I would do if he stopped. Each time I learned about a different religion, I made a bargain with their god, too, just in case. Once, when I learned what paganism actually meant, I made a bargain to become a farmer and worship Mother Nature if Daddy quit drinking." He looked at her—through her—and his eyes were hot enough to make her shiver. "The time for me to be a farmer has passed, but it seems like I would still be keeping my promise if I sold you the farm."

Max searched his face for sincerity. She found it, but she didn't know how much to trust it. Still, this was a gift horse and looking it in the mouth would be stupid. If he wasn't sincere, she wouldn't be any worse off and maybe she could use the time to convince him of the farm's worth.

"I'll still need to look over my finances before I agree."

This time it looked like he was assessing her face for sincerity. Whatever he found made him nod. "Okay. I'll even give you a week to fully explore your options before telling me yes or no."

A week to research other financing options and then nine months to buy the farm. She could do this. It wasn't in her plan, but she could still do this. She marched over to be directly in front of him and stuck out her hand. "Done."

When the side of his mouth kicked up this time, she knew it was with pleasure. He looked her straight in the eye, took her hand in his firm grip and gave a steady shake. "Till next week, then."

Despite the jolt his hand sent down her spine, she was also shaking on the finality of a relationship based on anything other than friendship. It was simpler this way, less risky.

Trey turned back to the woods, to whatever path had brought him to her packing shed, leaving Max with the uncomfortable feeling of missing the warmth of his hand in hers.

CHAPTER TWELVE

TREY SAT IN his office at his computer. The intensity with which he stared at his screen probably made it look like he was doing work. But instead of researching statistics from the home state of the congressman whose staffer he was meeting for lunch, he was looking at the Carolina Farmers Association website.

At his request, Max had emailed him some financial information so he could evaluate the options available to her. She was right—she didn't have enough money to get a mortgage by December. Included in her email had been a link to a *News and Observer* article about farmers trading work for equity.

It was a nice idea, but he didn't want to wait out three years with her paying him rent, nor did he want to wait out the time it would take her to earn equity in the land. He wanted it gone.

So why was he spending so much time looking at a farming website and thinking about the farmer?

Trey clicked over to his email and scrolled down to the first message Max had sent him. The picture of her and the farm popped up on his desktop and he maximized the image so it took up his entire screen. Bullshit about deities he didn't believe in aside, Max was the reason he wasn't going to sell the land to the developer—and that was if he was being polite. If he was being honest, he had seen enough of her body to want to see more, without clothing hindering his view.

Helping Max buy her dream lessened the sleaze-ball feelings that had crept down his neck when fantasies of taking off her clothes had interrupted his plans to sell her life away. Now he could pretend to forgive his father, help a small farmer gain more security and undress Max in his mind.

Trey understood conflicting motivations and how emotions and good intentions could be manipulated by shiny objects. Max was Trey's shiny object. He never would have believed that he'd be lusting after a woman in muddy work boots, but he also never would have believed he'd want to make the five-hour drive from D.C. to Durham to spend time on the family farm. But here he was, sitting at his desk thinking about driving to talk with her, rather than doing all this by email like a sane person. If he wasn't honest with himself about his attraction to her and how that attraction could alter his decision-making process, he would act against his better interest.

Trey clicked the link for a Durham credit union.

The credit union offered favorable rates and had a low barrier for entry, not to mention that their entire purpose was to help local businesses like Max's Vegetable Patch. But Max still didn't have what she needed. Even if Trey didn't charge her rent until December, she probably wouldn't get there. Her income seemed decent, if not steady. She kept her costs down, but both her income and her costs were variable. Trey had winced when he'd seen her tractor repair bill from last year.

Maybe he could extend her lease. He didn't need the money and she was a low-maintenance tenant. She would sign the document and he'd be able to ignore her while collecting a monthly rent check. Not needing the money meant he could lower her rent and she'd be able to buy the land sooner. Not by December, but sooner than three years. He sat back in his chair and clicked over to the picture of her again, before hurriedly clicking back to the credit union's website, angry at his own hubris.

He would never be able to ignore her.

Being a manipulator of people's emotions and interests didn't make him immune from being manipulated by his own. He was determined to act *only* in his own best interest, but he didn't know what his best interest was anymore. Max's smiling face and the teeming greenery behind her made him wonder if she *was* his best interest. But she came with the farm.

Selling the farm over to Max meant accepting a complete break in their relationship. He wouldn't have any excuse to email her or go down to North Carolina. His best interest, Max's best interest, ended their relationship, which he didn't want, either.

Making him a whiny child unwilling to let go of a toy he didn't want any longer.

His best interest was to stay true to himself. He could sell the land to Max, feel like he'd done the right thing for the little person and get on with the rest of his life.

He needed to find another way for Max to raise money.

WHEN TREY'S PHONE buzzed in his pocket on his way to his apartment from the metro station, his first inclination was to ignore it. This week felt like it had been a month long and he still had tomorrow's shit to deal with. Sure, tonight's fund-raiser sounded like fun—and probably would be fun—but it was also work. Since he'd gotten back from North Carolina, everything seemed like work and all work seemed like a chore. He needed to shift his focus back on his goal—keeping out of North Carolina—not on some freckled farmer. Responsibility got the better of him and he dug his phone out of his coat pocket.

The 919 area code was unexpected.

"Trey Harris," he answered.

"Trey," Jerome's voice boomed through the phone. "Kelly didn't think you'd answer a phone call from the Triangle area code. He owes me five dollars."

"Jerome, hello." Trey stopped his trod through the slush. He and Jerome emailed occasionally, but they were not in the habit of talking to one another over the phone. "I didn't expect to hear your voice on the other end of the line."

"I'm fixin' to offer you basketball tickets."

"Oh, that's great, but I really can't get away from work right now."

Jerome chuckled. "What, you're washing your hair *that* weekend? You don't even know what I'm offering."

Whatever it was, Jerome's offer required crossing into North Carolina. "Basketball games are great but…"

"Duke at the Dean Dome."

Trey leaned against a nearby building and tried to parse what Jerome was saying. "You're inviting me to the Carolina-Duke game in Chapel Hill," he clarified. It was the biggest game of the basketball season, aside from the Carolina-Duke game played in Durham. "What's the catch?"

"Why does there have to be a catch?" Jerome asked after a moment of silence, which meant there was definitely a catch. Probably a grappling hook. Or a harpoon.

"Both teams are good this year, so even assuming you have seats behind a giant screen in the upper deck, you could sell those tickets for at least five hundred dollars. But you're calling me out of the blue to offer them to me. Do you need a kidney?"

"With your dad dead, you have no reason to visit North Carolina until Kelly gets married—whenever that happens." Having to wait on the state to repeal an amendment banning gay marriage meant Trey might never have to visit North Carolina after he sold the farm. And he could do all the farm paperwork from D.C.

"I didn't visit North Carolina when my dad was alive."

If Jerome heard him, he ignored him. "I thought I'd use basketball tickets to bribe you to visit Chapel Hill, and Alea didn't think you'd take anything less than Duke tickets. So Duke tickets it is. The game is next Friday, 9:00 p.m."

Trey didn't need to be told when the game was. Duke-Carolina games were a part of his circadian rhythm. "And Alea doesn't want to go?"

"She's seven months pregnant and has no interest in small stadium seats or watching college kids sweat."

"And she thinks I'll drive down for the Duke game?" Who was he kidding? Of course he'd drive down for the Duke game.

"If you want to argue with Alea."

"No, I'm not stupid. Especially not when she's pregnant." Jerome's wife had been a lawyer before deciding to stay at home with their kids, and the only thing she loved more than her family was a good argument. Debates, she called them. Trey had only met her a couple of times and, if he was being generous to himself, their *debates* had been a draw. The only one Trey could even pretend he might have won was the one on education reform.

Jerome chuckled. "It's agreed, then. You can park at my house. We'll get dinner and take a bus to the stadium."

Trey had been efficiently backed into a corner and rewarded for it, but he still couldn't believe he was driving south for another weekend. Still, he'd have to make sure he stopped at the farm on his way and check on his tenant.

CHAPTER THIRTEEN

Two WEEKS AFTER deciding to buy her land, Max was unloading bales of straw from her truck with her new intern when she saw what looked like Trey's car come down the road. It was all she could do not to drop a bale on her foot when the sedan eased to a stop next to the farmhouse. She went back to her straw bale, still doubting it was Trey but not knowing who else it could be.

"Aren't you going to see who it is?" Sean asked.

"If it's who I think it is, he'll come find me."

Sean gave her a curious look, but didn't press the matter. He'd only been working here a week, but that wasn't the reason he allowed her privacy. Sean was a nut no squirrel could crack, and he offered Max the same opportunity to cling to her secrets. Sidney and Norma Jean—her third intern, an older woman who was thinking of starting a farm with her husband—generally chatted while working, but Sean had no use for small talk. Or any talk. Max knew he had big plans for his future in farming because she'd asked about them during the interview. But short of being required to share information to get a job, he wasn't going to expose any part of himself.

She preferred his silences when they were comfortable, but he was a hard worker and had found his hustle by day three, so she didn't begrudge him the uncomfortable silences, either. Farming didn't require conversation skills and he'd not yet broken her rule about not being able to get along with an employee.

Max wiped moisture off her brow with a handkerchief from her pocket. The sky was overcast and the air was cool, but she'd worked up a sweat unloading hay bales.

Ashes announced the arrival of Trey, who was walking toward them. Half a Friday at work plus several hours in the car and Trey still looked like a men's magazine cover model. Through his open coat she saw that his suit was a dark navy with a subtle pattern to it, though there was nothing subtle about the magenta check pattern on his shirt. Instead of looking fussy, he managed to look sleek. And as out of place on her farm as a banker coming to foreclose.

Knowing that he yelled at the television during basketball games and hid in the woods when he was upset, even as an adult, meant that she knew intimacies about him beyond the expensive clothes. Vulnerabilities that made the self-assured man striding toward her more impressive, because she knew the confidence had come through hard work and the composure through careful study.

Max greeted Trey and introduced him to Sean, who shook Trey's hand before going back to his work as though both of them had disappeared from his consciousness.

"What are you down here for?" she asked Trey. She shoved her dirty hands into her pockets before she could give in to her desire to touch his arm. She shouldn't feel this pull toward him, especially when they hadn't shared anything more intimate than her spontaneous kiss of his cheek.

"A friend offered me Duke tickets."

Clarification was unnecessary. A person would have to be living in a chasm not to know about the game. Or keep themselves purposefully ignorant. While getting gas this morning, she'd had to wait to pay until the customer in front of her and the clerk could finish their conversation about defensive strategy against the fast break. Both had been Duke fans, so at least she hadn't had to wait for them to debate which team was better.

"Anyway, I thought I'd stop by to see how my—what was it you called this piece of dirt?—my *ancestral landholding* was doing." His neck stretched a little when he lifted his head to look around. His strong jawline was slightly darkened with stubble from the day.

"Do you want another tour?"

"What?" He jerked his head back to her. "No, I thought I'd just look around."

That's what a tour would be. She bit her tongue.

"It doesn't look much different than it did when I left."

Max blinked several times at how easily he had wiped away her hard work. Then she looked around and tried to see it from his eyes. Everything she'd planted was in the greenhouse waiting for transplant. The fields visible from the driveway looked different to her than they had just two days ago, but that was because she'd started preparing them for planting. To her eyes, the soil looked eager.

"It's not going to look like it did in the picture until summer."

"Yeah," he drawled with an embarrassed smile, "as a country boy, you'd think I'd know that."

Maybe that was what was bothering him—he'd been removed from this land for years, maybe since he was a teenager, and suddenly it was his. Trey didn't strike her as the kind of person willing to be ignorant of anything he had a hand in—even if he was trying to take his hand out.

"The offer of a tour is still available."

"No, I should get going. I need to find a place to stay."

"You're not staying with Kelly?"

"Kelly has a one-bedroom apartment." He shook his head. "No, I'll get a hotel room."

"You could stay here." Max gulped, but the words were said and couldn't be unsaid. She looked at him out of the corner of her eye, trying to get a read on how he took her invitation. Given that weeks ago when she'd been working up the courage to kiss him he'd walked off her front porch and driven away, he wouldn't take her words as anything more than an invitation to sleep in the guest bed. Which was how she'd meant it. But now…her fingers twitched inside her pockets.

She shrugged and tried to fake nonchalance. "It may be too far a drive from the farm to Chapel Hill, but I've got a spare bedroom. It used to be your room, in fact."

Again she wished she could take back the words and replace them with something else—in this case a more explicit invitation, good sense be damned. Just because she'd gone back to the dark ages in farming technology didn't mean she couldn't be a modern woman and just come out and put the moves on a man she was attracted to. *Hey, Trey, last time you were here, I didn't invite you up to my bed like I wanted to and I'd like to correct that mistake.*

Maybe she should say something less direct. "It's still the same bed and mattress, but there are new sheets and I'm calling it a guest room."

God help her, she was a coward.

Trey's phone rang, saving her the embarrassment of having him turn down her offer. He seemed like a polite man; he probably wouldn't have pointed out that the hotel room would offer him a more enticing bed than a fifteen-year-old full-size mattress with new sheets. Maybe she should have pointed out that she bought new pillows.

He was sighing heavily as he put his phone back into his pocket, but his eyes were bright and interested. "How would you like to see some hustle tonight?"

"What?"

The side of his mouth lifted in a wry smile. "Jerome has a stomach bug that's apparently sweeping across his campus. I now have tickets to the hottest game in town and no one to go with."

Huh. "Wouldn't Kelly want to go?"

"Kelly's an NC State fan. He'd root for the court to develop a crater and for all the Duke and Carolina players to fall in. At least you're a mostly neutral party."

Max knew pretty much every native North Carolinian had an allegiance to one of the big basketball schools. Even the ones who didn't care about basketball came from a "Duke family" or a "Carolina family." She'd thought Kelly didn't care about basketball and Max hadn't been interested enough to ask, though she knew Hank had been a State fan.

"Can I wear my Illinois T-shirt?"

Trey's responding laugh was incredibly satisfying, relaxing his entire body as if the pressure of being back on the family farm had been lifted from his shoulders.

"I was just going to buy you dinner," he said through his smile, "but we'll stop somewhere along the way and buy you a Carolina shirt, too."

THE SKY-BLUE Carolina T-shirt looked terrible with Max's orange hair. If Trey was going to be poetic, he'd say it was like the sun in a summer sky. If he was being honest, he'd say it looked like a child threw blue paint on a canvas and then spilled the orange paint on top. As absurd a color clash as she was, the enjoyment he felt sitting next to her in the stadium was more ridiculous. When he'd handed her the shirt, she'd promised to be the loudest, proudest Carolina fan in the stands. And her follow-through was amazing; she was putting the college kids to shame.

Every time she jumped to her feet to cheer, he had a moment of panic that her nachos or drink would spill onto his lap. The one time he mentioned his fear to her she followed an elbow to his side with "Watch the game. Let me worry about my snacks." But she held his gaze for longer than necessary before she turned her attention back to the game, leaving him to wonder if she also thought the energy in the stadium was more than just about the excited crowd.

He tried to be attentive to the action on court. The

problem was that watching boys barely out of high
school run held no competition to the color explo-
sion bouncing up and down next to him. If Carolina
was lucky, they'd score layups over the Duke de-
fense. If Trey was lucky, Max would turn to him, a
smile on her face. Those eyes were just as stunning
when she was clapping her hands in the midst of the
heat of the stadium as when she'd been defying him
to question her presence on the farm in the chill of
a sunny winter's day. A couple times she stood up
to cheer and her breasts bounced right at eye level.

What the hell am I doing here?

Imagining those eyes fixed on his while she
straddled him, her breasts bouncing in his hands,
was enough to make him wish *he* could dump her
cold drink on his lap.

What the hell am I doing here, thinking that?
Nothing but complication lay down that road. He
was going to sell her the farm and be done with anyone and anything south of Richmond. D.C. was full
of attractive women. He'd concentrate on thinking
lustful thoughts about them. On Monday.

The students sitting next to him pitched forward,
their fists in the air as they leaped to their feet and
the Dean Dome erupted with jeers. A foul had been
called on Carolina.

Small scuffles erupted on the court as players
jostled one another a little too roughly. Beside him,
Max whistled and booed, stamped and clapped. All

he could think about was when she was going to brush up against him again.

The game was close. This was the last year playing college ball for some of the star players on the court and they seemed determined to make this last home game against Duke a game to remember. Trey's coworkers, no matter which college basketball team they rooted for, would ask how the game was. And Trey's response would be "Fine," while thinking, *The woman next to me was amazing!*

He had to look at one of the big-screen TVs to see why the crowd leaped to its feet this time and why Max held her hands over her head, the cotton of her T-shirt catching on the underside of her breasts and peaking at her nipples. Fortunately, they ran the replay twice. A Carolina player had attempted a high pass, which was blocked by a Duke player and went in for a Carolina basket. The euphoria following such an unexpected play carried through a steal for another Carolina basket. Chapel Hill's downtown would be packed with drunken students. He was glad not to be in his twenties and to be heading back to the peace of Max's farmhouse instead of to the post-game drunken celebration on Franklin Street.

Trey couldn't wait for the last five minutes of the game to finish.

When the game was finally over and he was singing the alma mater while walking down the stairs behind Max, Trey considered how the evening would end. He knew how he *wanted* it to end. Despite her rapt attention on the game, he was pretty sure how Max wanted the night to end. And not because she'd invited him to sleep at the farmhouse tonight. He had tried but been unable to forget how the color of her eyes had changed as she'd stared at him as he stood on the barn porch.

Or maybe he was making shit up so there would be a pleasant aspect to sleeping in the farmhouse tonight.

They crammed on a bus with what felt like a million other people, everyone hyped about the win over Duke. What space wasn't taken up by bodies was taken up by excitement, tinged with anticipation. For the thousands streaming toward Franklin Street, the night was just beginning. Durham, eight miles down the road and home to Duke University, would be silent.

Trey remembered how much fun wins over Duke had been and how eager he'd been to be a part of the jostling crowd. One morning after a game, his mama had called him at 5:00 a.m., pulling him into a hangover he'd been trying to sleep through, to yell at him for jumping over a bonfire. She'd seen him on the nightly news. He'd been young and certain of the righteousness of his desire to get the hell out of Carolina, confident he'd never come back.

The bus bounced over a pothole and Max bounced into him. He wrapped his arm around her waist to steady her and lowered his face to her knit hat. His raised arm keeping *him* steady on the bus was falling asleep and with the heat of the masses and his winter coat he was roasting, but the feel of Max held tightly against him was worth the burn.

The car ride home gave him plenty of time to think about the significance of wanting Max. On one level, his desire was easy to explain away. While her skin was too freckled, her hair was too orange and her eyes were too pale to be called pretty, she was mesmerizing, like some kind of fierce farmland sprite. She was fun to hang out with and he respected her work ethic. He'd be a lonely fool for the rest of his life to want anything more in a woman.

But the wanting was ill conceived. She wasn't some woman he was picking up in a bar and taking home for mutual pleasure. She was living in the farmhouse and farming land he owned. Whether they wanted it to or not, their relationship would last long past the orgasms. She might have expectations of him. Hell, he liked her enough personally to have expectations of himself.

If they were going to have sex, it was going to be complicated sex.

He downshifted to a stop, looking both ways for cars and deer. He should really do the right thing and go up to the guest room and toss and turn on the ancient mattress with new sheets. Max's mattress was probably no better, even if it did have Max on it.

They parked beside the farmhouse and he waited with Max while she let Ashes out into the yard. The dog came back in, went up to Max for a pat on the head and returned to his bed in the living room next to one of the baseboard heaters. When Max looked at him, eyes warm and wanting, he knew he would make the wrong decision. If she asked, if she even stepped forward with her hand out in invitation, he would end up in her bed instead of his own.

CHAPTER FOURTEEN

MAX HEARD ASHES huff as he collapsed in a heap on his bed. *Now or never, Maxine.* Tomorrow Trey would get in his car and drive back to D.C. She had let her cowardice get the better of her once and he'd walked away. If she wanted to wake up in the morning, look at a handsome man in her bed and think, *Look who I did,* she had to make more of a move than she'd made before.

She wasn't asking him for forever.

When he turned to face her, good-night forming on his lips, she took a step forward, reaching for him. This time, instead of turning away from her, he took a step toward her, too, his arm out and mirroring hers. Neither of them said a word. He lowered his lips to hers and the decision was made.

His skin was warm in the chill of the farmhouse. Despite the hard planes of his face and the scratch of his stubble, his lips were soft. His grip was firm on her waist, his fingers digging into the muscles of her belly, though the pressure was pleasurable.

He pulled back a couple inches and she leaned into him. Right now, she wanted to follow him wherever he would take her. He put his fingers to her lips before she pressed them against his for another kiss. "I want you." He paused. "Wanting you doesn't change that I will sell this farm and never return to North Carolina again."

She pushed his fingers away from her face with one hand and dug the other into the hair at the nape of his neck, pulling him back down to her. "I know. That's one of the things I like so much about you," she said, kissing him. He opened his mouth again—maybe to say something, maybe not—and Max ran her tongue around the edges of his teeth.

Together, they stumbled through the living room to her bedroom, barely missing Ashes and banging into one of the doorjambs along the way. Walking while kissing and trying to fumble with the buttons on Trey's shirt was going to get one of them hurt, but she didn't care. Especially when she got access to his undershirt and, with one yank, had his shirts off and full access to the hot ridges of his stomach.

The backs of his knees hit the bed and he fell backward, with her on top and a loud "oof" escaping his lips. "I should complete the Tar Heel fan fantasy and leave your shirt on," Trey said while pulling her T-shirt up and over her head. "But I've been wondering about a certain line of freckles since you stood in the kitchen wearing that low-cut top."

Once her shirt was off, he rolled her over onto her

back so that he was on top. A rush of cold air blasted her chest—bare except for her bra. She wanted this. She wanted him. Her bedside lamp flickered on and she blinked into the sudden brightness. Trey kissed a freckle in the indentation at the base of her neck. She tensed with anticipation. "If I don't follow that path of freckles," he said as he kissed his way down her sternum to the line of her bra, "I think I'll be lost forever."

The warmth of his lips against her cold skin sent shivers down her spine. The silliness she'd enjoyed in him while watching basketball was evident as he kissed patterns in her freckles around her chest and stomach, naming each one. A butterfly. A baseball bat. A crocodile. Like finding constellations in the sky, he said. She'd be irritated that he was so focused on her freckles except the expectations building in her blood made it hard to concentrate on any feeling other than desire.

When Trey stopped kissing the freckles on her stomach and started tracing lines with his tongue, her hips bucked. While he was licking his constellations into her freckles, he moved his hands to the fly of her jeans. A pop of the button and a rasp of the zipper and his hands were lifting the elastic of her panties.

She opened her mouth to speak, but all that came out was a sigh. It had been a long time....

He looked up at her. His lips were moist and his

eyes hot. "Was that a good sigh or a do-something-else sigh?"

One finger was under the elastic, the edge of his nail resting at the bend of her leg. When she moistened her lips to respond, the finger edged a little closer to her folds. A little closer to where she wanted it. Wanted him. She coughed. "It was a good sigh."

He pushed a second finger under the elastic and walked them up her hip until he hooked his fingers around the fabric and pulled her panties down a little. "More?"

Max nodded, happy to have him read her mind. Not that she had much of a mind left to read. Like the rest of her body, her brain was a pulsating mush of "I want" and "right there" and "a little to the left would be perfect."

She lifted her hips so that he could slide her underwear and jeans over her butt. His hands were warm as they guided her jeans down her legs and off her feet. As he walked his hands back up her calves, his grip was strong enough she could feel it in her toes. He paused at her knees and started kissing the inside line of her legs. He slowed midthigh, the tingles of his mouth shooting up and down her body.

"I love the strength of your legs." His breath was hot on her skin and her heels dug into the mattress, lifting her butt a little off the sheets.

He ran both his hands first up one of her legs and then up another. "Seeing you in a skirt was one of the bright spots of the funeral." Then he ran his tongue up the lines of her muscles until his mouth was on her sex.

She clutched the sheets so hard that her fingers hurt. He pulled away a little and she scooted closer to him. He chuckled. "Tell me what you want."

She lifted her chin and looked up at the ceiling. The words *I want you inside me* were on her lips but she couldn't utter them. This should be easier than asking for the farm, and she'd said that repeatedly. Trey wanted to do this. *Just open your mouth, Max.*

"Here?" A warm puff of air hit her sex as he blew gently, running his finger along the crease where the inside of her thigh met the skin of her labia.

No. Oral sex was nice and she might want his mouth there later, but she wanted to feel the weight of him on top of her. To have the hair on his chest tickle her nipples and the length of him push into her. She wanted the feeling of fullness and warmth that his fingers couldn't give her.

What was she worried about! This was sex; she couldn't make a mistake. Everything was going to be good. Him on top and inside her would be better....

Instead, she nodded.

Even in the dim light of her lamp she could see the pleasure flood his eyes at her assent. He sucked and nibbled and licked and she moaned, but she wanted him to grasp on to her waist as he pushed into her while she invoked the heavens.

She'd stopped feeling and started thinking and, after that, the sex just went south for her.

When he pulled away to take his jeans off, she dug in her nightstand for a condom, but it was too late. When he finally pushed into her, the moment was gone. She could feel the pleasure of him sliding in and out, but the tingles had disappeared. Nothing but frustration was about to burst out of her. He cried out, bucked and then pulled out.

While he looked for a trash can to dispose of the condom, she banged her head against the pillow. She was pissed as all hell at herself. *This should have been easier than asking for a farm, Maxine.*

He lifted the covers and they both slid under them, though she didn't scoot over to snuggle against him and he didn't reach out for her. In the instant before he turned off the lamp, she saw the confused concern on his face. Just as well the light was off; she wouldn't know what to say to him. *You were okay, but you could've been better and it was my fault. Maybe I'll ask you for the farm again. I managed to talk myself* into *that.*

MAX'S BACK WAS probably as freckled as the rest of her and Trey might never get to enjoy it. Sometime between him stripping off her pants and his orgasm, something had gone seriously wrong. He didn't know what it was, and her back to him wasn't helping. Lothario he wasn't, but he knew enough to ask what a woman wanted and act on it. He'd asked, she'd nodded and fireworks hadn't gone off.

Perhaps he was expecting too much out of both of them. Maybe he was expecting too much out of sex. Which meant the joke was on him and his fear that Max would have expectations.

He ran his hand over his face, pulling his skin taut. The room was dark. There was no reason to hide his frustration. The part of him that had always found his father's jokes about women distasteful wondered if he'd missed a "no, get off me."

He replayed the evening in his head. Max hadn't been scratching her nails down his back and biting his shoulder in pleasure, but she hadn't been beating against him in pain, either. If she hadn't been an *enthusiastic* participant, she'd at least been an *active* participant up to the end. He'd prefer enthusiastic.

The whole episode had turned into a buzz kill that made him want to slide out of bed and go… go where? Was he going to get out of her bed and walk upstairs to the bed he'd slept in when he was a teenager and sex involved his hand? Sex with his tenant in the farmhouse had been a mistake. Lying in bed wondering where he'd fucked up the fucking was his punishment.

When the sun came up tomorrow, they would

wake up landlord and tenant. Seller and buyer. He either let the darkness bind the awkwardness to them or he defused it now. He turned onto his side so that he faced her back. "Whatever we did seemed to only work for one of us."

She took so long to respond that he didn't think she was going to. Finally, as his eyes were adjusting to the spare bits of moonlight streaming in through her window, he saw her pale back muscles shift. She sighed, then turned to face him. The moonlight wasn't bright enough for him to read her expression, especially since her hair was wild about her face.

"I'm willing to try again," he said. "I'm pretty open to ideas. It's the house I grew up in, so pretty much any sex we have here is going to feel dirty to me."

Moisture off her teeth sparkled when she smiled. It wasn't a wide smile, but it was better than talking to her back. "It was fine."

Fine? His dick shrank by half. Apparently, neither it nor he was going to get another chance to do better than *fine*. Being the worst lay of her life at least would have meant he was memorable.

He may have trouble reading her expression, but his must have been crystal clear because she backtracked. "I mean, it was great, really. I didn't, well, you know, but I could've and…"

But I could've. It was a good thing shrinking by half meant there would always be some left, because otherwise his dick would have disappeared completely.

He snaked a hand through the sheets until he could rest it on her waist. Her skin was soft, and he wished his hand wasn't their only point of connection. He liked the feel of her soft skin covering her hard muscles. Feeling the contrast between the two against the length of his body once wasn't enough. He wanted to do it again. "Do you want to continue talking about this?"

"No." Her tone left no room for argument, which was fine because he didn't want to argue with her.

"Are you tired?" he asked.

She sighed and he could feel her start to roll over under his hand. He tightened and released his grip. "I'm not asking so I can be *fine* again." Next time he was going to be better than fine, though he couldn't believe he wanted to try for a next time after this conversation. He blamed his continued desire on freckles he still hadn't seen. "Maybe we can talk about something else."

She stayed where she was. "No, I'm not tired."

"Why Max's Vegetable Patch? Why not Max's Vegetable Farm or Vegetable Garden?"

It had seemed a safe topic until she responded with a sigh and her hair blew away from her mouth in the shadows of the night. "My name is Maxine Patch Backstrom."

Ah. It wasn't a bad name, though a little cutesy for the Max he knew. "A family name?"

"No." She rolled onto her back and he took the opportunity to slide closer to her, wrapping one arm around her. Just because the sex was *fine* didn't mean they couldn't enjoy lying in each other's arms afterward. His body was warm, his face was cold and she was soft. Their *fine* could be a lot worse.

"My dad met my mom while he was hiking the Appalachian Trail. She was living in the mountains at the time and had been out hiking with friends." She tilted her head closer to him, her hair tickling his neck and chin. As an experiment, he draped one leg over her, keeping the weight off and waiting for her to push it away. When she didn't, he relaxed and felt her legs sink a little.

If he wanted to keep his mind off sex, it was a stupid move. Her wild hair was tickling his face and he knew there was a patch of copper just above his leg that had tickled his chin when he'd tasted her.

He could do better than fine.

"…Harmon's Den." Though if he wanted a chance at doing better than fine, he needed to pay attention when she was talking. "Mom was so sure I was going to be a boy that she didn't even think of another name for me. Apparently, Max Patch is close enough on the trail to Harmon's Den and Maxine was close enough to Max to satisfy her whim. Though they did name my brother Harmon."

Trey slipped her hair off his chin while his mind caught up with what she was saying. "The name suits you." He'd hiked Max Patch once and the view had been awe-inspiring enough to silence a bunch of college students and their black-bear jokes.

"I guess it does. As a kid I hated it—but mostly because teachers insisted on calling me Maxine and at least once a year some boy would think it was funny to call me Patchwork."

"Probably because he had the hots for you." If she had pigtails, he'd pull them right now.

When she laughed, the side of her breasts bounced against his chest. In the battle between his wounded ego and his libido, his libido was winning. Her hand touched his leg and gave it a gentle squeeze. His ego didn't stand a chance.

"My mom said the same thing, but it didn't make the name Patchwork any less irritating."

"My aunt calls you Maxine."

"Yes, and trying to correct her is like trying to dig through lava rock with a plastic spoon."

Her perfect description of his aunt made him laugh. He tightened the arm he had around her a little, pulling her closer. However mediocre—*fine*—the coital part of the night had been, the postcoital cuddle had been so pleasurable Trey fell asleep forgetting that he was in the farmhouse.

CHAPTER FIFTEEN

TREY WOKE UP in the morning hard and ready to be anything other than fine. Only the sun streaming through the windows wasn't an early-morning sun and he was the only one in the bed. The chickens were up and so was Farmer Max.

He found his clothes and padded through the living room and dining room into the kitchen for some coffee. The worn wooden floors weren't so bad, but the linoleum in the kitchen was cold, even through his socks. His entire life the kitchen had been the wrong temperature. In the summer it was too hot. In the winter, too cold. Like the rest of the farmhouse, the kitchen was heated—it just wasn't heated well, and the fireplace had been a death trap even when he'd been a kid. Surrounded by outside walls or unheated rooms, the kitchen was hopeless. Between the peeling linoleum floors and the cracking laminate counters, it was also ugly.

There were no mugs in the cabinet he opened. Max had rearranged the kitchen. He blinked a couple times and looked around. It was the same ugly kitchen—and yet it was different. She'd engineered some sort of planters on the wall that were filled with herbs. The trestle table against one wall was the same trestle table that had been in the kitchen for as long as he could remember, only now it was painted a bright white. And the peas he'd shoved in its cracks as a kid were probably gone. There was a clock above the sink with songbirds at the numbers. And Max had removed the dingy tractor-pattern curtains his mother had made when he'd been five and replaced them with a cheery check pattern. The same kitchen, only brighter. More alive.

Had it been like this when he'd come here to search for the will?

Trey spotted the mugs on a mug tree near the coffeemaker. He poured himself a cup of coffee. Sitting down at the table with the mug in his hands, the coffee didn't look good. It was thin, with an oily black color and smelled like coffee dust. *Next time I come down, I'm bringing my own coffeepot and stopping at that small grocery store for a bag of* good *coffee.* Right now, all he wanted was breakfast.

After one sip, he considered himself fortified by the caffeine; he wasn't about to take another drink of the foul brew. Trey cleared papers off the table so he would have a place to eat the cereal he'd found. One of the papers fluttered to the floor and it wasn't until he was setting it on top of the pile that he realized it was a bank statement. And that Max had *thousands* of dollars more than she'd let on. Maybe even enough for her to get a mortgage for the farm. Definitely enough that she didn't need another three years to save.

He took a large gulp of the coffee and grimaced, the sour coffee and his anger burning a channel down his esophagus. Was she playing him? No. He shook his head in answer to his own question. She had no reason to play him and every reason to buy the farm. So why did she insist that she didn't have enough money?

No answer came to him as he sat at the table, not quite awake. He was angry, but the more he sat contemplating the bank statement and his soggy cereal, the more confusion overrode the anger. Max was a forthright person who wanted to buy this rotten piece of land and he wanted to sell it to her. Why wasn't she dumping all of her money into the purchase and be done with it?

His coffee was cold and cereal warm when Max walked into the kitchen, trailed by a panting Ashes. "Oh. You got yourself breakfast. I was thinking of making omelets. Would you still want one?"

He looked down into his bowl of cereal, where the flakes were disintegrating and becoming one with the milk. The whole mess would have to be tossed. He hated wasting food. And wasting time, which is what this entire I-don't-have-enough-money act was—a waste of his time.

"I saw your bank statement," he said to her back

as she was pouring herself a cup of her disgusting coffee.

"What?"

He waited until she'd turned back to face him before he spoke again. "Why did you lie about how much money you have?"

"I didn't lie." Her face puckered with confusion.

"I. Saw. Your. Bank. Statement," he repeated. "I know how much money you have saved." He had to take a deep breath to keep from yelling. "It may be enough for a down payment."

"Why were you going through my stuff?"

Trey squelched the temptation to say, "I asked you first," saying instead, "The bank statement was on the kitchen table, right out in the open for anyone to see."

She blinked, but still didn't answer his original question, so he repeated it. "Why did you lie?"

"I didn't lie." Though she held her coffee cup over her mouth, he could see the nervousness on her face. "That money's not for buying the land."

He ran his hand over his face, pressing hard into his cheekbones and hoping the pressure would override his irritation. "Max, what's more important than buying the land?"

"WELL, I…" WORDS STALLED. Max coughed. The movement cleared the way for speech, but still the words wouldn't come.

"What's the money for?"

She cleared her throat again. "I'm saving some of it to renovate the other tobacco barn, so I can provide housing for two interns."

She knew what he was going to say before he opened his mouth, because she had the same argument with herself every time she checked her bank account. Coming out the winner of those arguments didn't mean she'd come out the winner of this one.

"If you aren't able to buy the farm, you won't have a barn to renovate. Nor interns to hire." The air in the kitchen collapsed around her as he shifted in his seat.

His argument made perfect sense. Without a farm, the money was useless and she'd only have to use it to try to buy another farm. Pick up her life, leave her soil behind and go somewhere else. The very thought made her soul hurt.

"If I put all the money into buying the farm, I'll have nothing left if something goes wrong." She put her mug down on the counter before her sweat made it slippery. Then she wiped her palms on her pants. "It's putting all my eggs into one basket. It's dangerous."

That sounded reasonable. Sensible. Unlike pouring all of her money into the farm and being left with nothing if disaster struck. Like her mother moving halfway across the country for a man, only to end up divorced and far from all her friends and family.

I could lose everything.

All she needed was a broken tractor to make spending all of her savings buying the farm dangerous. With the remains of her spring crops rotting in the sun and no way to plow them under to prepare for fall. Crops that needed to be transplanted stuck in her greenhouse, stunted in the little seedling cells because she had no place to put them. And no cash in the bank to hire a mechanic.

The mechanic didn't work on the barter system.

She shoved her hands in her pockets, hoping to warm them.

Trey was talking again. She saw his mouth moving, but his voice wasn't loud enough to penetrate the objections and fears rushing about in her head. *What if...?* He must have sensed her confusion because he stopped, seemingly midsentence, and waited until she shook the noise from her head. "You," he drew out the word, "might not have a basket to put eggs in."

"If you could wait another three years..."

He leaned forward, crossing his arms on the table and caging her with his gaze. "I'm not going to wait another three years. I'm selling the farm by December. If you're not buying it, then someone else is."

She felt sick to her stomach. Sex had changed more than she'd expected it to. And it had changed nothing at the same time.

She swallowed and the sound echoed through her

body. She pictured her hand writing out that check and then the sight of her bank statement with nothing in it when she found out her water pump wasn't working. When her truck broke down. When fungus decimated her tomato plants and she had to buy more seedlings or not have any tomatoes that season.

She swallowed again. The CSA's entire purpose was to mitigate those risks. She could buy the farm in December. CSA participants paid her in January. That would only be one month of an empty bank balance. And the chances that something catastrophic would happen were slim. And the extra money she had saved was to fix up the tobacco barn anyway.

It wasn't that much of a risk, was it? The bigger risk was losing the farm completely. She was either all into the farm or all out. She looked at Trey. "I don't know" was all she could muster, and the irritation on his face changed to something closer to pity.

"How did you manage to leave your dad's farm behind in Illinois and come here? That must've been a huge risk."

"My brother got married and he and his wife moved into the farmhouse with my dad. Then my stepmother brought home this one guy who talked about how much he loved his farm and his harvester. I think she was trying to set me up with him, but all I wanted to do was go back to one of my summer jobs spent on the small farms and dig in the dirt. I was browsing ads for farmland when I saw your mom's ad." Typing the email had been one of the most freeing things she'd ever done. "Durham didn't look that far away from my mom on the map, so I just sent off the email. I didn't think about it."

He blinked, took a sip of his coffee and grimaced. "That's it. You didn't think?"

She shrugged. "Thinking gets me into trouble."

Everyone she knew—including herself—had been amazed when she'd packed up her bags and moved south to start a farm. If life were to present her with the same choice again, she wasn't sure she'd be able to make the move. Not because she didn't want to or it was a bad decision, but because she'd replied to the farm posting without a single thought until she'd hit the send button. By the time the panic and doubts had hit, she'd felt committed to moving and all her mental energy had gone to talking herself into why North Carolina was a great idea. She'd not done anything so freeing before that moment and she hadn't since.

At the time, she'd agreed to the lease with a handshake because it had seemed less risky than tying herself down to a life decision she'd given no forethought. After a couple years she and Hank had agreed to a three-year lease. They'd talked about when she would be able to buy the land from him and how much he thought he'd ask for it. The investments into the farm had been made, decided on and purchased together. The reach for permanence had been such a logical thing to do. The risks had been minimal. "The worst that could happen" seemed to shrink every passing day. Now either way she looked at her present situation, she feared losing her farm.

"Stop thinking, then." Trey looked so reasonable— all stubble faced and sharp jawed with enough strength to cut through all her doubts.

"It's too late." The words came out with a weary sigh. She'd been staring at the money sitting in her bank account since Trey had offered her the right of first refusal. The numbers beat down on her shoulders with a force at odds to their size and she had to stiffen her knees to prevent herself from buckling under. And every time she'd decided to contact the bank for a mortgage, the what-ifs came back in force. She looked down at her feet, but any answers there were hidden in her boots.

The worries about her tractor breaking again, the water pump dying, illness, injury, a storm… Those weren't the worries that stilled her hand. More powerful was the constant beat of *what if I'm wrong?*

Chair legs scraped against the floor. Light footsteps shuffled until she could see the toes of Trey's socks alternating with her work boots. Her worn flannel shirt was soft against her skin when he rested his hands on her biceps.

"What are you so afraid of?" He started to rub her arms. Friction of hands and cloth against skin created a warmth that crept, slowly at first, up her arms and through her body until it burst into her toes.

"My mom jumps from interest to interest with seemingly little thought. It's fine because she's in Asheville now and surrounded by people who share her spirit, but she just up and decided to marry my father after that one meeting. No thought. No planning and then—bam!—she's got two kids and a marriage she doesn't want, living in a place she doesn't want to be." Max pulled her hands out of her pockets and he folded her into his embrace. As her head rested against his shoulder, the unease in her stomach subsided.

She didn't know how long they stood there together, nor who pulled away first, but she did know that she felt stronger when she looked up into his face. She smiled. "I guess you won't give me an extension now, will you?"

"No." He chuckled and put his hands back on her arms, in affection and support rather than concern. "This is different. You know it is. Since that first day, I've seen you as a fighter and you want this place enough to fight for it. I care about what happens to this land—which I never imagined I would—but I *don't* want to own it. I don't want to be a part of it. That hasn't changed."

"I guess we won't know which way I will fall until December is upon us." She wished she could see the same fighting spirit in herself as Trey did. "Whatever I'm feeling most—fear or hope—will mean I sign the mortgage or I don't."

"I hope you won't let your fear make the decision for you."

He kissed her softly on the mouth. It tasted like goodbye.

CHAPTER SIXTEEN

Trey turned out of the farm's driveway onto Chicken Bridge Road and began the long drive back to D.C. On Old Oxford Highway, where old and new North Carolina sat across the street from one another, he thought he passed Kelly headed in the other direction.

The side of the road was already greener than it had been a month ago. The trees had an optimistic bend to them as they prepared to bud out. Birds swooped and danced with a sense of promise, prepared to forget the lean winter season. Fields were plowed. Persephone was not yet on the move, but she was awake and the world knew it. Nature was prepared to help her pull herself out of the darkness. He would have to pull his head out of his poetic ass if he was going to be any use to anyone at work.

He left the country scenery behind and drove through the city of Durham. Many of the gas stations and fast-food joints had been here when he was growing up. The *tacquerias* and *tiendas* were new. Durham was not the town it had been when he'd cheered his own escape, though he was grateful the small grocery store Max had shown him had survived all the changes, so he could stop in and buy a tub of pimento cheese on his way out of town.

When he pulled onto the interstate and shifted into fifth gear, Trey had time to think about the woman who'd enticed him down to Durham. How Max's fear managed to keep a grip on her.

The Max afraid to take a risk didn't match with his image of the woman standing, holding a rifle and shooting tin cans.

Like all things Max, this contradiction should be a sign that selling the farm to her—or someone else—come December was the right thing to do. Instead, Trey's mind drifted south to the farm as he drove north. He wasn't able to force his mind back to his work until he hit the D.C. suburbs.

MAX WAS BUSYING herself cleaning the kitchen when Kelly walked through the door. "Was that my brother I passed on the road?" he asked, helping himself to a glass of water before sitting down at the table.

Neither brother seemed to have noticed that someone other than their father lived in the house now. She should move the table and see if one of them tried to sit in the empty space.

"He came down for the basketball game. His friend Jerome had tickets."

Behind the rim of his glass, Kelly's brows were raised.

"What?"

He lowered his glass. "Why was he leaving *the farm?*"

"I guess he wanted to see his property," she said peevishly.

The old wood of the trestle table swallowed the sound of Kelly's glass hitting it. "My brother has the hots for you."

Both Harris boys could jump off a cliff.

Kelly seemed unperturbed by her dirty look. "Speaking of hots, who's the guy sitting on the porch of the barn?"

"Sean, one of my summer interns."

"He got a boyfriend or partner that you know of?" Kelly rolled his glass between his hands, a hungry look on his face.

"He just got out of the army."

"Doesn't mean he can't be gay." He stopped rolling his glass long enough to give her a "don't be stupid" look. "Just means he had to be silent about it for most of his career."

Max thought about arguing with him, but stopped herself. She didn't know anything about Sean other than that he was serious about farming and had spent all of his twenties and a healthy part of his thirties in the army. He could be gay. He could have a wife and kids. Both could be true. They didn't affect his ability to hoe weeds and he hadn't volunteered the information, so she hadn't asked. "Gay, straight or bi, he's a man with secrets, and I don't know that he'll let you or me in on them."

Kelly raised a brow at her, looking so much like his older brother that her heart hurt. Kelly was comfortable. Kelly believed she should own the farm. Even if he were straight, Kelly wouldn't interest her at all. Trey was a risk. She wanted him and she was afraid to even *try* to have him.

"Got anything I can use to strike up a conversation?"

"No. I'm not helping you hit on my intern. You want him, you work for it."

"I contested a will for you."

She sighed. "You could ask for a tour of the fields. Say I'm too mad at all the Harris boys to give you one."

Kelly laughed, then caught the look on her face and stopped. "What'd I do?"

"You were born." His concerned look made Max feel bad. "I'm not really mad at you. Or Trey, even. I'm mad at myself. If you want a chaperone, take Ashes."

Kelly stood and came over to rest a hand on her shoulder. "No. You need the dog more than I do."

Then he gave her shoulder a squeeze. "I'm off to go get me a man."

She chuckled, having to stop herself before she gave him the satisfaction of laughing outright. "Oh, shut up. The act doesn't suit you."

"But I made you laugh."

"Yes, yes, you did. Thank you, Kelly."

Almost as soon as the door closed behind Kelly, Max's landline started ringing. She answered quickly.

"Maxine, honey," her mother said, "how are you?"

Since returning to her home state, Max's mother had gotten her Southern accent back. Or maybe it had never really been gone, only hidden under the pressures of trying to be a Midwestern housewife and then a single mother living in a land where she'd never been comfortable. Maybe losing her accent had been a protective measure, a way to pretend marrying a man she'd known for the time it took to walk from Harmon's Den to Max Patch hadn't been stupid.

"Big money for easy work," she said, then winced. "Sorry, Mom."

"What are you sorry about? I was married to your daddy for eleven years and bore him two children. Hearing his words come out of the mouth of my beautiful child doesn't trouble me."

"I know, but…"

"But?"

Max didn't know how to finish her protest. Knowing how happy her mother was to be back in North Carolina, she couldn't understand how as a young woman she'd packed up all her bags and married an Illinois farmer.

No, that wasn't fair. There were photo albums with picture after picture of her mom and dad gazing lovingly at each other, and her dad was still handsome. What Max couldn't understand was how her mom didn't look back on that decision with regret. In one move, her mom had thrown everything she'd had behind one decision that had ultimately left her stranded.

"How's the new man in your life?" Her mother always had a new man in her life. And a new hobby. And new friends. And a new favorite restaurant. She had been a dying plant in Illinois, come alive and vibrant under Asheville's care.

"I'm still with Howie. He wants me to meet his kids." A *tsk* came through over the phone. "I don't know. I'm not sure we're serious enough for that yet." She paused, and Max waited to see what else her mom had to say. "He wants to come with me to Durham and meet you."

"Oh." Meeting a new potential step-parent wasn't new, though Max couldn't remember how her father had introduced them to Tina. One day his father had a girlfriend at their house cooking them dinner and the rest is history. Being thirty-two and introduced to your mom's boyfriend felt different, especially because her mom was open about having flings— not serious love interests.

"Mom, do you ever regret marrying Dad?"

"What? Honey, where did that come from? Of course I don't regret marrying your father. I loved him. Marrying your daddy gave me you and Harmon. How could I regret that?"

The sincerity in her mom's voice didn't match the memories Max had of her parents' marriage, which seemed to have mostly consisted of arguments. "You gave up everything to be with Dad and it didn't work. Aren't you happier now?"

"Tricky thing, happiness. Moment to moment it relies on such insubstantial things and in the long term, it's about having people you love in your life. Being a farmwife wasn't for me, but I was surrounded by people I love, so I wasn't unhappy there."

Silence was the only response Max had. Her mother's answers didn't help her own decision-making process.

"What's this about?" her mom asked.

Again, Max didn't immediately respond. Her mother had raised them all to believe in their dreams and go for what they wanted, which was easy when your dreams were easy and there wasn't much risk. But what about when failure meant losing everything? "I've just been thinking."

"Is this about the farm? If you need money, I will help you buy the farm. And I'm sure your daddy will help, too."

Guilt blew through her body with a sudden gust. Her parents were willing to risk their shaky finances to help her achieve her dream. But she had the funds to do it. And if she risked everything she had on this one dream—and failed—she knew she wouldn't be alone. She'd still be surrounded by people she loved.

"No. I don't need your money, Mom, but thanks. I've just been weighing the risks."

"Honey, sometimes the risks aren't worth weighing."

But how do you know when *those times are?* Max didn't ask her question. She listened to her mom talk about learning to throw pots; she talked about what they were planting on the farm and her new interns, then hung up the phone still weighed down by the risks.

CHAPTER SEVENTEEN

TREY WAS WORKING in his apartment when his cell phone rang. The number on the screen was one he'd known by heart since childhood. Despite knowing that Max was on the other end of the line, he had to overcome instinct before answering. And still, her voice instead of his father's was a surprise.

"I'm…I'm going to buy the farm." The fear in her voice had a simmering quality to it. Her anxiety was no longer making her decision for her, but neither Max nor her nerves were comfortable with the change from tyranny to rule by reason and law. "Only, could we wait until later in the year to make it official? My workload increases in the spring and in the summer I'll barely have time to think, much less to find a mortgage and a lawyer and…"

"Fine."

"Fine? You wanted to get the farm out of your hands as soon as possible."

"I also gave you until December. You still have until December." He still had until December to drive down and memorize her features.

"Okay, then." She paused. "You're not worried I'm going to back out?"

Her relief at his acquiescence seemed more substantial than her fear had been. And while he had a hard time merging the woman confidently standing in the yard shooting cans with the woman afraid to put all her eggs in one basket, they were the same woman. And the Max he'd met first wouldn't back down.

Of course, when he'd met that woman, he wouldn't have been willing to wait until December. But they were both different people than who they'd been the day they met, and her fierceness was more interesting now that he knew she fought for it. "Have you checked your email?"

"No."

"Check your email. Then call me back."

While he was waiting, Trey got up from his desk and got himself a glass of water. Then got out some crackers and the tub of pimento cheese. He couldn't face the work he had to do. Not while his head was still in Durham.

Finally, his phone rang again. "What do you think?" he said by way of an answer.

"Um, you can't use Kickstarter funds to buy real estate."

"You're still thinking in terms of can't. Think in terms of can." The coup d'état in her emotions wasn't complete yet. "What projects *can* you use the Kickstarter funds for?"

There was a short moment of silence on the other end of the line. "I can," she said the words slowly as the possibilities were coming to her, "use the Kickstarter money to renovate the old tobacco barn."

Trey wished he could see her face as the potential hit her. The white of her skin under her freckles would brighten and her eyes would take on a deep green color as the power she carried with her internally took over. "And if I have money left over, I need a new tractor and refrigerator building. I could do this."

The wheels in her head rolled over the phone line and through the cell signal, mowing down all the obstacles in her way. Max had been waiting to grasp on to her future, and something had given her the go-ahead.

And he wanted to be a part of it. More than suggesting Kickstarter and watching from the sidelines, more than helping her find a mortgage. Trey wanted to be an integral part of her strength. He'd been drawn into government and then lobbying because he liked the fight. Arguing to hear yourself yell was okay. Debating to win was better. Fighting for the slightest change that gave someone an opportunity or incentive to better themselves was the tops.

It had been a long time since he'd been a part of one person grabbing on to a better future.

"What can I do to help?"

"I've never done much with Kickstarter other than donate to some of the businesses in Durham. Maybe we can brainstorm ideas. I can set up a Google docs folder for us. If we do this, I don't want to *not* have the project fully funded. I don't want to get my hopes up with each penny only to watch it all get returned."

Trey considered her practical suggestion. She could do the research that needed to be done in North Carolina. He could supplement from D.C. But then he wouldn't have such a hand in the project. Or the excuse to count her freckles.

"I'll do you one better. I'll come down next weekend. We'll draft a strategy for this money-raising business." Trey smiled to himself. "I'm good at convincing people to do things."

MAX HAD JUST gotten out the dust rag when Kelly and Sean stepped into the kitchen. Sean looked happy and as relaxed as she'd ever seen him around another person. Kelly was looking at Sean like he was the sun, the soil and the rain. Max shoved the rag behind her back, then decided that move was too obvious and reached for the dust spray.

"Who ya' dusting for?" Kelly may be stupid in love, but he wasn't blind.

She could either lie outright, or admit to herself that she was cleaning the farmhouse because Trey was coming to visit. She was about to say, "Miss Lois," when Sean said, "It looks to me like she's cleaning for a lover."

Kelly's gaze shot from Sean to Max and then back to Sean. "So not only does Trey have the hots for you, but you have the hots for him, too."

"We're going to discuss a Kickstarter campaign."

"Is that what the heterosexuals are calling it these days?" Sean asked with a raised brow. Max wished he'd go back to being silent and borderline sullen.

"Your brother will never move farther south of D.C. than Alexandria, Virginia. Any relationship we have is casual and won't go anywhere." Though she was wondering if she should clean the floors and vacuum under the couch. She had imagined them having sex on the couch as soon as Trey walked through the door. Making it to the bedroom would give her too much time to *think*.

Kelly slipped his hand into Sean's and started swinging them. She was pretty sure he didn't even realize he was doing it, though Sean seemed self-conscious about it. Cleaning up for Trey's visit now felt hollow. She'd agreed with him that this relationship couldn't go anywhere—but she always wanted hand-holding.

"You know—" Kelly's voice brought Max's thoughts back to the present "—Trey grew up in this house and my mom was too busy to clean. Hell, Dad only cleaned when stuff started to stink and

Aunt Lois made Trey clean that bathroom. He ain't gonna notice a little dust."

"But *I* live in this house now." And it would be *her* house by the end of the year. And she intended to take pride in every clean crevice. "Something neither of you Harris boys seem to ever notice."

Kelly shrugged. "Should I start knocking?"

"No." Riling up an infatuated man was impossible. "Ashes will bark and I'll have to come let you in."

"Then what are you so upset over?"

"Nothing, I guess." Or nothing she would admit to Kelly. In truth, she was terrified that Trey *was* coming down to work on their Kickstarter and nothing else.

MAX PACED THE front porch of the farmhouse, watching the main road for Trey's car. The confidence she'd felt yesterday had dissolved, but she'd made a decision. Waffling now would spell disaster. She reached back to pull her hair into a ponytail and was rewarded by the hairband breaking and snapping the inside of her wrist. After she shoved the broken band into her left pocket, she reached into her right pocket for another. And broke that one, too. Between her anxiety and her curls, she'd break every hairband in her house if she wasn't careful.

She dug the first broken hairband out of her pocket and turned toward the door. At the first stomp of her feet, she took a deep breath, then another, more controlled step. When she stepped out of the bathroom, five new hairbands in her pocket, Trey was standing in her kitchen, drinking a glass of water.

"I didn't hear you come in."

"I know. You were muttering to yourself about something."

She'd been cursing her hair, Hank, Trey, her nerves and herself—but mostly her hair. Looking at Trey, confident and helpful in his suit and tie, cursing him seemed spiteful. After she got her hair into a ponytail without breaking the hairband, even cursing her hair seemed silly.

His gaze was hungry and intent as he put down his glass, but he didn't take a step toward her. He didn't have to. The way he looked at her was enough to make her belly tingle, and it wasn't until one side of his mouth kicked up in a smile that she realized her hands were still up about her head. She lowered them, feeling desired, desirous and silly all at the same time.

"You don't have to lower your hands on my account," he said as he stalked over to her. He didn't touch her, but she could feel him just the same, the sensation of his closeness overwhelming her silliness and leaving nothing but longing in its place.

The dangerous wanting pushed her back until she hit the wall. Trey looked relaxed. Comfortable.

And also feral. He caught her wrists, one in each hand and lifted her hands over her head, forcing her breasts out against her shirt.

"There," he said with satisfaction. He gathered her wrists in one hand, sliding the other down her arm until he had hold of her waist. His gaze was intent on her breasts, like he could see through her shirt. "The view is better up close."

It didn't matter that his dark brows and thick lashes hid his eyes from view, their heat flushed her skin first a pale pink and then a dark red as the burn sank from her breasts to the juncture of her thighs. When he raised his face to look at her, the warmth spread through the rest of her body.

Bubbling along with her desire was the thought that between her freckles, carroty hair and now flushed skin she must look a fiery mess.

She leaned forward to kiss him.

CHAPTER EIGHTEEN

SHE'S AS HOT as she looks, Trey thought when her lips touched his. He gripped Max's waist and wrists tighter, unwilling to let her go for fear that she'd start thinking and he'd end up *fine* again.

But she didn't pull back. She pushed her breasts forward, her arms straining against his hold of her wrists. His thumb was caught between the firm muscles of her belly and the leather of his belt. The uncompromising strength of a person—a woman—who made her money through physical labor was pressed against him and he wanted, desperately, to be a part of her.

She cocked her head and slid her tongue inside his mouth, running it along the edges of his teeth. There was no hesitation in her now. This was the woman who'd stalked across *his* land, a rifle in her hand, demanding a justification from him for why he was there. This was the steel he'd sensed inside her. The silly freckles and soft, wild hair hid the hard core, but when she let her guard down, let him really look into her eyes, he saw determination, not fear.

And she was letting him hold her hands above her head. She was backed up against the kitchen wall, and instead of fighting him, she was inviting him in.

Trey slid his hand back up the side of her body and along the underside of her arms until he again had two hands on her wrists. As his fingertips had tickled her underarms, her shivers had echoed through his bones. He was hard, straining against the fly of his pants.

He pulled away from her, just enough so that he could speak. "I didn't come down here for this."

"What did you come down here for, then?" She smiled and closed the gap between them again, daring him to argue with her.

To help you strategize, his mind said, lying to both of them. He could strategize with her over the phone and by email. He'd come here to be with her. "Okay. I'd be lying if I said I hadn't *considered...*" The words stopped when she licked her lips.

She twisted her wrists and he released her hands. Despite her attempt at a ponytail, her hair had exploded about her face and her eyes matched its fire. Her hands landed on his shoulders, her grip strong. She took a step forward, pushing him along in front of her until his backside hit the kitchen table. He turned and half sat, while being half pushed into a chair by Max. Only when she'd trapped him as thoroughly as he'd trapped her did she pull her hands from his shoulders. Her eyes were wide and fearless as she sat astride him, fumbling with the buttons of his shirt.

"Let me help…"

She swatted his hands away before he could finish his sentence. "You have better uses for your hands."

He obeyed, pulling her T-shirt out from between them where it had gotten caught and running his hands along her soft skin. He imagined he could feel her freckles under his fingertips, guiding him along the contours of her body as her thighs tensed around his. Her eyes were half-closed and her mouth was open, her tongue resting between her teeth. She looked *wanting*. Instead of thinking about his erection pressed against the seam of his pants, he focused on the sensations of her skin against his hands, determined to let her have all the control.

She'd reached the end of his shirt buttons and had to scoot back before she had access to his fly. A pop of his button and a rasp of his zipper and his erection was released. He closed his eyes and sighed. His pleasure was short-lived. Max's weight shifted, then her warmth was gone from his lap. When he opened his eyes, her backside was walking away from him.

"Um," he said, not certain what had gone wrong last time and not wanting to repeat that experience. He was sitting in his family's farmhouse kitchen, his pants undone and his erection pushing the fly of his boxers open. Despite feeling vulnerable, he didn't want to move in case Max came back.

When she came through the doorway, she held up a little square of foil and smiled wickedly at him. But she didn't walk immediately over to the chair. Instead, she put the condom between her teeth, reached for her jeans and wiggled out of them. For all that he was able to move, he might as well have been tied to the chair. Her pants pooled at her feet, followed by her panties. She stood in the doorway of the kitchen, her T-shirt brushing the top of her dark red thatch of hair, with nothing but white skin and freckles below it.

He was afraid to move—afraid this might be a dream. She was a hot, dirty fantasy and she was walking toward him.

Her intense, catlike eyes locked on his and he couldn't lower his gaze to appreciate the glory of her naked legs even if he wanted to. Even though she was the one moving toward him, he felt like he was the one being reeled in like a fish.

The muscles in his thighs tightened in anticipation when she stood in front of him, her pussy just below eye level and the smell of her overpowering him. He gripped the side of the chair, levering his hips up as she pulled his pants and boxers out from under him. His clothes fell around his feet, as effective as shackles keeping him there. If she ran, he couldn't catch her, though he'd probably trip and smash onto his face trying.

She brought the condom back up to her teeth. The sound of the foil tearing trembled around his head and through his blood, the anticipation of what was to come making him harder. When she finally rolled the condom down over him, the way her skin brushed lightly against his seized the air from his lungs. She straddled him. The tendons at the juncture of her hips shifted and the muscles in her thighs pulsed. If he could let go of the chair, he'd lift her shirt up over her head and lick her freckles. But he couldn't lift his hands.

She lowered herself onto him with a groan, her arms balanced on his shoulders and her hands grasping onto the back of the chair behind him. Her muscles tightened around him. Oxygen wrenched from his throat in a loud gasp that released the pressure keeping his hands adhered to the chair. He shoved his hands under her shirt and rested them on her waist, her skin slipping and sliding against his palms as she rode him.

In response to his scooting forward in the chair and changing the angle of their connection, she leaned back into his fingers with a heavy moan. Her breasts jutted up against her T-shirt. He was no longer able to resist her nipples, which were hard and visible through the thin cotton of her shirt and whatever bra she wore. With a slight push of his fingers, she was forward enough that he could take the peak of one of her nipples in his mouth. He sucked in, hard, and her entire body bucked against his. His balls tightened. Any blood that had been left in the rest of his body rushed to his dick. He clenched his teeth against his coming orgasm. When he came, it was going to be so hard he wasn't sure he'd be able to move from this chair to put his pants on even if the ghost of his father walked through the door.

Her legs tensed and gripped his. Her breaths started emerging in short bursts. She lifted up a little off the chair, stiff, with her head falling back and her mouth open in pleasure. With her close to release, he tightened his butt muscles to push himself up higher and pulled down on her with his hands, plunging himself deeper into her and making her suck in her breath. She shivered. First a gentle shiver and then a shudder passed through her until she went boneless. Her head fell forward, but she caught herself before hitting her forehead on the back of his chair.

He held his breath for several seconds, concentrating on the movement of her nipples under her shirt. Finally, her head shifted in his peripheral vision and her tongue brushed against his neck. He pulled her shirt over her head, then leaned back in his chair to feast his eyes on the way her mottled skin flushed under his attention. Then he pressed his face between her breasts so he could smell the sweat on her skin and came in rolling, hard waves.

When he could finally take a breath, he said, "I'll admit I came down here with something more than strategy in mind, but I don't think I could have imagined that."

She chuckled. The vibrations rumbled through her, providing enough sensation that he stiffened inside her again. "Kickstarter was a good idea."

"Up." He put his hands under her arms and lifted her off him. "I've got to dispose of this or it ceases to be useful. We can do that again tonight and I can hold you afterward. Also, my legs are starting to fall asleep."

The movement of her lifting off him released a spicy, earthy smell into the air. The scent of sex, strong and soft at the same time, much how he imagined Max to be.

EMPTINESS RUSHED INTO her as she pulled herself off Trey. It wasn't just the loss of his fullness inside her, but physical energy had been drained out of her.

What did I just do? As she walked naked across the kitchen to her pants, she was conscious of the open curtains. The lights were on in the kitchen. Dark was falling outside. Any one of her interns could have come by to say goodbye and seen them.

"Don't think so much," said a voice from behind her. "This doesn't have to change our original agreement if we don't let it." She whipped around to face Trey, who was standing next to her, his pants on and zipped, though his shirt was still unbuttoned. How long had she been standing there holding her clothes?

And she had been worried about being caught having sex! Being caught in the act was far preferable to being caught afterward, clothes clutched in her hands and bewilderment on her face. Max turned back around and shoved her pants on, leaving her panties for later. The soft cloth of the T-shirt hit her shoulder. Trey let out a soft harrumph when she yanked it from his hand.

This time when she turned around to face Trey, she opened her mouth to let loose the reassurances while preparing her mind to stop the self-doubt from gaining a foothold in her mind. But no reassurances came out of her mouth. Nor did the self-berating creep into her mind. When they crawled into bed tonight, she was going to crawl all over him.

"I'm not thinking too much and I wasn't worried about *that*." Even though the last part was a lie, the words came more confidently now that she had clothes on. "I'm thinking about what to eat for dinner."

"What do you have?"

"Eggs. The only fresh veggies I've got now are greens and sweet potatoes. I was thinking that tomorrow we could go downtown to talk with some of the other food folks in Durham who've done a Kick-starter. Then we could get some ice cream and a nice steak for dinner. Maybe a loaf of polenta bread."

"Since when did downtown Durham have places to buy ice cream, steak and polenta bread?"

"Your hometown has changed a lot since you've been gone. It's changed a lot since I've been here." When she'd moved to Durham, the downtown area was mostly boarded-up buildings with good bones and attractive facades, and the farmers' market had been in a parking lot. Now the downtown area was bustling with bars and restaurants. There was a new performing arts center and pedestrians were out at all hours of the day and night. More important for her, the farmers' market had a permanent home. Summer Saturdays at the market were a social occasion with people chatting up their favorite farmer, browsing art at the market across the street and eating their favorite items off the food trucks.

"Hmm…" and a slight cloud passing over his face was Trey's only response. "If you put the sweet potatoes in the oven, I'll start washing the greens. We can fry some eggs for the top and call it dinner."

Two male voices yelling outside interrupted her reply. As was her new usual, Max closed her ears to the noises. Instead of trying to be heard over the squabbling beyond the walls, she nodded her agreement and headed to the bathroom to wash up, tossing her panties in the hamper on her way.

When she came out of the bathroom, Trey was standing on the enclosed porch. Without the thicker walls of the house, the argument happening in the driveway was clearer.

"Fuck you and this entire silent act you've got going" rang loud and clear through the drafty wood. "And don't think I can't smell the booze just because it's vodka." A car door slammed. Tires peeled out, gravel pinging in all directions as the rubber spit the small rocks out like rotten food.

"Was that my brother?" Trey asked, a confused look on his face as he stared in the direction of Chicken Bridge Road.

Max sighed. Sean had never once been late or shirked any of his work, but he also drank more than he should. And was sleeping with her landlord's brother.

A frustrated yell reverberated off the porch walls, followed closely by the sound of something hard being kicked. The noise woke up Ashes and he yelped in the living room.

"Yes, that was Kelly." She'd been pleased when Kelly and Sean had struck up a romantic relationship until she'd noticed Sean's pile of beer cans. Now she wasn't so sure what she thought. "Didn't you see his car when you drove up?"

"Yes, I..." Trey stopped talking, a sheepish look on his face. "I thought I'd find him in the kitchen. Then I found only you and I forgot all about Kelly."

"Yes, well…" She would be upset that he'd had sex with her thinking his brother could walk in, but she'd been the one to shove him onto the chair and strip off his pants. And she'd known Kelly was around and liable to walk in the door at any moment. Of course all coherent thought had fled her mind for higher ground when Trey had looked at her with desire hot in his eyes.

"Kelly and Sean are…" Another sentence she didn't know how to finish. "Involved," she said, picking the best word she could find. The word *dating* implied that they went out together, which Max had never seen. And Kelly seemed more infatuated than Sean, which, when added to the drinking, meant Max worried about him. How do you tell a grown man not to give away the milk because then men won't buy the cow? Especially when she was involved in a relationship of questionable sanity herself.

Trey had been looking at her while she'd been talking, but his gaze eased back to the direction of the main road, where his brother had gone. "As far as I know, Kelly hasn't been in a serious relationship since Mom died."

"Would you know?"

Instead of looking insulted, Trey appeared to be honestly considering her question. "If any of his boyfriends had gotten serious? I think so. His last serious relationship ended at my mother's funeral. Dad was drunk and spouting shit. Kelly's boyfriend—hell, I don't even remember his name—made some crack about choosing that homophobic bastard over him. Kelly told him to leave and never come back."

Trey rubbed his hands over his face as if he were trying to scrub away the memory. "I emailed him a couple weeks after the funeral to ask about the boyfriend. Kelly said they were through." He shook his head. "I told him that I agreed with the guy but Kelly insisted Dad was coming around. He always manages to see the best in someone, and I don't know if that's his gift or his curse."

The kitchen was silent for several seconds while Trey looked in the direction of the intern barn. "What was that about the vodka?" he finally asked.

"Sean drinks. Probably too much."

"And you don't do anything about it?"

"I don't…" Max stopped. Trey had asked the same question she'd been asking herself for a couple weeks. "Sean deserves his privacy and it's not affected his work."

"Yet. What about when it's ninety-five degrees outside and he collapses in your fields because he's dehydrated?"

She sighed and internally cursed both Kelly and Sean for ruining her afterglow with reality. "I know. There's a line somewhere between micromanaging Sean's every movement and granting him the same privacy he would get if he lived in town. I'm not sure where that line is."

Trey's raised brow made it clear he didn't buy her argument. "He's a drunk. He'll push and push and push until you fall over. Give him a line in the sand and fire him if he crosses it."

"He's my employee, and I'll manage him how I see fit," she replied, piqued that Trey would question her management style and annoyed that he was right.

"Okay. You're right." His face contradicted his words. "You know both Sean and the farm better than I do. And when I sell you the land, none of this will be my responsibility. If Kelly's dating a drunk or you're hiring one, I won't have to be down here to see it."

His words hurt, even though they shouldn't. She'd agreed to their time-limited relationship and his desire to get rid of the land was in her best interest.

"Sorry for snapping." If he could make a gesture of peace, she could, too. "Hank… Well, Hank was good at discipline, but he had trouble remembering that I was the boss of the interns, not him."

"I am not my father."

"I know that." She rubbed at her eyes with the palms of her hands then shook her head. "I've given Sean an ultimatum, but I doubt my will to enforce it. It would be easier if he didn't have such an expression of peace on his face when working, and I worry that the ultimatum did more harm than good. It's not fair to Kelly, but I'm hoping the relationship gives Sean a reason to cut back."

"You're right. It's not fair to my brother." Trey's words were softened by the warmth and pressure of his hand on her back. "But Kelly isn't a child. He can take care of himself."

Max turned away from Trey to look in the direction of the intern barn. Could Kelly find the good in Sean before Max had to fire him, they killed each other or both? "Wash up. I'll go start dinner," she said.

Trey nodded but didn't move from his stand by the door.

CHAPTER NINETEEN

THE NEXT MORNING, Trey rolled over in Max's bed, pushed his toes out to meet hers, and met only empty space. He sighed—with contentment instead of mild frustration like the last time he'd woken up alone in Max's bed. Though he did wish she was still under the covers with him. But the life of the farmer was up with the chickens.

In the kitchen were Max's ancient coffeepot and a nearly full pot of her awful coffee. He ignored them for a trip out to his car. Back inside, Trey set up his own coffeepot, grinder and coffee next to hers. While he waited for his coffee to brew, he set out his legal pad and began to make notes for Max's fund-raising. The coffeepot ding interrupted his work, which was fine since he'd prefer to do the planning with Max. He poured himself a cup, put on shoes and a sweater and headed out the door in search of the farmer.

He found her looking over the field closest to the pond. The rising sun bouncing off her hair made it glow in a halo around her head. She was drinking out of a thermos mug, her feet wide apart and her back straight. Ashes sat next to her. She looked like a warrior queen of all she surveyed, needing only a staff to complete her Boudicca impression. He smiled at the thought.

She caught sight of him and smiled in invitation. Ashes's tail kicked up dust as it wagged across the ground.

"I like to come out in the mornings, when it's just me and the birds," she said when he reached hearing distance. A chickadee whistled a greeting, then a cardinal. Off in the distance, a mockingbird topped them both.

He took the hand she offered to him as he approached. "Isn't it always just you and the birds?" He said the words with a smile so she would know it was a gentle tease. Seeing the farm through her eyes was a different, wonderful experience. The farm was a place of promise and growth, with none of the hard-edged disappointment it had when he blinked and the view changed back. He blinked again, but Max's magical farm was out of his sightline.

"The interns are here now and, while we're not yet far enough into the season to work on Saturdays, Sean lives here. Before Sean, there was Hank."

"And now me."

"And now you. But you're okay." He grunted, not trusting the light in her eyes or his reaction to them. "I'll even invite you to finish my walk with me."

Their hands pulled apart when she reached down

to pick up her thermos. Would he be able to see the magic in the farm if they weren't holding hands? In the tilled fields and small seedlings not yet recognizable as vegetables, he still saw the waste of his childhood. But out of the corner of his eye, if he didn't try too hard, the picture morphed into the fecundity of Max's Vegetable Patch.

As they walked together, Max pointed out what was growing in which field and where she would begin planting summer crops soon. Trey listened with half an ear. Mostly he took in deep breaths of the crisp, spring-morning air and sipped his coffee.

As they passed the packing shed, Trey noticed a small house on wheels. "What's that?"

Max stopped her musings about planting more peas next year and her gaze followed the line of his pointing. She snickered. "That is a chicken coop Hank designed. It was supposed to be pulled behind a tractor and moved from field to field. 'A chicken tractor for the tractor,' your dad said."

"A chicken tractor?"

"Sure. Chickens are good at picking bugs out of fields. They also both fertilize and dig their fertilizer in. If you have a movable coop—a chicken tractor—you can move the chickens to fresh patches of earth. The run doesn't get fouled, the fields get extra nutrients and the chickens produce tastier eggs." She smiled. "Hank read about the idea in some magazine and wanted to try it."

The short moment of seeing his father through Max's smile instead of his own memories was nice, but disorienting. "Did it not work?"

She shrugged. "Because the chicken wire isn't dug into the ground, it's not as secure as the coop, so we had a lot of loss to coyotes, foxes and who knows what else. Hank was going to make repairs, but some of the newly proposed farm rules would make chickens in the fields a violation, so it doesn't seem worth it."

"I'm not sure I want chicken poop on my vegetables."

"But petroleum-based fertilizer doesn't bother you?"

He grunted. Max had a way of upsetting his worldview that he appreciated, even when it wasn't comfortable.

They walked along the tall grasses and brush between the last field and the deer fence. Ashes had been plodding along, but something caught his eye and he woke up with a bound for the end of the field. Standing outside the renovated tobacco barn was Sean.

Max introduced them. Even through what Trey was guessing had to be a wicked hangover, Sean had a tough army look. His hair was still in a buzz cut and his choice of T-shirt was fatigue-green. More disturbing, though, was the anger lurking behind his bloodshot eyes. Trey recognized the look. His father had worn a similar expression—hangover included—all of Trey's childhood. Another twenty years, poor diet choices and chain smoking would turn Sean into his father.

Trey offered his hand and shook Sean's firmly. After years of working in Congress and then as a lobbyist, Trey was good at reading handshakes. Sean wanted to be alone with his sins. He wanted everyone to pretend they didn't notice his blood-shot eyes and the puffiness of his face. Sean was fit enough that, probably, in two hours, no one would be able to tell he'd spent the night participating in a home embalming experiment.

In his college partying days, Trey had seen his ability to rally as a sign he wasn't his father. Until the day he'd woken up, stumbled to the toilet for a piss and seen his old man looking back at him in the mirror.

Trey looked at Sean and saw his father at the same age—the weight of service in an unpopular war on his shoulders included. Sean was trying to find a goal for himself outside the bottle, so Trey gave him credit for that. On the other hand, the intern had spent the previous night yelling at Trey's younger brother while standing on their family land. Loss of points there. But Sean didn't try to win a handshake contest—the shake was confident, if not inviting—so Trey called the exchange even and decided he'd talk with his brother about it.

"YOU GRADUATE FROM college and flee North Carolina like you're selling 'shine and the feds are on
your tail and now you're daring to play big brother
and tell me that I should be careful who I spend
the night with?" Kelly's face was mottled with
rage, though he was hissing, rather than yelling,
the words. "Who the fuck do you think you are?"

Trey had seen Kelly turn into the driveway after
breakfast and told Max he was going out to talk with
his brother about Sean. Max had informed him that
they were grown men and so long as Sean didn't
endanger himself or the farm, she was going to stay
out of their business. When she'd first seen the beer
cans, she'd told Sean where she would draw the line
and kick him out of the program. Being drunk for
work was over the line. Being in a romantic relationship with her landlord's brother wasn't even on
the page.

But Max wasn't Kelly's older brother. Max hadn't
grown up in the same household, hiding from the
same father. She couldn't see how right Trey was,
and that irritated him. Kelly couldn't see how he
was reliving their childhood and that made his blood
boil. "Who the fuck do you think *you* are? Mama?"

Kelly stared at him, his mouth gaping open
and then shut like a bass caught on a line. When
his brother finally found a reply, Trey wished his
brother had kept silent. "Maybe I am. Maybe I'd
throw away my education and youth on some angry,

drunken fool to pop out two kids who'll one day ignore me because they think I'm weak. But it still means I'm not our daddy. And I'll take being Mama any day."

Kelly flipped Trey the finger and stalked off away from the farmhouse, in the direction of the drunken, angry man he was currently obsessed with. Leaving Trey stuck in the driveway wondering what the hell the crack about being their father was about. Trey had a good job. He had an education. Hell, he didn't even drink. He was nothing like his father.

MAX CLIMBED INTO the passenger seat of Trey's car, strapped on her seat belt and pointed in the direction of town. The farm and its boozy past and present were wearing on him, so he was ready to shift into gear and drive away, even if it was just into town. But if he was headed back to D.C., Max wouldn't be sitting next to him talking excitedly about their plans for the afternoon and all the people they would talk to.

He followed her instructions, content to let her direct him, even though he'd grown up in this town. Since he'd moved away, some of the traffic patterns had changed and his mother had never let them come downtown when they were kids anyway.

The brick mill buildings looked much the same from the outside, but the city was missing the sweet, almost grassy smell of tobacco that had been its hallmark. The tobacco mills had smelled good enough to make him forget smoking was bad for him, no matter how many antismoking campaigns had been aimed at him. But his dad had smoked, so that had been reason enough to never pick up the habit. Near the Durham School for the Arts, Max had him pull into a small parking lot by what looked to be a day spa and a butcher shop that also sold pastries.

Max knocked on the door and they were let into the shop by a young man with a beard and glasses. The woman he introduced them to was his wife and the pastry chef. Max knew them from the farmers' market and she apparently regularly bought their caramels when she was in town. She started in with her questions about their Kickstarter campaign.

The couple talked about collecting videos of support from other local Durham food ventures, including some farmers, chefs and a local brewery. A lot of what they said echoed the instructions on the Kickstarter website: Be specific with what you will spend the money on and know your budget. Sell your venture and your creativity. The video is important. Be clever in the rewards you choose. Your network is important.

The information wasn't new, but Trey could see how the idea of success was overtaking Max's fears. Her eyes got brighter, a true spring-green, and excitement flushed her freckles darker. The slope of her shoulders lowered and her face softened. The serious-sounding Max Backstrom and the lighter Maxine Patch was a woman with many interesting facets and freckles.

At eleven, the butcher shop opened for business. Max and Trey ordered some sandwiches and headed out for Main Street. "There's some tables at Five Points now where we can sit and eat. Then we have one more stop for ice cream and more Kickstarter pointers."

Construction equipment was blocking the sidewalk in front of one of the tobacco warehouses. Others that had been empty during his childhood were now restaurants and apartment buildings. There were people out walking their dogs and pushing strollers. The morning had been cool, but as the spring sun rose in the sky, people began understanding the weather according to their own sense of temperature. Max had taken off her sweatshirt and was walking around in a T-shirt and jeans. Trey kept his sweater on. Some people they passed were in shorts, while others had on jackets. He remembered one of his high school teachers saying, "If you don't like the weather in North Carolina, wait fifteen minutes." Everyone they passed seemed to be hoping for different weather.

After they finished their sandwiches, they went into the ice cream shop and each ordered a cone. Max chose Vietnamese Coffee. Trey looked at the menu and wondered if this was really the same town he grew up in, but he decided against one of the more unusual flavors and ordered plain chocolate. The proprietors of the ice cream shop said much the same thing about running a Kickstarter as the butcher and his wife had said.

As they left the store, Max wondered out loud if they should talk to people who'd run a Kickstarter in Durham and *hadn't* been funded.

"Why?"

She slid onto a bench and took a lick of her ice cream. Goose bumps appeared on her arms, making her freckles look three dimensional. He turned his attention to her mouth and the consideration she was giving both his question and her ice cream. "So we know what not to do." She shrugged. "So I know what will happen if this fails."

"If this fails, you will be in the same place you are now, only with a little more awareness of your goals. Plus, we're not going to fail."

"What's it like, being so certain in yourself and your decisions all the time? I overthink everything."

"Like your flavor of ice cream?" He took a big bite of his and felt the cold on his back teeth. The ice cream was rich, sweet and smooth. Leaving his sweater on had been a good idea, though it was possible the shivers in his spine were due more to watching Max enjoy her dessert than the iciness of his own.

She wrinkled her nose at him over her dwindling cone. "Don't be ridiculous." Then she considered the last bit of ice cream she had left. "The roasted banana and coconut did sound good, though."

Trey leaned back in his seat. The spring day was cool, but the sun had warmed the black metal chair and he felt its heat through his sweater, taking some of the edge off the ice cream. "Are you enjoying your ice cream less because you're thinking about how the roasted banana would have tasted?"

"No. That would be silly." She popped the last bit of cone in her mouth and then wiped her hands on her napkin. "I *am* thinking of going back for a pint of the banana, though."

In the corner of her mouth was a little drip of coffee ice cream. He lifted up in his chair and leaned over to kiss her, swiping the ice cream with his tongue. She was flushing when he sat back down. "Now you're thinking bigger, rather than letting some idea of failure force you to think smaller. And that's why this Kickstarter is going to work. You're going to think bigger and I'm going to help you create a strategy to make it happen. I'm good at that."

For a moment, she looked like she was going to argue with him, but stopped herself. "Okay. What first?"

"Both your friends said making a budget and asking for the right amount was important. Get out your little notebook and let's create a budget for this barn. You know how much the last one cost, right?"

"I have some idea. This barn is in worse repair and your dad covered a lot of the costs of the other barn." His disbelief must have been clear on his face, because she continued, "It was part of your mom's wishes."

Trey had to be still so that what Max was telling him could sink in. His mother crafting a more elaborate plan for farming than just "rent the land to this farmer I picked out," fit about as well with his memory of the worn-out woman as his father's care of the chickens fit with his memory of the drunk.

"I wish I could have known your mother. She seems like such a strong woman. I interacted with her a little via email, but she'd died by the time the lease was finalized and I couldn't make it to her funeral. She had such great plans for the land. I think she'd have been pleased with this Kickstarter idea."

He'd come down to visit his mother a couple times when she'd been sick, and she'd gone from diagnosed to dying so fast that he hadn't felt like he had time to do more than just tell her he would miss her. She'd said she had this great idea and that they should get together as a family to talk about it. The thought of sitting down to talk with his father about *anything* had convinced Trey that he shouldn't keep visiting.

Suddenly, the bright spring sun seemed to darken

and remorse took the place of its comforting warmth. In his determination to avoid his father, he'd missed out on getting to know his mother at what might have been her finest moment. He couldn't look back and see the woman with strength and vision the way Max could. And probably Kelly, too. He could only see the woman trapped in a loveless marriage by poverty and kids. What else about his family had he missed?

He smiled at Max, but those thoughts didn't fully go away. "Note my mom's wishes in your notebook and let's make sure that gets included in your video." He wasn't sure if doing that was capitalizing on his mom's memory or abusing it, but at least brainstorming pushed the thoughts of his mama into the background. "Right now it's budgeting time. Think big. If you could make that barn into the best intern housing available, what would it look like?"

CHAPTER TWENTY

TREY TURNED INTO the farm's driveway at ten in the morning on the next Saturday. To say his boss had been upset that he wanted another weekend off to drive to North Carolina was putting it mildly. After much arguing, they'd finally come to a compromise. Trey could have the Saturday off, but he had agreed to attend a dinner last night and was scheduled to play golf tomorrow. He'd promised Max that he'd give her the whole weekend to come down and plan the Kickstarter with her and her interns, but now that promise was only worth about half of what it should be.

He opened the car door and looked at the looming white memories of the farmhouse, dusted with a heavy coating of yellow pine pollen. Another weekend and he was here instead of in D.C. But he was only here for a day—no sleeping over. No waking up in the middle of the night with Max curled up in his arms and her hair in his nose. The only thing on the agenda today was getting Max one step closer to feeling comfortable buying the farm and him one step closer to cutting his ties with Durham.

When he'd emailed her about his change of plans. Max had said she was sorry but that they could re-schedule, since they had until September when the Northern Piedmont Farm Tour was happening to plan the Kickstarter. But Trey had promised, and so here he was. The clouds were spitting into the chill of a cloudy spring day, threatening to do worse.

He reached over to the passenger seat and grabbed his umbrella, then started through the drizzle to the front door. Once inside he wove his way through to the kitchen, where Kelly and the angry intern were sitting at the trestle table. The intern—Trey had no interest in calling the man by his name right now—ignored him. Ashes greeted him with a wag of his tail, though didn't move from his adoring pose at the intern's feet. Trey got grudging affection from the dog; the angry drunk got worship. Kelly greeted him with a cold "Hello," and gestured to the pot of coffee.

Trey let both slights roll off his shoulder. Kelly shouldn't be getting involved with a drunk. But if Kelly wanted to stick his head in the sand and let his ass hang out to be kicked, Trey couldn't stop him. His brother was a grown man.

"Where's Max?" Trey asked when he sat at the table with his cup.

"She's at the farmers' market selling," Sean re-plied, with a derisive rise to his eyebrows. "It's how she makes her money. Selling produce."

Trey opened his mouth to snap back, saw the pain on Kelly's face and stopped. Sean's eyes were bloodshot. His face was puffy and his eyes had the tight look of a man who'd tied on twelve last night—and then tried for a baker's dozen. Picking a fight with a man in such a state was almost as stupid as picking a fight with a drunk.

They sat around the table in uncomfortable silence until Sean finally stood and said he was going to take a nap. Trey's better sense told him not to call, "They're not called naps if you do it hugging the toilet." Besides, the person Trey really wanted to smack was Kelly; Sean was only in the way.

"What the hell do you think you're doing?" Kelly asked as soon as the porch door banged shut.

"Me? What the hell do you think *you're* doing? That guy's a fucking waste of space."

"He needed to relax last night." Trey took a good, long look at his brother. Kelly had puffy eyes and there was still sleep in the corner of them, but he didn't smell like alcohol. He looked worn down.

"Listen to you, defending that drunk like Mom defending Dad. What's Sean's excuse for finishing a fifth of liquor every other night?"

"You tried that argument last time you were here. It didn't work then and it won't work now. You don't really care who I spend my evenings with. You've never cared before. Maybe Sean's only the most recent in a long line of drunks. Maybe I like fucking drunks. Maybe we both have daddy issues."

Trey smashed his fist into the trestle table. The thick wood had absorbed many fists over the years it had been in the Harris family, and the coffee in his mug barely shimmered. "At least I'm trying to do something other than repeat our parents' mistakes."

"Fuck it. I'm not sticking around for this shit." Kelly pulled a folded piece of paper out from his pocket and threw it on top of the table. "Tell Max I'm sorry I couldn't be here, but I've jotted down our ideas. And Aunt Lois's."

Trey picked up the note. "Does Sean even have ideas?" he asked, regretting the words as soon as they were out of his mouth.

Kelly snatched the paper out of Trey's hand and stomped over to the counter. He grabbed a pen from a drawer and scribbled something on the page, then balled it up and tossed it at Trey. It landed in the middle of the floor. They both stared at it, then their heads shifted in tandem and they stared at each other. Neither moved to pick up the paper.

Kelly blinked first, though he walked past the balled-up paper. He stopped at the table.

"Don't forget that you're playing the benevolent landlord and lover to the cute farmer today—the last Harris generation to own this farm and *so* happy to turn the farm over to new hands. Give the farm new life and all that shit you don't really believe in. Make sure you've got that anger boiling up inside you buried deep enough that it doesn't explode. Wouldn't want Max to see through the facade to the scared little boy cowering in a corner." Then his brother walked out the door.

Trey waited for the sound of a car starting that never came. His brother had gone back to the barn to be with his drunk.

Trey stood, got himself a second cup of coffee and picked up the paper on his way back to the table. The scribbled item was to "highlight the land's farming tradition." He snorted. If growing beer cans in the woods was a farming tradition, then Sean was following fine in Trey's father's footsteps.

Aunt Lois's idea was to show parts of the house and farm "where history had happened," as if this was Bennett Place and Confederate troops had surrendered to the North en mass instead of Hank Harris's farm, where beer cans had been the only thing to fall in the line of service. History had definitely happened here and was repeating itself.

Trey should get himself a calendar and circle the date when he was able to sign the land over to Max and never have to worry about it again. He took his cup of dusty, oily coffee outside and sat in one of the rockers on the front porch. The sun was breaking through the clouds, but another storm was threatening on the horizon. There would be rain for his drive home. He took a deep breath. The spring chill cooled his lungs and his anger, but he wished for the silence people imagined in the country instead of the drone of insects and birds. The country was never silent.

The refrigerator truck came into view. Max was home. She turned down the drive. He couldn't see her face for all her hair and he didn't think she noticed him sitting in the shadows of the porch as she drove the truck around to park it by the packing shed. He set his coffee on the floor and walked to meet her. When she caught sight of him, a smile burst out on her thin, pale lips. Suddenly, the farm felt like a different world. The house was no longer a place of angry drunks with good Southern heritage, but a fairyland where a Midwestern sprite transformed water, dirt and sun into food.

Only this sprite wasn't some figment of a drunken peasant's imagination. Her footsteps kicked up dirt as she walked toward him. Her arms were strong as she wrapped them around his waist. And her lips were warm when he leaned in for a kiss.

When he pulled away, the wind had picked up, speeding in the storm that would hassle his drive north. The small, new leaves on the trees danced in the air. Max's hair whipped around her neck but didn't dare cover her face. His sprite controlled the currents of the earth.

"You look pleased with yourself," he said.

"Where's Sean?" She looked around, puffed up

and excited. "I sold out of vegetables at the market. Sidney and Norma Jean are putting away the crates so I can go account for the money before our brainstorming session."

"Sean's in the barn with Kelly." For one fleeting moment, the temptation to spare Max the knowledge that her employee was hungover when she needed him awake and ready to work passed through his mind. But that would be a momentary kindness, which would exacerbate the problem later. Plus, this Max could take Sean. "He's sleeping off a hangover."

A shadow skittered across Max's face. "He promised me he was cutting back. That it wouldn't affect his work."

"You shouldn't believe the promises of a drunk."

She made a noise in the back of her throat—of acknowledgment, of agreement, of denial, he couldn't tell.

"Why are you and Kelly so willing to overlook Sean's drinking problem?"

"I can't speak for Kelly, but Sean's a hard worker. Working the land nourishes him and he nourishes it in return."

"He's a drunk. Drunks don't change."

The frustration on her face turned to pity when she looked at him. "We all hold the capacity for change, Trey. Some of us just take longer than others." His arm grew warm as she rubbed her hand against his shirt. "I'll talk with Sean later. Could you make another pot of coffee? I have some treats from the farmers' market for us to eat while we're brainstorming."

CHAPTER TWENTY-ONE

MAX GAVE TREY the first-of-the-season carrots to cut while she made a dip for them and the radishes. Neither broccoli nor cauliflower was in season, so her vegetable tray would be on the red side of the spectrum. But that couldn't be helped. In the winter, when she was sick of greens and sweet potatoes, she'd go to the grocery store for out-of-season vegetables, but not now when she only had to wait another couple weeks for all the spring vegetables and another two months for tomatoes.

She looked out the kitchen window to the willow tree being whipped around by the wind. Another rainstorm. If the storms don't quit, there will be no tomatoes or squash or eggplant. She squelched that thought. Of course it would dry out. This wasn't Portland.

Trey took the vegetable tray, which also now had apples and grapes on it, and put it on the table. When he returned, Max was cutting up the pastries. "What are those?" he asked.

"Empanadas and pigs in a blanket. Plus some

doughnut muffins. I've got some cheese, too, and a loaf of bread."

"All from the farmers' market?"

"Well, yes. Don't they have farmers' markets in D.C.?"

"I'm sure they do." He looked sheepish for the first time since she'd met him. It was a cute look on him—made his cheeks look rounder and softened his eyes. Boyish, without the anger rolling in him from his childhood. This was how he would have looked with different parents and a different life.

Max pushed those thoughts out of her head, too. While not a religious woman, her mother had always said that God never gave anyone a burden they couldn't handle, and rather than wasting time wondering if you did the right thing, you should accept the decision and make the best of the future it gave you. Max didn't have too much argument with her mother's advice, but accepting past decisions had never been her problem—feeling confident you were making the correct decision in the present was. Like her father, she made pro and con lists in her head. Seemingly unlike her father, Max got trapped in those lists.

Trey had clearly made the best out of his past and he seemed comfortable with the decisions that he was making in the present. To wish a different past on him was to wish a different future on him as well, and that seemed to diminish his successes. Instead, she'd just be glad to catch a glimpse of the boy.

"But you've never been to one," she finished for him.

"I eat out a lot and have never seen the need."

"You should come to the Durham market with me one weekend." Max picked up the plate of pastries and set it on the table alongside the vegetables and dip. "See what's there and how Durham has changed."

He chuckled. "My aunt Lois sent me an email the other day that said something very similar. She's still hoping I'll move back down here. Are you two working together?"

"I'm not…" She stopped herself before she spoke a lie. Was she not trying to convince him that Durham had changed? Even more worrying, was she trying to convince him to move down here? That seemed like a definite no. When he came to Durham, they shared a bed. She enjoyed his company and the decisive way he approached life. She liked how he could walk around her farm in a suit and not get a speck of dirt on him. But their entire relationship was based on his selling her the farm and severing all ties to his North Carolina past.

"Don't be silly, Trey. Our relationship is temporary—that's one of its pluses. Besides," she said, "convincing you to move back to Durham would be self-defeating after I worked so hard to convince you to sell me the farm."

This time he laughed out loud. "Don't worry about that. Even if moving to Durham entered my mind, I would never move back to the farm."

Well, that settles that. "You should still come to a farmers' market. At least see the money-making side of this enterprise we're trying to fund." She put a light tone in her voice to cover up her irrational disappointment.

A knock on the kitchen door announced the arrival of Sidney and Norma Jean. She gestured at the two interns to sit at the table, smiling and pretending like nothing was wrong. *Nothing* was *wrong.* She had fresh bread, local cheese and her own vegetables to nosh on. Company she enjoyed was seating themselves around a table in a farmhouse that would be hers in December, barring disaster. And they were going to plan a fund-raising campaign so she could fix up the second barn and have two live-in interns through the winter. She'd be able to run a winter CSA and sell at the winter market. Everything was rosy.

"Where are Kelly and Sean?" Sidney asked.

Max checked the watch on her belt loop. "Um. Trey said that Sean needed a nap and Kelly went with him. So I'm not sure if they're coming back."

Trey cleared his throat. "That's right, but I have their notes and ideas here." He pulled a folded piece of paper from his back pocket and smoothed it out on the table. There were both creases from the folds and creases from where it looked like the paper had been balled up.

She sat at the table next to Trey, trying not to notice the tingle that ran down her spine when his leg brushed against hers, or that their hands grazed against each other when they reached for carrots at the same time. Instead, she got out her pen and concentrated on making sure her notes would be readable later, when she had to turn the brainstorming into something tangible.

Trey repeated what they'd learned from the butcher and the ice cream store owners, both for the interns' benefit and as a refresher for him and Max. Then he leaned back in his chair and let the interns speak.

Sidney and Norma Jean looked at each other and offered a couple of their ideas for which CSA members might be interested in doing a video. Max took notes and offered her own ideas, but eventually she stopped actively participating and just started watching Trey interact with her two interns.

Despite Sidney being a young woman and Norma Jean being an older one, Max acted as teacher to both of them. Their interaction with Trey was completely different. They'd been hesitant at first, but it didn't take long for Trey to get them talking. He asked questions, encouraged, poked and challenged and they responded. Max learned more about her interns' skills outside of farming listening to them talk to Trey than she had in a month of working closely with them.

Norma Jean liked to make woven bracelets on the side and offered some as a gift for donors, which Max thought was a great idea. And Trey pushed Norma Jean even further until she grabbed the notepad from Max and was sketching out how the weaves would reflect the seasons of the farm.

She drew out a pattern inspired by what their squash and melon field would look like in the summer, the vines twining together and little bits of the fruit peeking out from under the large leaves. There was one of the tomato field, with the bright yellows and reds of the tomatoes and purple of the eggplants. And there was one of the fallow field, the crimson clover brilliant in the spring sun. Each bracelet would come with a picture of the farm and a story of the inspiration for the pattern.

The bracelets had been Norma Jean's idea, but the push for it had come from Trey. Trey had given her intern the encouragement to think bigger and more creatively. To say he was *letting* the interns shine wasn't accurate, because it wasn't about them seeking permission—it was about Trey creating the opportunity for success. And he looked pleased with himself, as well.

His shoulders and jaw were relaxed. There was

a slight smile on his face that made his eyes bright. He looked like how she felt when she saw the first sprouts of spring, full of the pleasure she experienced knowing that she had created the environment that let the plant do what it did best.

This was not the bitter man of this morning. *This is a man I could love.*

CHAPTER TWENTY-TWO

MAX KNOCKED ON the barn door late Monday morning. Kelly's car was gone, so Sean wasn't enjoying a cozy sleep-in with his lover. Sidney and Norma Jean had headed out to the fields over an hour ago. If she had to guess, Sean was hungover. She balled her hand into a fist and pounded on the wooden door before a sense of kindness could convince her to knock softly. She was his boss. Kindness didn't enter into the equation.

Sean's appearance shocked her into saying, "You look like shit," as soon as he opened the door.

He leaned against the doorway, a slow smile on his normally handsome face. "Good morning to you, too."

Then he scrubbed his face with his hands and the smell of stale booze and cigarettes hit her. She sniffed again. *Was that pot?* If he was growing pot on her farm... No, she didn't want to think about that now. She had steeled herself for one difficult conversation and she wasn't yet ready to have another.

"I could ignore that you're an hour late, but you

aren't in any condition to work right now." The wrinkles in his face from whatever piece of fabric he'd slept on would need a belt sander to get out. Then there were the bloodshot eyes, and the way he couldn't focus on her face for longer than a couple seconds before he had to look away. "I can't see how you could be out in the fields in less than an hour without vomiting all over my plants."

His Adam's apple bobbed as he swallowed once. Twice. Then a third time. "Bad dreams, that's all."

"Play the wounded-vet card on Kelly. He seems to eat it up. I'm not interested. I hired you to have a strong back and tender hands—and I wanted those for my tomato plants, not for me." Before she said her next words, Max took a steadying breath. "You have a week to find yourself a rehab program to attend. I'll give you time off for meetings. I won't even tell Vets to Farms that you're drinking. But if you don't find a program, or you slip and miss a meeting before the season is up, I will fire you without blinking. You'll be out of a job and you'll be out of housing."

Sean was either eyeing her for seriousness or trying to focus on something that would help him stay upright. "Kelly will take me in."

"Will he?" She looked directly into his eyes as she asked the question; Sean looked away first. "That's what I thought. If you need today off, you can have it, but not again. I have too much work on the farm to accommodate drunkards."

Before she lost her nerve, Max turned on the heel of her boot and marched off the porch, Ashes at her side. Once they were behind the house and out of sight of the barn, she collapsed cross-legged on the dirt. Hank had been a misogynist and would probably have made a terrible boss, but he had also happily taken care of the discipline problems among her employees. Not that she'd had very many, but there had been a couple. Hank had enjoyed laying down the law—Max didn't. The division of labor had happened so naturally that she hadn't noticed how much she'd relied on the old man until he wasn't here to be her enforcer.

Her moment of self-indulgence over, Max stood, wiped the dirt off her clothes and headed back to the fields. She'd take the .22 out after the farmwork was over and shoot cans. Of course, since Hank was dead, she wouldn't have an endless supply of targets. Hank had been an asshole, but his death had left a hole in her life that wouldn't be easily filled.

MAX HAD BEEN so lost in her thoughts while hoeing weeds in the carrot fields that Sean's cough startled her. She looked at the watch on her belt loop, then up at her intern. He was presentable—mostly. He either actually smelled better, or the fresh scent of dirt and spring vegetables covered up the stink of alcohol. In any case, if he had come to the fields like this on time, she might not have laid down her ultimatum. "Can you work?"

He started to nod, then turned a pale green. After taking a deep breath, he nodded again, this time with more confidence. "I've had two bottles of V8 and half a bottle of aspirin. If I keep drinking water, I should be fine."

"You're lucky it's only the beginning of May. If this were July, I'd ban you from the fields for the day out of fear that heat exhaustion would kill you. As it is, I'm going to keep a close eye on you. If you start to wobble, you're done for the day."

Sean nodded again, apparently chastened by his weakness.

"I expect to hear about a rehab group by next Monday."

"I'll have it to you by Friday." He said this with a force she didn't fully believe could be sloshing around under all the alcohol.

"Oh?"

"Kelly's deadline before he left was Friday."

Knowing Kelly was also on her side—and on Sean's—gave her more courage. "And the pot?"

Sean had the grace to blush, making his skin match the blood she suspected was shooting through the whites of his eyes. He had on dark sunglasses, but the tightness around his mouth was a dead give-away that he was one loud noise or bright flash away from barfing on her plants. "It won't happen again."

"Are you growing it here?"

"No."

She lifted her sunglasses up off her head and looked at him. When he didn't meet her eyes, she reached out, pulled his glasses off his face and stared until he met her gaze. "There's some growing in the woods, near the creek, but I didn't plant it. There's a good crop of it. Probably been there for years."

Just as she was mourning Hank's death... "After we're done for the day, you'll show me where it is and I'll make sure it disappears. I can't have a drunk—" he winced at the words "—working on my farm, and I definitely can't have pot growing wild on my property." God knows what would have happened if it had been discovered during an inspection. The very thought made her heart pound and her breath shorten.

She wondered how long Sean had known, and if he'd ever planned to tell her. The trouble with drunks was that they are hard to trust. The trouble with this particular drunk was Max had kept her blinders on for too long. Fear of getting through the summer season short a worker. Hope that Sean would pull his shit together and be the farmer he wanted to be.

Ugh. Well, this is one more lesson I'll have learned this summer.

"Pot goes in the same category as drinking. Go to meetings. If I catch you, you're gone."

"Yes, ma'am." He tensed like there was a salute coming, but his hands stayed by his sides. Or maybe that twitch was a precursor to an upset stomach. Either way, she wanted to be far away from him until she reined in her urge to beat him senseless.

"Go take over from Sidney in the greenhouse. Work as long as you can. If you have to quit for the day, I'd rather you tell me than I find out tomorrow. Do I make myself clear?"

He nodded. After she turned her concentration back down to the carrots, he started to walk away. Walk was a polite term. Sean shuffled like a man both deathly ill and chastened. Hopefully he could give her enough work to help her get through this season. She needed a full staff and perfect weather if she was going to feel comfortable writing Trey and the bank a check at the end of the year.

She pushed at the hoe too hard. The tool slipped and she nearly cut the top off a carrot. A good summer required her concentration—the more energy she spent being stressed out about all the changes in her life, the more carrots she'd behead.

THE NEXT DAY, Max walked into the house to a voice mail from Trey. "I'm thinking I'll come down this weekend. See how the Kickstarter planning is going. Take you to dinner. I'd like to stay at the farm, if that's all right with you. Though we could take a vacation to Kelly's apartment, which I understand is still empty most nights."

The last bit made her chuckle. Trey hadn't been able to hide his dislike of Sean. He'd tried not to be the big, older brother upset with who his younger sibling had gotten messed up with, but he was only fooling himself. More amusing, Trey was obviously torn between trying to warn Kelly off a man he considered bad news and respecting that Kelly was a grown man who could make his own decisions. Playing the role of older brother for the first time in years was probably hard enough. Trying to do so when you weren't sure what the rules were for warning your brother away from a man was going to tax all of Trey's charm and energy.

Thinking about Trey's predicament was easier than addressing her mixed feelings about the man. The more time she spent with him, the more time she wanted to spend with him. She respected his advice about her business. She looked forward to seeing him, even if the way he challenged her wasn't always relaxing. She loved seeing his smile. And she definitely wanted another go at sex with him.

But the more time she spent with him, the clearer it was to her how foolish expecting anything other than a fling would be. He was angry at his father and he hated the farm. He lived in D.C. and wasn't moving back. He'd never expressed any interest in this lasting longer than the time it took for her to buy the property.

He is a man I could love.

She could tell him that she wanted their relationship to last beyond their business dealings—just open her mouth and blurt out all the feelings milling about in her heart. But what would be the purpose? She wasn't moving to D.C. for him; why should she expect him to move south for her?

He is a man I could love.

It wasn't fair for her not to tell Trey how she felt, but Max didn't think she had enough energy right now to risk being fair....

She returned his call. "No minivacation at Kelly's, but I'm looking forward to seeing you."

"Great. I'm sorry I couldn't come down last weekend. I had a bunch of work I'd been putting off, plus some events that I had to attend."

"Must be nice to attend *events* as part of your job," she said with a smile.

"It's better now that I can escape to the farm for a break from everything."

Did he realize he'd referred to the farm as a break? She wished she could see his face and all the meaning in his eyes. She also wished she could shake her head and get rid of the "is all I am a country vacation to you" thoughts from her head. They weren't fair to him. As long as she wasn't willing to risk asking him for more, she shouldn't be hurt by feelings he might not have.

"Just so you know, I have to work the farmers' market on Saturday morning."

"Besides seeing you, the market is one of the things I'm most looking forward to. I want to see the farming revolution you're a part of and that my family's land will be connected to."

Max tucked the phone in the crook of her neck and gestured to Ashes to follow her into the living room. "Not that long ago you were ready to sell this land to a developer and only decided to sell it to me under duress. This is quite a change of opinion."

There was only silence on the other end of the line for a long time. "You're right. One of the first rules you learn as a professional convincer is not to fall prey to your own marketing, and I've fallen prey to everything we're going to tell people in your Kickstarter. I believe in Max's Vegetable Patch."

She fell into Hank's old recliner—it was much more comfortable than the kitchen chairs. "Thank you."

The words weren't adequate—especially considering the week she was having. Sean seemed to be making the most of his last week of drunkenness. She hoped he took to sobriety with the same enthusiasm. "Really, from the bottom of my heart, thank you."

"Is something wrong on the Patch?"

It was Max's turn to be silent.

"I don't believe in Max's Vegetable Patch so much as I believe in you, Max."

Should she heed Trey's warning and be careful falling prey to her own marketing, even if the positive press was out of Trey's own mouth? He was a sympathetic ear and gave good advice. In the long run, she needed him to sell her the property—not be a believer. A good listener was more important. "I've had to give Sean an ultimatum." Then she told him the rest. Like that first week when Trey had asked for a tour, her insecurities poured out of her until no pile of sandbags existed that could stop them. "I'm not sure Sean's relationship with Kelly or me will survive his last week of alcohol."

"This is harder on both you and Kelly because you let yourself develop a relationship with him."

"I'm his boss," she said, deliberately misunderstanding what he was saying. "Of course I'm going to develop a relationship with him."

Trey ignored her. "And he disappointed you, as drunks always do."

"I'd rather risk disappointment than keep myself closed off from someone with wonderful potential. And, drunk or not, Sean still has the potential to be a great farmer—even a great partner for Kelly."

"Okay."

"Okay?" Trey was a man with strong opinions

and once he'd committed to the fight, Max had been sure he'd follow through until she cried exhaustion.

"I don't want to fight with you about Sean in the little time we have together before December."

"Oh." Trey's sudden capitulation didn't feel so good anymore.

"You said before that Max's Vegetable Patch was your farm and you would manage it how you wanted. I said I supported you. I gave you advice and acknowledged you knew both the farm and Sean better than I did. I still disagree with how you handled it, but if I really support you and The Patch, I shouldn't play Monday-morning quarterback."

With one hand, life hands you a man who can both disagree with and support you. With the other hand, life informs you that this man won't be staying around long, so don't get comfortable with him. "Thank you" was all she could say in response, wishing he was next to her instead of on the other end of the phone.

"However, if you ask me how I feel *before* you discipline Sean again, I'll argue with you until we're both blue in the face." His tone had lightened and she managed a laugh in return.

"Plus, you and Kelly are both right that Sean isn't my dad."

"Ugh, your dad. I can't believe Hank had pot growing on the farm."

"Don't blame my dad for that."

She blinked. "Did you just excuse your father for something?"

Trey snorted. "I guess I did. But my dad hated hippies and anything he associated with hippies, including pot. He's never forgiven them for, well, for the sixties."

"He had gotten better. At least—" she had to be honest here "—he got better about some things and learned to shut up about the rest."

A grunt came over the phone. "Tell me what you plan to do about Sean."

"I thought you didn't want to argue about him."

"I don't. But I think you need someone to talk to. I can give advice without arguing." He paused. "I think."

With a smile, Max told him. Trey made all the right noises. He clucked and hmmed and she could feel him nodding from five hours away. Finally, when she'd laid out all her staffing problems, he said, "You'll figure it out. No matter what I think, you need to feel that you made the right decision." The struggle in his voice was clear, but she appreciated his effort to lend her support and not criticism.

"Maybe I should fire Sean." She shrugged at Ashes, who was too busy sleeping to concern himself with her conversation. "I *can* function with only two interns." She would work from sunup to sundown, but it was possible.

"Maybe." Disappointment pinched. Had she

meant the words as a test of Trey's faith in her? "But the question isn't whether you can, but whether you should." There was a pause. "Do you know what I imagine when I picture you?"

"Mud and red hair?"

His laugh was full and hearty enough to travel to Durham and swell her heart without the help of a phone line. "Specifically, yes, though not always the mud. Sometimes freckles and the hair. Sometimes your hair, the fields and no mud and no clothes."

She leaned her head back in the recliner and pictured that, too. There was a nice flat spot between the first and second fields, down by the ponds. She could ignore the chiggers and ticks if she let her mind come back to that image tonight. And she'd include a picnic....

Then she shook her head clear. This was why a relationship with Trey was risky. So long as she could tell herself this was a time-limited fling, she could hold herself steady. But as it grew to mean more to her, Max knew she was just holding her heart out, waiting for it to be crushed. "Okay. Besides the red hair, what do you see?"

"A woman who stood on *my* property and dared me to question her place."

Was that what she had been doing?

The temptation to prevaricate, to be humble at his words, gushed into the room. Max ignored the flood. "Then I will dare Sean to disobey me. And if he leaves, I will hire someone else."

"That's the woman I remember. She's a bit foolish because she still believes in Big Ten basketball, but she stands by her pronouncements, and I admire that."

Max got up from the recliner, calmer than she'd been when she sat down. "I have to cook dinner and if I stay on the phone with you, I'll just get a big head."

"You could give me a big head."

She snorted. "You need practice with your dirty talk."

"I can't practice on the politicians. They don't appreciate it, at least not from me."

"You'll be down this weekend. You can practice on me." That was enough future for now.

CHAPTER TWENTY-THREE

IF TREY WAS going to be in a relationship with a farmer, he was either going to have to start waking up when the sun winked at the horizon or get used to waking up alone. No lazy weekend-morning sex with Max so long as she was up and out the door to be ready for the farmers' market when it opened at eight in the morning.

Relationship? The word flashed in his head before he could stop it. If this ended in December as they'd both agreed, then it wasn't a *relationship* in the heavy sense of the word. When her Kickstarter was over and he had sold her the land, they'd have to redefine whatever it was they were doing. He didn't know how they could maintain a long-distance relationship when they both understood that neither would move, but he also knew he wouldn't want this to be over with the new year.

However this relationship ended, he was going to be awake tomorrow morning for morning sex— even if he had to set an alarm and bring the coffeepot into the bedroom.

In the kitchen, his coffeepot was out, along with

a bag of coffee and the grinder. A Post-it stuck on it read, "I thought about making coffee, but I didn't know how much to use. There's my swill on the counter if you want it. Breakfast at the market."

He smiled. Tonight, he'd prepare the coffee and the first one up would only have to press a button for something other than swill. Maybe he'd even be awake enough to bring Max coffee in bed.

TREY HAD NEVER been to a farmers' market in D.C., so he hadn't known what to expect. He had figured there'd be people, but the crowds were a surprise. So were the food trucks and the woman selling yarn. He knew Durham's food scene had boomed, and that small farming was giving new life to North Carolina's agricultural economy. But this was not just new life.

Bounty was the word that came to mind.

If he had stayed in North Carolina, could he have been part of this dramatic shift in his hometown? Trey scratched at the back of his neck. He couldn't have stayed. If he had stayed...

Stopping at a booth that sold pies distracted him from the question. He bought several empanadas, a trio of pigs in a blanket, those tasty doughnut muffins and a whole lemon chess pie that would be delicious with some of Max's fresh strawberries. Then his wallet was almost empty of cash. He shouldn't have blown all his money at one booth when he could also see cheese and meat sellers down the aisle.

"Trey Harris? Is that you?"

The unknown voice surprised him, and he turned in a full circle to find its source. His high school girlfriend was walking toward him with a baby on one hip and another child holding her hand. His mind tracked all the ways she looked different than she had when he'd last seen her between their first and second years of college. She'd gained some weight, her hair was now cut to just below her ears and the blond had darkened to nearly brown. But her brown eyes were still shining and her smile was still warm. She looked happy, and prettier than he remembered.

"Patty, how are you?" He stuck out his hand for a shake and was instead enveloped into a hug. She smelled like baby powder and Irish Spring soap. The baby didn't seem to mind being squeezed between them.

"I *was* fine. Now I'm flabbergasted. I never thought I'd see the day when Trey Harris walked around the Durham Farmers' Market. Isn't there a force field at the border that keeps you in Virginia?"

"Hah." His laugh was hollow, but Patty didn't notice. "Dad died. I'm selling the farm."

"That red-haired woman farms his land, doesn't she? Max's Vegetable Patch? I have some friends who get their CSA from her."

"That's the one. If everything works out, Max will own the land and your friends can continue to get their CSA from her. In fact, she's going to be launching a Kickstarter in September and it would be great if they all donated money."

Patty listened to his sales pitch with a half smile on her face and promised to come by for the farm tour in September. Before she continued on with her shopping, her eyes softened and she said, "I'm sorry about your dad."

"Thanks" was all he could muster up. Then he carried his largesse to Max's booth before Patty could say anything else.

When he came up to the booth arrayed with spring vegetables, Max was weighing some carrots and Sean was giving someone their change. "Oh," she said when she saw him, "did you buy us some treats from Scratch?"

Trey passed his bags over and Max set them in the back of the truck. After she and Sean had rung up a few more customers, Max gave her intern some cash and sent him off for some coffee to go with their breakfast. "You can sell vegetables while Sean and I eat our breakfast."

"Where are the other two?"

"Sidney and Norma Jean?" She put another pint of peas out to replace one that had just sold. "It's supposed to rain this afternoon so they're trying to finish the last of the weeding before the ground gets wet. When you hoe in wet soil all you do is push the weeds over."

"And him?" Trey gestured with his head in the direction Sean had gone.

"I can keep an eye on him better this way. I apologized to Kelly for dragging his boyfriend out of bed so early on a Saturday morning, but we both agreed it was in Sean's best interest. He was red-eyed this morning, but he didn't smell like a distillery floor, so I think he was just tired."

"And," he lowered his voice, "the pot?"

Sean returned with their coffee, so Max didn't get a chance to answer his last question. She and Sean sold more vegetables and talked with customers about the farm or what variety of carrot or radish they were buying. Trey chatted up people in line, asking them about the market and what they planned to do with their produce. A couple people looked at Trey in his dark jeans and dress shirt and seemed to know he was decoration. They waited for Max or Sean to answer their questions, though he did take money from a few customers. He scoped out a couple people Max seemed especially friendly with who also had enough presence that he thought they'd do well on a video for the Kickstarter. At his urging, Max wrote down their names so she would remember to ask them when the launch was closer.

The small part of him that was still in D.C., still trying to get the education bill passed, whispered,

Ask everyone to call their senator and congressman about the bill, but Trey silenced the voice before it got any traction. Besides coming to North Carolina for Max, he was doing it to get away from the education bill—he was sick of it. The Triangle reps to the House were all for the thing and the senators were entrenched in their positions—one yay and one nay—so it would be a waste of breath, even if he was willing to dirty Max's own campaign with his.

Not that anyone would listen to him talk about anything other than Max's farm right now. Some of the people bought their vegetables and left, but those who stayed to chat were clearly interested in Max and the farm. When he'd researched how to sell Max's Kickstarter, he'd quickly discovered that the local food movement was plastered with the adage "know your farmer." Max's customers knew and loved her.

"When do you want to start on the video?" Trey asked after the crowds had cleared from the market and they were eating their empanadas in between loading their stuff.

"Ugh," she said with her face wrinkled in disgust. "I know I have to do the video, but I'm not looking forward to it."

"Contact a couple people from your CSA and we'll do their video first. Invite them to the farm for lunch. Give them a tour and we'll film them talking about how much they love you." Convincing people to laud a business whose product they liked and business ethic they believed in sounded like the easiest thing in the world.

"The McKenzies'll do it for sure," Sean said. "They get a regular CSA delivery on Wednesdays and buy vegetables every Saturday."

Max swallowed her bite of food and wiped her hands on her jeans before speaking.

"I'm going to whine once and then I'll put on my big girl britches and do it, but I wish I could just grow vegetables and people would buy them. I like selling carrots. I hate selling myself."

"Done?"

She wrinkled her nose again. Some of her freckles disappeared, but most seemed to grow bigger as the wrinkles linked one freckle with another. "Yes," she said finally. "I'll keep the rest of my whine to myself."

"You can share it with me, but I'm not going to sympathize." Trey collected their food wrappers into the paper bag, which Sean took out of his hand before heading off in search of a trash can.

Max watched her intern march off and shrugged. The man wavered between attempted friendliness and standoffishness. It was like there was some barrier he was trying to break through—probably a thick layer of alcohol.

Max turned her attention back to Trey. "I don't

really want sympathy, because sympathy might convince me not to do it, but I don't want the nerves
bundled up inside me, either."

"I'll come down for the video and we'll do it together. I can't come down next weekend, or the
weekend after that, but I can come down… When
is that?"

"Memorial Day?"

"Great. I'll drive down after work on Friday and
teach you to make a sale on Saturday. You can practice selling things to me all weekend. I'll even play
hard to get," he said with a waggle of his eyebrows.

She gave him a long, hard look before she answered, "Sure."

He hadn't expected to have to sell her on his help.

CHAPTER TWENTY-FOUR

MAX SAT ON the folding chair under the roof of the pack house. The day was sunny, with a nice breeze, both of which should help dry out her fields after a week of straight rain. At her feet were crates and crates of onions to clean, which would then go in the greenhouse to dry out for storage.

She tossed an onion into the crate before looking at the watch on her belt loop. Sean was two hours late. The other two interns were out in the fields, trying to hoe the weeds out from under the tomatoes, but Max had assigned Sean to onion-prepping duty. Despite his preference for being out in the fields, she wanted to talk with him about how his meetings were going.

The past couple weeks Sean seemed to have blossomed—as much as a silent, stoic man can. He talked a little while working, even with Sidney. The drinking seemed to have been the cause of most of his fights with Kelly, because those had settled down, too. Max was beginning to see the engagement with farming that she'd witnessed in Sean's interview.

But now he was two hours late, and she was assuming the worst.

Living on the same property as her workers was fine when they didn't have a private life. She'd not really considered how she would handle the issue of employee privacy when they were living on *her* land and working on *her* farm. She'd just been excited to be able to offer the barn for housing. More convenient for the intern. Cheaper for her.

She cut the brown bits of stalk and skin off the onion and tossed it to the side. She didn't usually have to wish that she'd overthought something and considered all the negative possibilities, but this was one time where she wished that she had. If she'd considered what to do with an alcoholic intern earlier, maybe she wouldn't be sitting here cleaning onions, obsessively checking her watch.

Sean could legitimately be sick, have a summer cold, food poisoning or a migraine. Max didn't want to wish illness on anyone, but illness was better than what she was afraid she would find when she knocked on his door. Another onion went into the crate, this time with more force than the vegetable deserved. *It* hadn't done anything wrong.

If he's not here by the time this crate is empty, then I will confront him. She looked down into the crate of onions. There were only two left. Her immediate thought was to have the rule she'd just set for herself apply to the next crate, but she dismissed her cowardliness. While part of the attraction of small farming had been the smaller number of employees and less required management of people, she was still Sean's boss and she needed to act like it. She rushed through the last two onions, tossed her knife in the empty bin and headed for the barn.

Out of the shade of the packing shed's roof, the sun was warming the moist air. Max stopped her march to the barn to look up into the sky. Today was the first day they'd been able to be out in the fields hoeing weeds, and the clear sky teased that they might have a sunny day tomorrow, too. Which meant everyone would be out working on a Saturday, trying to get as much done as possible while the soil was dry. "Make hay while the sun shines," as the saying goes. Only Max needed to "hoe weeds after three sunny days."

And two days of sun wouldn't be enough to dry out her flooded cornfields. And she'd have to wait for the spent kohlrabi, broccoli and cauliflower fields to dry out before turning the soil under to prep it for planting. Again.

The rain had ruined all their work of last week.

But at least they'd managed to get some onions harvested and out to dry. The air wafting out of the greenhouse was tinged with the smell of onions. By late afternoon, if she could see the building, she'd be able to smell the onions; the heat of the sun tended to make them pungent. When she passed the farmhouse, Ashes came out from behind the side porch and followed her to the barn. He was less willing to work on the sunny days and had so far spent today napping in the shade.

Max knocked on the barn door. Ashes sat at her feet, his tail swooshing on the wood of the barn's porch, and looking at the door with a big, doggy grin. Sean was one of Ashes's favorite people. Though when the door opened, even her dog looked shocked. Months' worth of sun couldn't cover up the sick pallor of Sean's skin, and his entire body had the tightness of someone trying desperately to pretend they didn't feel like shit.

She and Ashes both sniffed the air, though for different reasons. Whatever her dog smelled, he'd keep to himself, but she didn't smell any alcohol. "Can I come in?" she asked.

He nodded once then stepped back. She hadn't been in the barn since March. When she'd lived here, the barn had been spare. Now it was Spartan. The same furniture she'd used was in all the same places, but any softness was gone. Sean had no decoration, no photos of his family, no detritus lying around the house. Everything was neat as a pin and just as comfortable looking.

He collapsed into the recliner, his body contracting like he wanted to curl up into a ball, but he straightened himself out and managed to look like he was sitting normally—if she ignored the strain that sitting obviously caused him. He shivered in the warm room, but didn't get up to get a sweatshirt or pull a blanket over himself.

"I have to poke around for alcohol."

He nodded again, still not having said a word since she'd knocked on his door. And she did feel bad. Everything about Sean bawled out sickness, but she needed to make sure. After all, hangovers were a type of sickness, too.

Ashes came over to her intern and rested his chin on the man's knee, both in support and in hopes of a pet. He reached out his hand as if to scratch behind Ashes's ears, but the effort seemed to be too much. His hand fell through the air, smacking her dog on the forehead. Ashes grunted, but didn't yelp. He moved his head back and forth under Sean's hand, content to pet himself.

She opened cabinet doors and the refrigerator, rummaged around in both the kitchen and bathroom trash and went upstairs to the loft to look around. It didn't look like the bed had been slept in, but that didn't surprise her. The bathroom was downstairs, and when she'd been sick in this barn, she hadn't wanted to risk the stairs, either. She didn't see any evidence of alcohol, nor did she smell booze lingering in the air. When she came back down the stairs, both Sean and Ashes had their eyes closed, though Sean's were closed in pain and Ashes's in contentment. Somewhere, her intern had found enough energy to move one finger and scratch behind the dog's ears.

"What's wrong?" she asked.

Sean didn't open his eyes. "Stomach flu, I guess." Normally, his voice was quiet. Now his voice was weak.

"When did you get sick?"

"Last night."

"Have you had anything to eat?"

"I couldn't keep anything down."

"What about something to drink?"

"Water." It looked like it took effort to open his eyes. "I couldn't keep that down."

"What did you eat?"

"The only thing I had." He gave her a little smile, then stopped when it clearly pained him. "Pringles. Sour-cream-and-onion flavor."

Her sympathy came out in a shudder and a laugh. "That must've been terrible when it came back up."

His answering laugh came out like a cough and his body contracted on the recliner. When he recovered enough to straighten himself out he said, "It wasn't great."

"I have ginger ale at the house and some crackers. I don't think I have saltines, but oyster crackers should do. I'll bring those over. Can you make it upstairs to the bed?"

He nodded weakly.

"You head up there. I'll bring what I've got over and get you a trash can. Then I have to finish the onions."

"If you bring some here, I can help."

"And get your sick self all over my produce? No, thank you. Plus, the smell would make you barf faster than anything."

His smile was more robust than any response she'd gotten from him so far. He pushed himself out of the chair and shuffled past her to the stairs. Ashes followed. "Do you mind if I keep the dog?" he said, one hand on the banister and one on the wall. He swayed a bit, but didn't fall.

"Keep the dog. I'll come over before lunch to let him out and check on you."

CHAPTER TWENTY-FIVE

MAX STOOD AT the crest of the hill behind the farm-house and looked over her drowning fields. Two weeks ago, Sean had been sick. Two weeks ago had been their last sunny day. The rain dripping off her hood obscured her vision, but she didn't need to *see* the fields to know what they looked like.

Her first field had two inches of standing water. At least that field was plowed under so she didn't also have to see her plants dying.

Rot crept up the stalks of her tomato plants in her second field, turning leaf after leaf yellow. The tomatoes fought the rot, producing what fruit they could, but the basil had simply folded and died. The squash and melon fields were no better. There the rot spread like the vines of the plants—not up but out until her field was gold instead of green. Any fruit those plants produced grew soft before collapsing altogether. Only the peppers seemed to be enjoying the wet.

She'd had to cancel two weeks of her CSA because she didn't have any produce to give out. They'd tacked those two weeks onto the end of the season and she had to hope the weather dried out enough for her to plant greens and other cool-season, quick-growing vegetables for her members. If it didn't, well, she didn't know what she'd do.

Standing around the fields all day in her rain gear was boring. Preparing a field for planting only to have the rain swamp it for a week so they had to prepare it again was disheartening. Watching her plants die in the fields was painful.

The geese didn't seem to mind the weather. They waddled through her fields, squawking and pooping. Ashes had declined to come out in the rain with her. And Max didn't have the energy to chase them away from fields that weren't productive anyway. Next year, maybe all their extra manure could simply be plowed into the dirt for richer soil and better vegetables. Next year, maybe it wouldn't rain so much.

And next year, maybe she wouldn't have a farm. Buying the land in December was getting riskier and riskier as her cushion got smaller and smaller.

Trey was coming down today to make her part of the video for the Kickstarter, which had seemed like such a good idea all those months ago. Now, instead of her coffers growing from market sales, they were shrinking. And to make matters worse, it was supposed to rain all weekend. She'd be standing out in the fields in the rain asking people to give money to renovate a barn when she didn't know if she'd have the money to buy the land the barn was standing on.

Mustering the energy or excitement for the video was a bit like plowing the hard, unworked clay that the soil had been when she'd taken over the farm five years ago.

She turned from her sodden fields to slug her way through the mud back to the farmhouse to find something to wear.

"OH, THIS LIGHT will be great for the video," Kissa, the college student Trey had found to do all their videos, said as she set up her camera on the front porch. Her straight black hair was in a bouncy ponytail and her dark brown eyes were as eager as always, despite the continuing threat of rain. The girl was going to be a senior at Carolina next year, majoring in journalism, and Trey had found her through a friend of his from high school. She'd been willing to tape and edit all the videos free of charge—experience, she said—but Trey was paying her anyway.

Trey had been at the farm when he'd called Kissa to negotiate the contract. The memory of him arguing with her over the phone still made Max smile. "If you're going to produce something of value, make people pay for it. You can donate your time and expertise when you're not a starving college student." Apparently, she'd then counteroffered with a quote that had made Trey balk, and he'd had to negotiate her down, with Kissa using his own advice against him. Kissa's fresh, eager face probably fooled a lot of people into thinking she couldn't be a shark if she needed to be.

When they'd originally planned to do the video, Max was supposed to be standing on the top of the rise with the farm, in all of its fecund green glory, behind her. However, most of her plants were yellowing and dying, and the only thing bountiful was the grass between the fields, which she couldn't mow down because the ground was too wet. So they'd set up on the front porch and changed the script a little.

"Are you sure you don't want to mention the bad weather on the video?" Trey asked.

"I don't want donations because I'm struggling. I want donations because I will be successful." They'd had this argument many times since Trey had learned how bad a season the farm was having. He thought they could get more money by pulling on heartstrings; Max had no interest in pity. Farming was dependent on the weather, and if she couldn't handle a bad year, then she didn't deserve to have the land.

"I think you should use all the weapons at your disposal, but it's your farm and your Kickstarter, so I'll support you no matter what." He leaned down to kiss her cheek near her ear. "It'll be great."

Kissa directed Max through her video, filming her saying the same lines on the front porch, in the packing shed, in the greenhouse and over by the unrenovated barn. As they dashed through the rain from place to place, the mud reminded Max of how stuck in her situation she was. Her reserves hadn't started shrinking—yet—but they weren't growing. Every penny she earned was going back into the farm and there was none left over for investment. Soon the farm would start cannibalizing itself. And she still had to fork over all of her savings as a down payment on the land.

Trey hadn't mentioned extending the lease for another year and Max hadn't asked. On the few sunny days they'd had this summer, when Max and all the interns were working from dawn until dusk and moving twice as fast as normal, buying the farm seemed like a possibility. On rainy days when she had nothing to do but brood, putting all her money toward buying the farm seemed a sure way to get herself bankrupt in three years.

Lois and Garner said they'd never seen a summer like this one, so the odds were good that next summer would be sunny and hot and perfect for growing vegetables. But what if it wasn't? After buying the land, she wouldn't have enough reserves to sustain her through another bad year.

Standing under an umbrella in front of the barn, Max talked about the benefit of being able to provide housing for another intern, how it meant she could widen her pool of applicants, how she could have two interns over the winter and provide a winter CSA and sell for longer at the market. She talked about some of the visions she had for her farm—grape vines, fig trees and blueberries.

By the time Max was done, the rain had stopped its downpour and the clouds were now spitting out the last of their water—until they could build up their reserves again. Max felt their desperation. And yet, as she watched Kissa and Trey set up for his part of the video, she didn't wish to change her situation. She wished it wasn't the wettest summer in decades. She wished she felt confident in her finances. She wished she'd been able to provide her CSA members with the abundance of tomatoes they'd come to expect from her. But if everything went as planned, she would own this land next year and there would be housing where a falling-down barn had stood.

And she couldn't regret that.

Trey stood in front of the farmhouse and talked about the history of the farm. Some of the historical events, Max was sure, were exaggerated for effect. He talked about how important it was to him and his brother for the land to stay agricultural and how Max had brought new life to the farm. His eyes were bright and encouraging. His face was open, with none of the tightness of anger that he usually wore when talking about the farm.

He was a professional convincer; she couldn't let herself forget that. As heartbreaking as his anger was, as ruinous as it was, it was also who Trey was at his most honest. Even knowing all this, Max still believed him. *Maybe because you want to believe,* the doubting voice in her head said.

After all the filming was finished, Trey, Kissa and Max sat around the kitchen table and talked about the final video. Kissa had gotten shots of the farm when it was green and glorious, before the rain had ruined everything, and she talked about how she would intersperse that with Max and Trey talking. The girl sorted through some images Max had of the farm and photographs Trey had of his family and the farm's history and picked some she thought would make a good backdrop. She gave them a date by which she'd have all the videos finished, said her goodbyes and left.

"I'll miss the drone of the cicadas," Trey said, reaching over the table to envelop her hand in his. She closed her eyes to savor the touch.

Max was so used to the cicadas that she didn't hear their whine unless she stopped to listen to it. The windows were open in the farmhouse and all the ceiling fans were going. The hum of the cicadas underpinned the symphony of the farm. "Miss it?"

She opened her eyes when the table moved a bit because Trey was shifting forward. He kissed the palm of her hand. "Sure." Then he smiled and there was mischief in his grin. He kissed her fingertips, starting with her index finger and moving down until he wasn't kissing her pinky finger, but had taken it into his mouth and was sucking it gently. She could feel his mouth in her bones and the depths of her stomach. Watching each finger disappear between his pale pink lips and come out glistening mesmerized her. When he stopped after moving back down the line of her hand, she found herself staring at her hand in his rather than looking at his face.

"Summer doesn't last forever," Trey said. She shook her head, whether to disagree with him or to clear the lust-induced fog from her brain, she didn't know.

He laid her hand back on the table, the mischievous smile still on his face. The fog in her brain was gone, but the lust remained in her marrow, heightening all of her senses. The wood of the table was rough under the pads of her fingertips. The buzzing of the cicadas vibrated the hair on her arms and she could see every uncertainty of her life in Trey's smile.

"No? Summer does last forever?" he asked at the shake of her head.

"It has to end sometime." Her voice was light and almost foreign in her ears. "But I find that doesn't matter."

She slipped her legs out from under the table and

walked to her bedroom, her shoulders back and her head held high, not looking to see if Trey followed her. Though she did stop in the doorway to remove her T-shirt—just so there would be no doubts of her intentions. The way the summer was going, the bedroom might not be hers after December. The man whose footsteps echoed down the hall behind her might not be hers after September. And rather than worry about the uncertainty of it all, she wanted to make use of both the bedroom and the man while they were hers to use.

CHAPTER TWENTY-SIX

MAX SAT AT her computer and pretended to type up language for a brochure to hand out at the farm tour in September. In reality, she was staring out the window through the rain at the dark windows of Sean's barn. She moved to check her watch on her belt loop, then remembered she hadn't put it on because they couldn't be out in the fields today, so she checked the clock on the screen. Eleven in the morning. Sidney and Norma Jean were under the protection of the packing-house roof seeding celeriac. Sean wasn't needed for anything, but he should still be awake and moving in the barn.

And maybe he was. And maybe he was hungover.

She looked back at the sentence she had typed. "Max's Vegetable Patch is five years old, started when Max Backstrom moved to North Carolina from Illinois." A perfectly fine sentence that was too boring to inspire anyone to invest money. Which was what happened when you stuck a woman who'd only ever wanted a job outside playing in the dirt at a desk with a blank page.

Why isn't he awake? Her suspicions darted about

in her brain, pirouetting and sticking their pointy, hard toes where they didn't belong.

The curtains hadn't so much as twitched in the hour she'd been sitting here pretending to work. And she really should be working, not sitting here worrying whether or not Sean was hungover. Because he probably wasn't. Since her initial ultimatum months ago, he'd not given her a single indication that he'd fallen off the wagon. And the one time she'd been suspicious, he'd had the stomach flu and been sick for three days.

Can the stomach flu hit twice in one summer? She could go over and ask him if he wanted lunch. She occasionally made lunch for the interns instead of them bringing their own. But then she'd have to make lunch for Sidney and Norma Jean—or at least offer it—and she didn't have the groceries for lunch for herself, much less four people. And that would be cowardly. She should have enough respect for him to just march over there, knock on his door and be open with her suspicions. He knew he was being monitored. Kelly was probably also watching him with the same guarded eye.

Her mind made up, Max shut the laptop and headed to the porch for her raincoat and galoshes.

When Sean opened the door, she knew she'd been had. He slouched against the door frame, puffy and shit-faced, not even bothering to shield the whiskey bottle on the table. Or the glass with amber liquid in it. He hadn't just spent last night drinking; he was spending the morning drinking.

She tried to have sympathy for his addiction and the struggle he faced to quit drinking. She tried to have compassion for the experience of a soldier with both the pressures of combat and of Don't Ask, Don't Tell. She tried to be pleased that he'd managed almost the whole summer without drinking. She tried to understand the world from his point of view.

But if she was going to feel any of those things, they would have to wait until tomorrow at the earliest. Because standing in the doorway staring at her drunken intern and a bottle of booze, all she felt was rage. With all his sins out in the open, he obviously wanted her to feel rage. She was playing right into the hand he'd dealt her. And even knowing it was what he wanted her to do, she said, "You're fired." He expected her to keep her word and she could do no less.

Sean's Adam's apple bobbed and he took a shuddering breath. Then he ran back into the barn and she heard the sounds of vomiting coming from the bathroom. How long had he been sitting in the barn, drinking and wondering when she would check on him? Spending all that time convincing herself Sean could be trusted meant he'd had that many more minutes to pickle himself. She hoped the cool porcelain on his cheeks was worth all the work he'd put into this little episode.

She didn't leave the porch. She didn't want to step into that barn and its alcohol-soaked filth right now. When he stepped back onto the porch, he had changed his shirt and splashed some water on his face. He looked more alive, but that was a hollow comparison to the puffy corpse he'd been a few minutes earlier.

His charming, mysterious smile fell flat. Whether repeated use had diminished its power or he wasn't sober enough to pull it off, she didn't know. The first time she'd stood on the barn porch staring at her hungover intern, he'd looked roguishly handsome. She wouldn't have wanted to wake up next to him, but she'd been able to credit his bad-boy appeal. Now she couldn't ignore the bits of vomit crusted at the corner of his mouth.

His half-assed attempt to clean himself up hadn't amounted to much. Neither had his promise not to drink.

She stood on the porch, her hand on Ashes's head, and waited for the excuses to come pouring out of Sean's mouth. She hadn't grown up with an alcoholic father, and Hank had stopped drinking by the time she'd moved to the farm, but she'd talked enough with Trey and Kelly to know what to expect.

It didn't take long.

"Last night wasn't my fault." His voice was hoarse. His voice box was probably also crusted over with puke. "I won't do it again."

She waited for the last in the trifecta of avoiding responsibility. This one took him longer to get out. Sean had enough pride to try to meet her eyes, but she could tell he struggled with it by the way he grasped on to the door frame for support.

"Give me another chance."

They both knew he'd set himself up to be fired, but he had played his role and so she could play hers. "This is my business and my livelihood, not baseball. There are no three strikes and you're out. There's only out." The words sounded like they came from another person. A stronger, angrier person who had a future to protect, who didn't waste time overthinking her problems.

"I got this phone call last night from my mom. She never was happy when I joined the army, but now I'm out and she wants to come visit and…"

"Stop." She held up a hand. "You've never shared your past with me before and doing it now won't change that you're fired."

She was sorry for whatever had happened that had caused the bender and his sudden desire to get fired. As they'd worked on the farm together, she'd seen him struggle with himself and the relief that manual labor gave him. She'd seen him work his body so hard he looked like he would fall over into the pepper plants, and she gathered from Kelly that Sean was trying to keep his mind away from his demons.

But those demons weren't her demons, and this

farm was her farm. Pity wouldn't get him to quit drinking for good. Pity would only mean she'd be spending another morning in the near future looking at her watch and wondering where her employee was. Pity would hurt them both.

He blinked, but looked more relieved than surprised. His shoulders drooped like a man beaten down by life and she was one more rock being thrown at him. Then she remembered how this morning had unfolded and decided that she may be the rock, but Sean was the hand that threw it. "If you're not working here, you can't stay in the barn. Do you have another place to go?"

"Kelly's." She must have looked doubtful because he continued, "No, really. Kelly said I could stay with him when I'm done here and looking for something else."

Max didn't think Kelly had planned on Sean showing up at his doorstep after being fired. "I'll give you until the end of next week to move out. If Kelly won't take you in, hopefully that will give you enough time to find someplace else to stay."

He nodded. The pride that had made him look her in the eyes while tossing excuses at her feet was powerful enough for him not to beg. She wondered if his pride was also what had brought on this bender. Better to sabotage yourself and know you had control over your fall than to trip over something you didn't see. Max understood that feeling.

"And next summer?" Sean asked.

Short one intern, scrambling to find money to buy the land and rainy weather meant next summer would be a miracle. If Sean could promise his own miracle, she'd take him back. "*If* you're sober and going to meetings. I won't be so keen to grant you more than one chance, nor will you have the luxury of privacy if I suspect you of drinking."

The sun had gotten high enough in the sky to light up the inside of the barn, even through the clouds. Though Sean had been living in the barn for the entire summer, the inside still looked empty. How do you start your life over when you don't have roots to keep you stable and feed you?

Just as she had to fight to keep her roots solidly planted in this Carolina clay, Sean needed to struggle just to get his feet on the ground long enough not to be blown over.

She didn't know whether or not to hope Kelly took Sean in. He needed something to hold on to, to give him the motivation to resist a bender. The prospect of working the land hadn't been enough. Maybe Kelly would be enough. Maybe rock bottom wouldn't have to break too much of Sean when he hit it.

"I'll be sober next summer," he said. She took his words with all the force of the promise every drunk makes, but she stuck out her hand and shook on it anyway.

CHAPTER TWENTY-SEVEN

THE HOUSE WAS silent when Trey let himself in after his drive, which was unusual; Max had been waiting up for him in the kitchen the past several weekends he'd driven down from D.C. She'd left the kitchen light on, so she was expecting him. He took off his shoes and left them with his bag at the kitchen table, then made his way through the house to her bedroom.

Ashes barely stirred as Trey walked past the old dog. If it hadn't been for the twitching of the dog's feet, he wouldn't be certain the dog was alive at all. In her bedroom, Max's dead sleep matched that of her dog's. Her hair was in its usual braid and—also as Trey was coming to expect—most of her curls had popped out of the braid and were wild about her face. In the moonlight coming through the open curtains, Max's hair was an otherworldly color.

Trey peeled off his clothes and slid under the sheets. Even though Max didn't wake up, she stirred enough to snuggle closer to him and throw an arm over his chest. He rested his hand on hers, feeling the lift of both of their hands with the rise and fall of his chest. He closed his eyes. His last coherent thought before falling asleep was to wonder whether he could dispense with the bag nonsense and just leave some clothes at the farm. Would that violate their understanding?

AT THE SOUND of stirring from the bedroom, Max smiled. She got out a mug and poured Trey a cup of coffee. It was her coffee, so he'd grimace. But if he wanted to be certain his first cup of the morning was coffee he approved of, he could beat her to the coffeepot.

She found it amusing that even after the many weekends he'd been staying here he couldn't wake up before she did. Though working the farmers' market with her on Saturday mornings meant he was getting closer. She'd told him once to prepare the coffee when he got in on Friday nights and she'd push a button in the morning, but he'd replied that he usually had more important things on his mind after his drive.

He'd been unzipping her jeans when she'd told him to make the coffee. He'd been pushing her onto the couch when he'd told her that he had better things to do.

She could learn to make coffee with his fancy coffeepot. If she was being honest with herself, she could also taste a difference between his coffee and her "sludge." But why learn to make coffee in a pot that will go away once she signed the mortgage papers? And why grow accustomed to fancy coffee she was too cheap to buy?

Max didn't share any of these worries with Trey when he stumbled into the kitchen, bleary-eyed and rubbing his face. He was here now. He had driven five hours after work to wake up early the next morning and help her buy her dream. For that, she would always love him. Even when he walked out the door, never to cross the Virginia–North Carolina border again.

He grimaced in anticipation when she handed him his cup, but his eyes perked up at his first sip. After he'd drunk about half the mug, he declared himself awake enough to make "real coffee"—as soon as he'd had his good-morning kiss.

Trey, who was so angry when he talked about his father, his childhood or the farm, could be so sweet when caught off guard. She'd sometimes catch herself wondering what he'd be like if he hadn't grown up with such hatred and resentment, but then she'd remember that his bitterness had given him his drive to succeed.

She took a sip of her coffee before her mind ran away with her. Philosophy was appropriate for hoeing tomatoes and eggplants, not so much for stale coffee on a rainy Saturday morning.

"What are you smiling about?" Trey asked as he turned around to face her after starting *his* coffee.

"Nothing. No, that's not true. Thank you for coming down to help me at the market and for pushing me to buy the land. And the Kickstarter idea." Not knowing what her life would look like after December was terrifying, but the thought of owning the land had taken on enough substance to dampen her fears—most of the time. "I just hope people invest in the Kickstarter. Otherwise, this whole plan is for naught."

"You have the resources to buy the farm, even if the Kickstarter doesn't succeed." She made a face, but Trey wrapped his free arm around her and dropped a coffee-scented kiss on her lips before she could argue with him. "And as far as the Kickstarter is concerned, you're only convincing them to pay for a product they already want, and I'll help you do that. Besides—" he pulled away far enough to take a sip of his coffee "—I've gotten something out of this summer, too."

Rid of the farm? Those were ungrateful words, sown in anxiety and fear about the future. She should eradicate them while they were still too small to spread. "Fresh vegetables?" was what she said instead.

"Well," he offered, "my vegetable intake does increase on the weekends I visit, but I come to see you. Working the farmers' market is just a side pleasure."

It was on the tip of her tongue to ask what would

happen to their relationship after she signed the mortgage papers, but they'd already talked about it, so she chickened out.

Max ate some cereal before they left, but Trey preferred to search out his breakfast at the market. After they were both full of coffee, Max packed into the truck with Norma Jean while Trey got in his car to follow behind. At the market, the three of them unloaded the tables and tents, then proceeded to set up the vegetables.

It was raining. Again.

"There's not a lot," Trey whispered to her when they started pulling the vegetables out of the back of the truck.

"I know." She tried to say the words with a layer of optimism, but the sheer sadness of the season encumbered her voice. "The rains have hit us hard this summer."

"But I was here just three weekends ago and there was plenty."

"And we didn't have one fully sunny day in those three weeks since." She lifted a box of green tomatoes onto the table and laid them out in baskets. All she had were green tomatoes because her first planting had been overcome by blight and her second planting wasn't ripe yet. Picking some of the tomatoes while green to sell would cut into future harvests, but she had to offer *something,* and with the way the weather had been going, she might not get red tomatoes out of her second planting anyway. To help sales, Max had printed out two recipes: one for fried green tomatoes and one for a green-tomato curry.

She had no melons to offer, no summer squash, eggplant or basil. The peppers had done okay with all the rain and the onions had been harvested before the worst of it started, but her winter squash crop had been cut in half. Everything was rotting in the fields—everything except the weeds.

"And I miss Sean," she said, not fully believing that she was confessing such a thing. Sidney and Norma Jean were fine. They were hard workers and they were both interested in learning about farming. But Sean had put his soul into the work; Max had felt it each and every time they worked the land together.

Trey stopped pulling vegetables out of the truck and pulled Max into his arms for a hug.

"I feel like I shouldn't miss him, because he got drunk knowing I would fire him and intending for me to do so. But I still do." She turned her face into his shirt, hoping her next confession would be lost in the cotton. "And I'm afraid to call Kelly and ask how Sean is, because I'm afraid he ruined that, too."

Max could feel the pressure of Trey's kiss through her hair, even if his lips never reached her skin. "You did the right thing. The hard thing, but the right thing."

"Maybe I should've never let him stay after that first time." It was so easy to look back and question past decisions, especially now that she could see the results.

He straightened his arms and she was able to look directly into his eyes. "When you let Sean stay the first time, you gave him a second chance. That was a hard decision, one I'm not sure I would have the ability to make. After all the weekends I've spent with you on the farm, I think you made the right one then. And you made the right one now."

She could feel the truth of his words in his grip on her shoulders. Trey didn't like Sean, had hated that he was dating Kelly and despised the man's alcohol abuse. He'd doubted her decision to give Sean another chance originally, so it was nice to hear a confirmation of it even after the consequences had become apparent. "Thank you."

Trey gave her a kiss on her lips, then went back to unloading the truck. After a couple minutes, sounding more like an afterthought, he asked, "And your finances?"

Max's heart sank a little further. In their daily—sometimes hourly—email and text exchanges, Trey hadn't once asked about her finances. She didn't want to tell him how tenuous this summer had made her bank account. She hadn't eaten into her savings account—yet—but she hadn't added anything to it, either. In the summer she ate mostly what she grew, and this summer there wasn't much to eat. The downpours had even done the impossible and made the chickens look depressed with their muddy feet and rain dripping off their beaks and combs.

"I'll still be able to buy the farm—" *so long as we get sunny days for the rest of the summer and I can get some quick fall crops in* "—if that's what you're worried about." Max was worried about so many things. She couldn't use any Kickstarter money to buy real estate and every time she looked at her bank statement, she saw how close her savings was getting to the breaking point. And yet, when the time came, she'd probably still try to buy the land, even if it took every penny she had.

When she looked up at Trey, his eyes managed to be both warm with sympathy and cold with anger. "I don't care about you being able to buy the farm. I care about you." The box Trey was holding dropped with a thud onto the table—luckily it held onions. "Why do you think I've been coming down to the farm on all my free weekends?"

"I don't know." Now, as people were starting to walk up to the various farmers for their vegetables, was not the time for this conversation. But Max had chickened out during all the appropriate times. "Sometimes I wonder if you're softening on your stance against moving. I know you'll never be a farmer, but I wonder if you could lobby at the

General Assembly or if that would be a step down. I wonder if you could stand to live in the farmhouse."

When Trey's eyes softened with pity and his mouth opened to politely turn her down, Max rushed to finish her thought. "But then I wonder if it would be my parents all over again. If the person you are right now is dependent on you living somewhere other than Durham. My mom may *say* she didn't resent moving to Illinois, that it was worth it for the two children she'd borne, but I don't always believe her."

Trey had closed his mouth and he was silent for several seconds. "Max, we agreed that our relationship was a temporary thing."

"I know. And I'm not trying to back out or renegotiate, I'm just…" What was she doing anyway? Trey hadn't yet given her an outright no, but he would if she pressed the matter—and no amount of unburdening of her soul was worth how she'd feel when he did. She smiled; it was a weak smile, but the corners of her mouth lifted and she showed teeth, so it counted. "You said I should think big and not worry about reality." She shook her head. "That's all this is."

"Max, I never wanted to disappoint you, and it's not about you."

"Can we not talk about this now?" she asked, interrupting him. "Customers are going to start arriving any minute."

Trey huffed and gave her a disgusted, disappointed look, but he said, "Sure." Then he put on his "I can sell a fur coat in the Mohave" face and turned to meet the crowd.

It had taken all of Norma Jean's merchandising abilities to turn the Patch's meager crop into something enticing. Bounty it wasn't, but neither did it look to be the last scraps before the apocalypse. Which was how it felt.

The financial loss wasn't only one problem. She also worried that she was losing the faith of her CSA customers, especially the ones who'd just joined this year and didn't have the previous years' experience of what she could provide during a normal summer. And then there was the simple emotional toll.

For most of the summer, all the work they had put in felt like a waste.

Max pulled herself out of her wretched and self-destructive musings long enough to notice Trey talking to someone. Not a customer, or at least not a regular one. The slight African-American man had a goatee and was wearing a Carolina T-shirt. Attached to each of his hands was a small child— a girl and a boy. The little girl was wearing a pink princess dress, complete with sparkles and lace, with enough confidence that Max felt underdressed. The man looked vaguely familiar, though she didn't recognize the woman holding the infant and standing at his side.

"I heard a rumor from my sister that you were working the farmers' market some weekends," the man said. "I told her that she was a fool and a liar, but now I see it's true. I'd make you give me some of the money I just lost in a bet, but I'm afraid it will scare you back North."

"D.C. is hardly North." Trey said the words with a smile and a Southern accent so thick Max could have painted walls with it.

"It may be a Southern city, but it's not exactly the South," the man said with a smile and a shake of his head. "Introduce me to the farmer who convinced you to come down without basketball tickets as a bribe."

Trey laughed. It wasn't the laugh he let loose when he was about to convince you to buy something; it was his genuine, "I'm happy to see you" laugh. This man was a friend. Trey claimed he had no ties to North Carolina other than Kelly and the farm he couldn't wait to get rid of, but that was a lie. However loose, this man was still a tie.

"Max Bergstrom, meet Jerome Harris. Jerome and I went to high school together. He's now a fancy professor at U.N.C. He's the guy I was supposed to go to the basketball game with."

"Oh, right." Max shook Jerome's hand. "The game was lots of fun. Thank you."

"Don't thank me. Thank the germs the students

pass around for making me intimate with my bathroom. I hope to never be that sick again."

"I'll thank them as I see them," she responded with a laugh.

"This is my wife, Alea, and my children, Danielle, Julian and Carissa." Alea shifted her weight and the baby so that Max could shake her hand. The two older children also gave her polite handshakes and said, "Nice to meet you, ma'am," though the girl said hers loud and proud and the boy mumbled his a bit.

"I saw you at Hank's viewing," Jerome said.

"Oh, yes, I remember now." At the funeral, Jerome had looked so serious and professorial she hadn't put the man in the suit together with the man in his casual clothes, smiling at his wife and kids.

They talked about this and that for several more minutes until the kids grew impatient and started pulling on their father's hands. "Don't be a stranger, ya' hear?" Jerome told Trey as his children were leading him away. "And let me know the next time you're down. We can get a drink or catch a baseball game."

Trey nodded. He was waving at the kids with an unreserved grin on his face. And once again Max started to wonder where his anger at North Carolina had gone.

CHAPTER TWENTY-EIGHT

NORMALLY TREY FELT fine when he got back to the farm with Max after a morning at the market, but this was not a normal weekend. In the past week he had determined that work was going to kill him—or he was going to kill one of the fools at the Department of Education who couldn't keep his mouth shut if world peace was on the line. One of the two.

Creating distractions hadn't helped. Yet instead of digging up more research to provide for the congressman from Indiana to use as counterbalance to the Department of Education's idiot, he was educating himself about the effects of the stalled farm bill on small farms and emailing his findings to a colleague who was working with one of the senators from North Carolina. Not his job. Not his area of expertise. And certainly not his area of interest.

But he'd also kept checking the Durham weather report. More rain and more ruined crops might make it impossible for Max to buy the farm, and then where would their relationship be? Where would his life be? After the summer and the comfort he'd found in Max's company, he couldn't keep his threat of selling the farm to some developer if she didn't buy it first. But owning the farm still caused him to cringe. Max made the land bearable. Hell, Max made the land *magical*.

Trey dragged his feet up the back steps into the farmhouse, each shoe feeling like an unwieldy concrete block attached to his foot. After spending all of yesterday scrambling to get done what he needed to finish before he could responsibly leave town, he'd climbed into his car without stopping back home for a bag and driven to Durham. When he'd crawled into Max's bed at three-thirty in the morning, he'd assured her that he'd be up and ready for the market, but that had been a hard promise to keep—even when Max had made him coffee with his own beans in his own pot. Now he was afraid that if he didn't get into a supine position on the bed soon, he'd find himself in a prone position on the floor.

Max had understood his offer to help her unload the truck as the hollow suggestion it had been and had shooed him to the door with a kiss.

Ashes took the opportunity to slip out the back door as Trey stumbled his way into the house and toward the bedroom. He'd just taken off his shoes and pants when his phone started ringing in his pants pocket. Tiredness might be responsible for his hallucinations, but he was pretty sure his pants were bouncing off the floor with each ring, like in a cartoon.

When he picked up the phone to turn the ringer off, he saw why the phone had seemed so insistent. Aunt Lois was calling. He debated making her leave a message, but his aunt had a way of persisting—oh, so politely and never without her Southern-ladyness. She would probably haunt his dreams.

"Hello, Aunt Lois." He hoped he sounded tired and she would get the hint.

"Trey, dear, I hear you've been coming down to help Max on the farm. Every weekend, I hear. And that the Kickstarter thing was your idea."

"Every weekend isn't quite right." Trey said the words slowly, not sure what his aunt's agenda was, though he was sure she had one. She never called him, much less to talk about how he spent his time.

"I've been expecting you to come over to Sunday supper when you're down. Tomorrow. Garner is doing ribs."

"Oh, Aunt Lois, I don't know. I have a long drive back to D.C. tomorrow." *And I'd hoped to spend the entire day in bed with Max.* Even if he couldn't define their relationship, packing the whole thing into two days every other weekend was difficult. He couldn't get enough of her in their short time together, which made him possessive of every little second.

Such a simple, ordinary, normal thing as actually

having enough time with your lover that you would *want* a small break seemed impossible to him. Other than Max's surprising thoughts the other morning, they'd only mentioned the future so far as to talk about a tour of D.C. when the busy growing season was over. And the farm's future seemed uncertain at the moment. A sexual relationship with his tenant was only bearable when the lease had a defined end point. If she couldn't buy the land and he didn't sell it to someone else, the small, petty fights could become real big and real hurtful real fast. And when Max bought the land…

The convenience of their relationship had gotten complicated. If he was being honest with himself, he had to admit that he could have foreseen the entanglements of the farm and their feelings. But also, if he was being honest with himself, he was glad he hadn't.

If only he could lie down, fall asleep and dream of Max without any complications or clothes.

Unfortunately, thinking about his future with Max meant he hadn't been paying attention to what his aunt was saying. Apparently, she'd agreed to have supper a little earlier and he'd agreed to come over with Max. Since his aunt wasn't a liar—she was far too forthright to lie and never seemed to need the aide of manipulation to get what she wanted, anyhow—he had to believe he'd actually said yes.

Which was fine. If he'd been listening, then he would have argued. If he'd argued, she'd have kept at him. Eventually, he would have given in, but he would've lost fifteen minutes of much-needed sleep. This was shorter, at least. They settled to have supper at three; he agreed to bring a side dish, and as soon as the phone clicked off, Trey stripped off his shirt and fell backward onto the bed.

TREY FOLLOWED MAX'S little sedan as she turned into his aunt and uncle's driveway. They'd driven separately because Trey had to leave for D.C. as soon as supper was over. Max stood by her sedan, waiting for him.

"Have you been to my aunt's for supper before?" he asked her, after greeting her with a kiss. The entire drive over, he'd looked to the passenger seat of his car, wishing she was sitting there instead of in her own car.

"I've been over a couple times before. She collects quite the variety of guests. I never know who will be here and what Miss Lois will have arranged the conversation to be about. It's like a bar and political forum all in one. And since today is Sunday, there'll also likely be a bit of the church feeling."

"Do you know who's here?" he asked as they walked to the front door.

"That car belongs to a county commissioner."

Max nodded to a blue sedan. "I don't know who the other two cars belong to."

Trey spun that little piece of knowledge around in his head. If his aunt had her Sunday suppers for the reasons Max implied, and if she curated her guests as carefully as he imagined she did, everyone here had a purpose and Aunt Lois's purpose was more complicated than just sticking her nose in her nephew's business.

Trey stalled Max's hand before she could knock on the door. "Do you know anything about the commissioner?"

"Not much. She's young. She's not originally from Durham, but has been active in politics since she moved here when her husband got a job at Duke. I voted for her." Max pulled her hand away and knocked. "What are you afraid of anyway?"

"Like any reasonable person, I'm afraid of my aunt." Max grabbing his hand and smiling at him wasn't as reassuring as he'd hoped. She was probably afraid of his aunt, too. But her attempt at encouragement meant he was smiling when his aunt opened the door.

"Oh, deviled eggs," his aunt exclaimed as she took the tray from Max's hand. "You do make some of the best deviled eggs I've ever tasted."

"I can't take all the credit. The chickens lay some good eggs."

Max stepped inside the house and Trey followed

her, bending down to drop a kiss on his aunt's cheek and receive one from her in return. His aunt's living room was spotless and comfortable, as always. Since his aunt and uncle had been the Harrises to keep up the family tradition of farming, it seemed like they should have the old farmhouse with rickety heating and wood floors. Instead, his aunt and uncle lived in a brick ranch house with carpet and a large back deck. As a child, Trey had envied his cousins their more modern home. Now, though he still saw the old farmhouse as the home of his father's failures, he'd come to look forward to hearing the squeak of floors at Max's steps when she got out of bed in the morning.

As soon as he walked out onto the back deck and saw the five people his age seated in deck chairs and drinking iced tea, Trey knew what Aunt Lois's purpose this afternoon was.

He was introduced to the young county commissioner and her husband; a second couple who had devised a way for small meat farmers to combine their resources, lower the cost of slaughtering and get their goods to the consumer; and last, a sheep farmer.

Only the sheep farmer was a native North Carolinian and he had taken over his parents' tobacco farm when he was twenty-five. He now produced most of the local lamb sold in the Triangle's very popular and well-regarded restaurants.

When Trey and Max approached the crowd, fortified with their own icy glasses of sweet tea, they were talking about a new chocolate shop opening off University Road and how this shop's hot chocolate compared with the hot chocolate at some other new place in town, which did single-origin bar chocolate. Durham was not the struggling mill town he'd grown up in, and Aunt Lois wanted to make sure he knew it.

When Uncle Garner pulled the ribs off the grill, Aunt Lois announced she would go inside to get all the fixin's, so everyone should be prepared to eat soon. Trey followed his aunt into the house.

"Aunt Lois, you're not being subtle." He held out his arms and she put a tray into his hands.

"I have never been subtle in all my life," she responded, her accent thick and slow—the true molasses in January. In the past, the accent had grated on Trey's ears, reminding him of his mom's unhappy servitude and his father's bigotry. Coming from his aunt, the tray in his hands getting heavy with plates, napkins, forks and a big bowl of coleslaw, the accent sounded soothing. "Mah life," his aunt had said, and some of the tension in his shoulders had relaxed.

His aunt picked up another tray loaded down with potato salad, cornbread, collard greens and pickled shrimp. Before she could walk outside, he called out, "I'm not moving back to Durham because there's now good chocolate shops here. Or because there's a well-educated population my age."

"No." She turned around to face him with a look on her face that made him feel dumber than a grasshopper who'd stumbled into the hen house. "I expect you would move down here because you're crazy about that girl and she's crazy about you."

"On my sixteenth birthday, I made a promise to myself that I would never move back to the farm. And unlike my father, I keep my promises."

"Trey, honey, I never thought I would say this about anyone, but you have grown into more of a fool than your daddy ever was." She balanced her tray on her arm and pulled the sliding glass door open. "Stop being stupid and go outside and make friends. You'll find these people are interesting, if you can stop staring at yourself in the winda' for one minute."

Scolded and not wanting to be caught standing at the open door with his mouth agape, Trey followed his aunt outside. Max had already sat down and was patting the seat next to her.

CHAPTER TWENTY-NINE

WHILE TAKING A break from giving tours of the farm, Max stood by the ice cream bus, enjoying her cone and watching Trey work. With some of the folks who stopped by the farm tour, Trey joked and y'all'ed. With others, he was a serious business-man listening to their questions and answering their concerns. Still others got the righteousness of the organic farmer treatment, complete with information about the importance of the water supply and keeping diversity in the seed population for every-thing from apples to zucchini. He seemed to be able to get the perfect read on the person as they walked up to the table and knew which persona to take on before the person even opened their mouth. What-ever he was doing, he was having more success than Sidney, who got people to pick up their Kickstarter brochure but failed to get them to take it home. Trey hadn't only gotten people to take a brochure home, but a couple people took advantage of the iPad Trey had provided to give a donation while on the farm.

Still, she couldn't complain about Sidney's work. Both Sidney and Norma Jean had come back to the farm for the weekend to help out with the farm tour. Norma Jean was taking a group through the tobacco barn while Max took a much-needed break. She was wondering if she should switch the interns' roles when the couple with Trey leaned over the tablet, presumably to enter a donation, and she caught sight of Trey's face absent of any guise.

He looks tired. But not only tired, he looked uncertain.

Max sucked vanilla ice cream into her mouth and let the cold freeze her back teeth. There'd been a brief moment a month ago when she'd felt like whatever relationship she had with Trey *wasn't* dependent on his feelings about the farm or her ability to buy it. Like they were a normal couple exploring their feelings for each other and the comfort they could provide. And then he'd left his aunt Lois's supper and come back two weeks later a different person. More reserved. Timid, even.

She could still feel his affection for her. He still smiled when he saw her and when they made love she felt his need for her. But after they pulled apart and were lying in bed together, no matter how dark the night was, she sensed him looking around the room. Tension radiated through his body, as if the room was pressing in on him.

And maybe it was. Maybe all the activity of planning the Kickstarter and tugging the farm through the hard summer had distracted him from his underlying hatred of the land, and when the mortgage papers were signed, he would have nothing more pulling him south. And once he crossed the state line—going north—for the last time, the lines that had appeared in his forehead would smooth away.

The couple finished entering their information. Trey looked up, caught her looking at him and gave her a big smile and a wink. Maybe she was wrong. Maybe the tension and withdrawing she felt was from her.

Finishing the summer with the same bank balance she'd had at the beginning of May had been a huge accomplishment, but not the accomplishment she'd wanted. And it didn't give her the confidence she'd hoped to have when they launched the Kickstarter. With the CSA over and her stints at the market winding down for the season, she had more time to panic over her future.

Maybe it's not him. Maybe it's me. That thought wasn't reassuring. Trey had come down early to help set up for the tour. He'd helped clean and was leading occasional tours for those people who wanted a more historical understanding of the farm. He was putting his whole self into this launch. If she couldn't put *her* whole self in as well, she didn't deserve him.

Later that night, Trey stood silent and focused as she flicked his shirt buttons open. She trailed her index finger up to his neck and then down through each new inch of flesh she revealed until she could place her palms on his chest and fully spread her fingers over his skin. When the rush of the day threatened to speed up her hands, she took a deep breath and concentrated her attention on the man in front of her. She took her time exploring his body with her lips and tongue, muscle by muscle and pore by pore until their desire had them shaking in unison. When he entered her, he filled her completely, leaving no space for the anxieties that had haunted her all day.

Her release soaked her in awareness of his body and hers. But the tenderness and time they had taken with each other meant she felt his retreat more completely than she ever had before.

"IS THERE SOMETHING WRONG?" asked a soft voice through the dark.

Trey had pulled Max tight against him and was enjoying the warmth of her back against his chest when she asked the question. His skin pulled back from hers, but he kept his arms around her, fighting to close the distance.

"No." His reply was both a lie and the truth. He could imagine no better feeling in this world than to lie in this bed in this farmhouse with his arms wrapped around this woman, and the willingness with which he would toss his life away to be here forever scared the shit out of him.

You're crazy about that girl and she's crazy about you. You have grown into more of a fool than your daddy ever was. Aunt Lois's words had followed him home, though with a different result than she'd intended.

"I know this relationship has an end point, Trey. I knew it when we started."

"Let's not talk about this now," he said, pulling her hair back from her neck and kissing the one freckle-free spot he'd found on her entire body. The full, four square inches of white skin was back behind her ear. Only someone lying in this position and pulling her hair away would know it was there. Thinking about this secret spot was usually a precursor to his research into farm legislation instead of education. For a chance to kiss this one spot he would drive five hours.

He pulled his lips away and smoothed her hair back over the spot. "I was just thinking of something my aunt said."

She stiffened in his arms, the same response he often had to his aunt, and he smiled, though his smile quickly disappeared at the defensiveness in her voice as she spoke. "I admire the work she does and don't know if I'd have settled into this community without her support, but she doesn't speak for me about this relationship. I've never spoken with her about it."

Had he lied when he'd told Max his withdrawal wasn't about her? No. He hadn't lied to her and he didn't plan to start. He also hadn't wanted to have this conversation here, now, *again,* but the opportunity was here. He should seize it. "At her supper, she was trying to convince me to move down here."

The bed creaked as Max rolled in his arms over onto her back. The moonlight reflected off her light skin and fell into dark freckles to create a brilliant pattern of bright versus hidden. He could spend the rest of the night exploring the mysteries of her face and know no more at 6:00 a.m. than he did right now. "You know I'm not moving back to North Carolina, right? Whatever this relationship is, I can't do that."

"Your hatred of this farm has never been a question."

She hadn't answered his actual question. "Even if it wasn't this farm, I still wouldn't move back." *I have a life in D.C., a good job, and...* He didn't say any of those things. Defending his stance implied there was a weak point she could exploit.

"I know you're not moving back, and that my buying the farm means the death of our relationship." Her tone was flat, but before he could press, she said with more pep, "But I've never been to D.C. and I'd still like a tour one day."

He ignored the false brightness of her tone to focus on her words. "I give the best tours."

Rammed in the future they'd agreed on, Trey closed his eyes and waited to fall asleep.

CHAPTER THIRTY

THE JOLLY GREEN Giant had been pressing down on Max's shoulders for months. Maybe even years. There'd always been that force sinking her shoulder blades farther and farther into her lungs. First it had been the fear of moving to North Carolina and starting a farm. Then it had been Hank and his odious personality, combined with the fear that he'd realize she was a woman and decide he couldn't lease to her. Feeling comfortable with Hank hadn't pushed the weight fully away, though it had lightened the load a bit. But his death had sent the full force of the giant crashing back down on her shoulders.

Now as she stepped out of Trey's car onto the gravel road that was hers, the giant was gone. His hands weren't even resting on her shoulders waiting to push down again. Max still felt pressure, but the force was pushing her forward to the future rather than weighing her down.

She took in a deep breath, filling her lungs with *her* cool, clean air. On *her* farm. Her gravel. Her old farmhouse. Her falling-down barn and her own matching chicken coop. Her deep breath was intended to calm both her fears and her excitement; it didn't work.

It had been clear early on that her Kickstarter would be fully funded, and since then everything else had moved so quickly. Even the mortgage-approval process had been smoother than she'd expected. And the avalanche, once started, wouldn't slow for any doubts. It bowled right past and over her. In Trey's visits since the Kickstarter launch, she hadn't even had time to think about how signing the mortgage would end their relationship.

Hadn't had time, or hadn't wanted to? No matter. Without the giant pressing down on her shoulders, the feeling of owning her own farm might carry her away off this earth.

Trey came around the car and took her hand. She let him lead her around all the other cars parked in *her* driveway. Honestly, she was never going to get sick of that particular possessive pronoun.

They walked hand in hand around the back of her house to where tents were set up. Kelly and Norma Jean were setting up the rented tables and chairs. The smell of smoke and pork filled the air. Garner had brought his pig cooker over in the back of his truck and was putting a final mop of sauce on the meat. There were two long tables lined end to end with plenty of empty space for all the barbecue that Garner would soon pronounce ready. Lois was laying out slaw, collard greens, cornbread, potato salad and corn pudding. And big jugs of sweet tea. Lois didn't truck with alcohol.

Max's stomach grumbled. "This looks fabulous."

Trey's hand was warm in hers. "Asking Aunt Lois to plan the party was a good idea, though I think the Christmas lights were Norma Jean's idea."

"I had great interns this summer." They'd not only worked hard on the farm, they'd also become invested in the success of the Kickstarter and Max's ability to buy the land. When Max had sent Norma Jean an email to thank her for all the help, she had said it was worth it because she was learning about hope through struggle. Norma Jean vowed that when she had a farm, she wouldn't let small trials get her down.

Trey squeezed Max's hand. "Even Sean?"

Max squeezed back. "Even Sean. While I had him, he was a good employee. And he taught me that I could feel sympathy without letting those feelings get in the way of the fact that I have to be the boss." The crunch of tires on the gravel behind her made her turn around. A car she didn't recognize was pulling into the drive. "I think that's one of the Kickstarter funders. I hope they find the party worth their investment."

He frowned at her words. "They didn't donate money so that they could have a party. They donated so that you could have a farm."

She opened her mouth to argue with him, but

stopped when she saw the intent look on his face. He turned so that they were facing each other and put his hands on her shoulders. "This party is for you. I gave you a shitty bargain in a shitty farming year and you succeeded. You beat all your own expectations, no matter what mine were. You deserve a party."

Seeing herself reflected in Trey's eyes warmed her through to her fingers on the cold November night. In his eyes, she stood tall and fearless in the face of challenges. They both knew self-doubt did cartwheels in her head, but that mattered less than the fact that she didn't let those doubts bust out. "Let's go greet our guests. Maybe they'll want a tour before it gets too dark."

Their first Kickstarter guests were a couple that owned a music production company in Durham, and as soon as Max shook the woman's hand, she knew who they were. Though the woman didn't stop to talk like many of Max's other customers, she came by the Patch's table every weekend to buy some vegetables. At their indication that they wanted a tour, Max led them up to the tables to get something to drink first and the party was started.

When she returned from her tour, the party was in full swing. Kelly ran up to her to shake her hand in congratulations. Lois walked, but there was a wide smile on her face. Garner shook her hand, but didn't say anything. Soon Kelly and Lois were followed by a host of Max's friends and neighbors. People she'd met at Lois's Sunday suppers. Other farmers from the market. Other Kickstarter donors. And her mom, who enveloped her in a warm patchouli hug and said, "I'm so proud of you." The only thing that would make the evening better was if her father and brother were here. But she'd bought the farm ahead of schedule and they were still busy with their own farmwork.

Across the backyard, Max caught a glimpse of Trey, his smile wide and honest. He looked happy. He was on his father's property—now *her* property— and he looked happy. Knowing he was here almost made up for her missing her father and brother.

Trey was pushing his empty plate away when Kelly sat down next to him. "I'm trying to eat for Sean, as well as for me," his brother said with a gesture toward his full plate. Kelly's second serving was larger than his first had been.

"Shouldn't you be sneaking some vodka into your tea, then?" Trey had more he wanted to say, but picking a fight with his brother at Max's party was in poor taste.

Kelly stopped eating to look at him, his fork halfway to his mouth. His brother cocked his head, pursed his lips and finally put the fork back down on his plate. "Didn't Max tell you?"

"Tell me what?"

"Sean is in Wilmington at a rehab facility. They offer a program specifically for veterans that he's participating in." Kelly picked up his fork again, considered the pile of barbecue and then shoved it into his mouth.

"How did this happen?"

Kelly took a big gulp of his tea before answering Trey's question. "Well, getting fired from the farm wasn't rock bottom. Sean had to crawl back up a bit from getting fired and got back into regular AA meetings—and then he dived into rock bottom. I reached out to his mother and together we got him into the Wilmington program." He scraped another pile of barbecue onto his fork. "Mrs. Yarnell really is a lovely woman, though her strident pacifism is hard on Sean." Kelly shook his head as if not believing what he was about to say. "It was hard to have a homophobic father and be gay. Mrs. Yarnell is as welcoming as she can be about Sean's sexuality, but she broke his heart by refusing contact with him when he joined the army. We all have our blind spots."

"And..." Trey stopped, not certain what question he wanted to ask first. The things he had wanted to say when Kelly first sat down were still bouncing around in his head, but their tone was different. "Why have you stuck with him?" Apparently, the question was shocking enough for Kelly to stop chewing. His brother held up his hand in a gesture of patience as he tried to finish his bite, not surprisingly a huge effort given the pile of food that had been on the fork. "That's what you get for taking such big bites," Trey said with a snort.

When Kelly finally swallowed, he said, "Because I love him."

"But..."

"But how could I love an alcoholic, especially after our father?"

Trey shrugged, fixing his gaze on some point past all the partygoers. He tried to pretend he wasn't here on his father's—now Max's—farm, having this conversation, but the music, smells and chatter drew him back to the present. He scanned the people under the tent until his eyes caught Max, who was laughing with one of the Kickstarter guests. This land was hers now. The fall breeze ruffling her hair was blowing away the last bits of his father and Trey's unhappy childhood. Not rebirth so much as new growth. Like Max's treasured compost piles, the old, rotting waste was providing nutrients for something new and wholesome.

What had his aunt said? *You're crazy about her and she's crazy about you.* She hadn't been wrong. She was almost never wrong, but she seemed to believe that Trey could be here without seeing his childhood in every tree and branch. Perhaps it was possible. Kelly's childhood had been equally awful, though in a different way, and he'd managed to return to the farm. And as much as Trey accused otherwise, Kelly and Sean's relationship was different than his parents' relationship, lacking the victim and perpetrator edge.

Trey turned back to his brother. "Yes. That is exactly the question I don't know the answer to."

"We all have our blind spots." Trey rolled his eyes at Kelly's answer. "Compassion. Sean is fighting a war that I don't understand. So long as he's fighting that war and not fighting me, I can have compassion for him. Dad's problem was that he spent most of his life fighting us instead of his own demons."

"I'm supposed to have compassion for our father?"

"Supposed to? I don't know. But you might try it and find out. Add Mama in there, too, while you're at it."

"Huh. I'm going to get a second plate." Trey stood and walked over to the line of food, trying not to notice that he got two scoops of the corn pudding that had always been his mom's favorite and that he passed up the potato salad his dad had never liked.

When he returned to the table, Max was joining Kelly with her own plate of food. "Not eating with the Kickstarter guests?" Kelly asked.

"I don't want to sound like an ingrate, but I need a break from being 'on.' It's exhausting," Max said.

"You don't look *on,*" Kelly said.

"She's wearing her interview clothes. Casual enough that no one forgets she's a farmer, but without the mud stains." Trey ignored the elbow to his side. "I recognize the outfit from when she interviewed Sean."

"You probably should've worn something nice to sign the mortgage papers," Kelly said, though the smile on his face made it clear he was teasing.

"I know, but I didn't want to look too flush. Besides, if I showed up to this party in a skirt, I would've been bombarded with people asking me to point out the farmer. Even the people who come to the farmers' market wouldn't recognize me. Hank called my outfit farmer chic, though I'm not even sure he knew what chic meant," Max said with a laugh.

Trey put down his fork. "Where would my father learn a phrase like *farmer chic?*"

"Well," Kelly said, "I think he learned *chic* because of me. There was a six-month period when Dad was trying to understand gay culture until I told him to knock it off." He made a disgusted face. "It was just weird and wrong and full of stereotypes that don't apply to me."

Max laughed. "Oh, he must've kept that learning experiment a secret from me. Though Hank did spend about a year reading up on modern organic farming techniques and emailing me articles. Some of it was helpful. Most of it I already knew, but it was sweet."

Trey scooted back to the edge of his chair as Kelly and Max reminisced about his father's misguided attempts to broaden his mind. Finally, he interrupted. "I can't imagine my father doing any of this."

"Oh, Hank wasn't *good* at it, or even comfortable with it. But he'd made a commitment with himself to learn and he was sober enough to try to stick with it. It's just that whenever he was trying on a new skin, he walked like his pants were too tight."

"Some of it stuck, though," Kelly said quietly.

Max shot a look at his brother. "Yes, some of it did. He built the chicken coop because he preferred the eggs I brought home from the market, though he couldn't bear the price of them. And—" Max paused and Trey felt the pressure of her hand on his leg "—he was starting to check out books on education from the library. He had just returned one from that former head of D.C. schools."

Her last sentence distracted him from the hand on his thigh. "My dad went to the library?"

"Dad was all kinds of surprising in those last years. You never knew what you were going to get out of him, good or bad."

Trey put his hand under the table and grasped

Max's. She gave his a squeeze, which was comforting, but didn't help realign his life with a world where his father went to the public library.

CHAPTER THIRTY-ONE

THE TIKI LAMPS provided so little illumination, Max wondered if they'd be better off working without them and using only the stars and moonlight to guide them. But they'd provided enough light to see Trey raise his brows at that suggestion, so the lamps stayed lit. Max leaned against the last folding table still standing, winding fairy lights around her arm while Trey carried chairs to the barn. The party had been blessed with crisp though not cold November weather, but the wind carried the tangy smell of a storm. The tents would join the chairs and tables in the barn until the rental company retrieved them. The fairy lights would be packed away in the attic, joining the Harris family crap neither Trey nor Kelly had removed yet.

Trey will at least have to come back for that. Only he wouldn't. The man she loved could drive to D.C. and make Kelly return to the farm for the boxes. And since she owned the land she was standing on, he wouldn't continue to drive five hours after work on Friday to "check up on his property." His excuse and his chain had been signed away today in an office with uncomfortable furniture and cheap art on the walls.

She'd let herself forget the less-welcome consequences of owning the farm during the celebration. Now with just the two of them left, those consequences were all she could think on.

They were going to walk into the farmhouse, have sex and then he would drive away. And even if he came back occasionally, this relationship would still have no future.

Trey was walking toward her, the moonlight and the tiki lamps casting shadows that danced across his face. No matter that the light was dim, Trey's smile was bright. "You're leaning against the last table." His eyes twinkled. Close up, she saw that the muscles of his face were relaxed and there was no evidence there had ever been uncomfortable lines on his neck. Watching their relationship slowly dissolve across the two hundred and fifty miles between Durham and D.C. couldn't be the only outcome to their situation.

His arm slipped around her waist. Warm, strong and about to exit her life. "We can't go to bed until all the tables and tents are put away. Your rules—" a playful kiss on her lips interrupted his words "—not mine."

She put the bundle of fairy lights in the box and stood. Trey hadn't stepped back, so when she was on her own two feet, she was also in his arms. It didn't matter that there was one layer of thick woolen sweater and one layer of thermal-lined sweatshirt between them, her skin remembered the feel of his body against hers. She tilted her face up to his and kissed him. His lips were warm. Then he tilted his head and the cool skin of his cheek brushed hers. She wanted to ignore the coming storm and the tents and go inside.

She wanted to stay out here forever so that morning never came.

His tongue tickled the edge of her lips and she met it with her own. Slippery, wet and warm in blissful contrast to the dry chill of the night air. He tightened his arms around her, pulling her close against him. She thrust her hands under his sweater, rubbing the cotton of his shirt against his skin, creating friction and heat under her hands. He moaned and shivered when she finally yanked his shirt out from his pants and touched skin to skin.

She wasn't ready to be finished when he pulled away from her. He reached his hand up and brushed some of her flyaway hair from her face. "It's warmer inside. The tents can be left until morning."

She dragged her hands out from under his shirt and smoothed his sweater back down. "No." Responsibility and reality were unwelcome. "I'm not convinced the weather will hold."

He nodded, stepping back far enough for her to grab the box of lights and slip away from him.

She didn't trust herself to find the courage to ask him to stay for her. But the longer the night lasted, the more chances she had to dig up some bravery. As she walked to the farmhouse to deposit her box by the door, the sounds of table legs being folded punctuated the conversation running through her head.

"Trey, would you move to North Carolina, back to the farm, to be with me?"

"But I have a good job, one that I care about, in D.C."

"But I just bought this farm. I can't move."

"But I hate the farm."

"But you love me."

At least she thought he did. He'd driven down here almost every weekend to be with her as she worked to buy the farm. He'd supported her. He'd encouraged her. And he hadn't done all of that just because he wanted to be rid of the land.

Her right foot hit the step and she fell forward, her box of fairy lights bouncing in her arms before sliding out of her grip and onto the porch. Luck was with her tonight because the box landed top up and she didn't have to spend the rest of her evening rewinding strings of lights.

"Everything okay?" Trey called from across the lawn.

"I'm fine," she called back. "I just stumbled on the steps." Only she was lying; she wasn't fine. She was driving herself crazy with her fear over asking one simple question. A no would hurt, but she'd survive. She would have her farm to absorb all her energies and she'd live to see another day. At least she'd know.

As they took down the tents and made small talk, all the reasons she shouldn't put her heart out there danced through her head. *Don't even try. You'll only fail. You'll lose what you have now. It's not worth it.*

"Are you sure you're okay?" Trey asked again as they were stuffing the last tent into its bag. "You seem...unfocused."

"I'm tired. And today's been pretty emotional."

He put the bag on the ground and stepped closer to her, wrapping his arms around her. Her body melted into his, only stopping from being a loose puddle on the ground by the resilience of her skin. "Tomorrow you'll wake up on your own farm with money in the bank to make it into the farm you've always wanted."

She chuckled into his sweater, then lifted her face to his. "I know. And that's a pretty emotionally exhausting thought."

"Then let's get all this stuff put away and get you to bed." His kiss was sweet. "Maybe we'll even sleep."

After they'd moved all the tents into the barn, they walked back to the farmhouse hand in hand. The backyard looked so empty without all the tents and people celebrating. She had enjoyed sitting at the top of the rise and surveying her fields. Hell, this was her land. If she wanted to build a patio at the top of the hill and sit on a chair with a beer after work and look out over her vegetables, she could. And that, more than anything, gave her the courage to ask Trey, "Will you move to North Carolina? To be with me?" as they crossed the threshold from the porch to the living room.

"I'm sorry?" he replied. She didn't know if it was too dark to read his expression or if he didn't have one. She also didn't know which of those options was better.

"Me. To be with me. On the farm. I can't move to D.C." She laughed at the irony of it all. "You see, I just bought this farm from the man I love because he didn't want it. But I want him. And I come with the land."

"You're tired."

She flipped the lights on and saw his expression for the first time. Fear. She hadn't expected that. He sighed when he caught her looking at him. His deep breath seemed to go on forever.

He was going to say no. She'd known he was going to say no when she asked, but she'd hoped… But she wouldn't have been able to look herself in the mirror tomorrow morning, or the next day, or the next if she hadn't asked. "I am tired. But that doesn't change what I'm asking. Or why."

Ashes lifted his head. His tail pounded the floor in greeting, but he didn't get up. Her old dog had tried to stay at the party all night; he'd only gone to bed when she'd noticed him falling asleep while standing and she'd put him in the house. She wished she could embrace exhaustion with the same dead man's flop as Ashes. Instead, she sat on the couch, her body ready to be catatonic and her mind racing around in circles. From the red shooting through Trey's eyes and the ginger way he arranged himself on the couch, Max wasn't the only tired one.

Neither of them spoke. They just looked at each other. Tension simmered, despite the drafts that prevented the room from getting hot. Ashes moaned from his spot on the floor. The silence reigned until the dog fell asleep, then the soft woofs and twitches of his dreams were all that kept the room from feeling like a tomb.

Just when she thought they would spend the rest of the night in ghostly silence, Trey scrubbed at his face with his hand and then spoke. "Do you know what you're asking me to give up?"

Her nod disoriented her balance and all her body wanted to do was fall asleep. But she'd asked the question now and she would get her answer now, even if all she wanted to do was curl up into a ball.

"I've worked incredibly hard to get where I am. My job is important, it pays well and I enjoy it." Not willing to try nodding again, Max blinked her understanding. "You're asking me to give that up. To move down to my dad's farm."

"It's not your dad's farm anymore."

"Every day of my childhood, I ate dinner at that table in the kitchen. My mother would come home from work, make 'real food' if we were lucky enough, and my dad would have a beer. And if we *were* having 'real food,' it was only because that was my dad's first beer of the night. More often, my dad already had a pile of cans building for the day and we were eating biscuits for dinner because he was drinking the grocery money."

Max blinked again. The tears were coming. If she moved her head, they'd slosh around in her eyes and the tight ball that was her heart might break into a million pieces.

"That same table is still in the same kitchen. And not even the new couch or the new paint colors can hide that it's the same house. You live here now and there are crops growing in the fields instead of weeds, but that doesn't change what this place is."

Being fairly certain of Trey's answer ahead of time didn't make it any easier to hear. And she had known. She had known and had asked anyway. She took a deep breath before sobs choked her. Her tears were hot as they rolled in streams down her face. "It's *my* farm. It's me."

The sadness on Trey's face only made his answer worse. "I know. I'm sorry."

He sat in silence. Max sat blubbering. Too tired to keep herself under control, her sobs were messy and loud. Fragments of her heart floated around her body, tearing muscle and bone as they brushed past. She'd had a choice of keeping the farm or keeping Trey and she'd chosen. Just because she wouldn't choose differently didn't mean she was happy with her choice right now.

The couch shifted as Trey stood and his footsteps retreated from the living room. He returned with a box of tissues. "Thank you." She had to cough the words out. She blew her nose. Once. And again. The pile of tissues grew to the size of her hand. Then her two hands fisted together. In the morning, she would be dry as a bone. Her broken heart was going to squeeze her dry.

But there would be no regret in the morning. She would wish she hadn't been so tired. She would wish his answer had been different. But she wouldn't wake up and regret having the guts to risk it all and ask him to stay.

She pulled one last tissue and wiped her eyes.

"Are you done?" When he had returned with the tissues, he'd sat next to her on the couch. Closer and also farther than he'd ever been before.

She nodded.

"I have to drive back to D.C. in the morning." She knew that. And that he wasn't coming back. "I'm going to bed. Are you coming?"

"I'll be there soon." The residue of her tears made her words halting, but she said them. Even though she knew they were a lie. Trey nodded, then left the living room for her bedroom. After she heard her bed creak, she let her head fall back on the pillow and closed her eyes.

TREY KNEW THE instant he woke up that Max wasn't in bed next to him. He'd lain awake for what felt like hours, waiting for her to come to bed. Knowing she wouldn't. Maybe he should have said he would sleep on the couch and prodded her to go to bed.

Maybe she shouldn't have asked him for the one thing he couldn't give her.

The temptation for his mind to scream, *If you loved me, you wouldn't ask me for this* nearly over-powered rationality. The problem with his self-pitying call was that his mind was also yelling back, *If you loved her, you'd move.*

Almost every morning he'd woken up in this bed, Max had gotten up earlier than he had and emptiness had greeted him. But those mornings had felt full of promise. But like everything else about this farm, this empty bed was nothing but empty promises.

He'd never promised her. She'd never promised him. And here they both were, disappointed. He preferred anger; regret was a harder emotion to get out of bed with. He swung his legs over the edge and put on his clothes, prepared to hike the fields to find her.

He didn't have to look that far. Max was where he'd left her, on the couch in the living room, only at some point in the night she'd lain down. She was curled up in a tiny ball—out of sadness or for warmth, he couldn't tell. He covered her with one of the blankets off the recliner. Then he walked to the kitchen with the intention of making himself coffee, but he couldn't get past the doorway. Memories of childhood mornings he'd stood in this very doorway skimmed his mind. He waited for the anger to come. When it failed him, he took a deep breath and pushed his blood to boil. He concentrated on the fear of being a little boy. On nights of hungry bellies, Kelly trying desperately to be noticed, while at the same time trying to hide his secret. On his mother coming in after working two shifts and having to clean the bathroom because his father didn't do women's work. On the smell of alcohol.

The dam holding his anger back broke and the rage soared through his body in a familiar rush of adrenaline and self-righteousness. *You are making the right decision,* his anger told him. *You could never be happy in this house.*

Trey walked back over to where Max slept and caressed her hair, which was coarse and springy under his hand. He would miss her hair. He would miss her freckles.

She stirred but didn't wake. He gave her hair one last squeeze, patted his pockets for his keys and wallet and headed out the door.

CHAPTER THIRTY-TWO

TREY USED THE first ping sounding through the audiobook he was listening to on his phone as a signal to increase the speed on the treadmill. At the second ping, he wiped his dripping face with the gym's towel. At the third, he increased the incline. If he kept going at this rate, he'd be too exhausted to read the texts from Kelly—because Trey was sure that was what those dings were. The fourth ping had Trey changing the program from straight running to interval. Even if he was able to read the texts, he would be too worn out to process them.

The towel was soaked with his sweat and fairly useless, but Trey tried mopping his face anyway. The only other option was to get off the treadmill and respond to his brother. But that would mean thinking about Max. And the farm. And Max. He raised the volume, letting the mind-numbing voice of the narrator ruin what would otherwise be an interesting book on inner-city education and drown out any thought of the farm. And Max.

Kelly had sent him some emails marked with a little red "important" exclamation point. Trey had ignored those. Then Kelly had changed the subject heading from "Dad and the farm" to "READ THIS!!!" and finally to "STOP STICKING YOUR FUCKING HEAD IN THE SAND." Trey had left all of those emails unread. He'd sold the land to Max; it was no longer his problem. His ties had dissolved when he signed those papers. Family had never been enough to tie him to his past, and that hadn't changed.

Max might have been enough. Max could have been enough. *Max would have been enough.*

The volume coming through his headphones was as loud as he could stand it without going deaf, so Trey turned his gaze from the television screens in front of him to the screen on the treadmill and ticked down the seconds in his head with each pound of his feet. *Two. One. Sixty. Fifty-nine. Fifty-eight.* If he could control his breathing, he could call what he was doing "meditating" instead of "avoiding."

The screen on his phone changed with the incoming call. From Kelly. When Trey forced his gaze from the treadmill screen back up to the TVs and tried to read the running headlines on CNN, he could no longer lie to himself. At ten o'clock in the morning on the Tuesday before Thanksgiving, in an almost empty gym, Trey could ignore the no-cell-phone rule. He lowered the speed of the treadmill to where he could huff out words and answered the phone with "What?"

"That answers my question about whether or not you even read my emails."

"The Harris's tobacco farm is now officially Max's Vegetable Patch. Why would I read emails about it? I don't care about it." *I care about Max.* He swabbed his face with the dripping towel, scrubbing as best he could while trying to run and talk on the phone at the same time, but the thought didn't disappear.

"I can barely understand you. What are you doing?"

"Running. I'll call you back when I'm not busy." Running while holding the phone to his ear was easier than he'd thought. He upped the speed of the treadmill.

"Dammit." Kelly's voice interrupted the movement of Trey's finger across the air to cancel the call. "You'll always find some excuse to not hear what I have to say, so I'll just get on with it. I found the will."

"What did you say?" Trey was only half listening.

"I found the will. Dad kept his promise to Max. He left the farm to you, on the condition that you offered her a new three-year lease."

Trey stopped running. When his heels curved over the back of the treadmill he lurched forward, smacking his fist down on the red emergency-stop button. The machine stopped with a jolt that rocked through his body. Only the tightness in his chest kept him from smashing forward. "What did you say?"

"Dad's new will. He'd shoved it into Mama's Bible. We only searched the attic. Neither of us thought about searching the box I'd taken home."

Trey left his towel hanging on the side of the treadmill. He'd come back later to grab it and wipe down the machine. What he needed now was a place he could talk without falling over. He headed into the empty yoga studio and sat in the corner on the cool parquet floor.

He couldn't keep one small promise to you.

"I don't care about where you found it. What did you say was in it?"

"He kept his promise to Max. The new will stated that you were to inherit the land on the condition that you offer Max another three-year lease."

"And what if I wasn't willing to?"

"Then the land would go to Uncle Garner and Aunt Lois."

Who would have offered Max another lease without being asked…. "I've sold the land. This shouldn't matter."

"I thought you'd want to know. Dad wanted Max to have the land." Why was his brother's voice so chipper?

"You thought I'd want to know that by forcing Max to buy the land instead of leasing it, I exceeded Dad's hopes and expectations?" Trey's teeth were tight around the words coming out of his mouth. "Why would I want to know that?"

"I don't know. I…"

"Does it piss you off? To know that Dad wasn't going to leave the land to you, no matter what? Even if I had refused to obey his explicit wishes and he was still going to leave the land to someone else because you were the 'gay son'?"

"Fuck you, Trey." The curse hammered at Trey's ears through the phone. "You think you know everything about me and everything about Dad because *you* have bad memories. You probably even think what you learned being at the farm with Max confirmed your beliefs about Dad. Sure, he wasn't a drunk, but he was the same old bastard he always was and the proof of that is that he wasn't going to leave the family farm to the *gay son*. Fuck you."

"What? Am I wrong?"

"While he was revising his will, Dad asked me if I wanted it. I told him that he should sell it to Max and use the money to pay for his medical bills when he got older. He said he'd think about it."

Trey didn't believe a word of it—and yet, the laughing stories Max and Kelly had told at her party floated around in his head. "You're telling me that when you challenged the will, you did so actually believing he left the farm to you?"

"No. I'm telling you that he liked what was being done with the farm and wanted Max to keep farming, but also that he was too set in his ways to sell the farm and be done with it. I didn't know if he left me the farm, you the farm or even if he willed the damn thing to Max. But for the first time in his entire adult life, Dad had a vision beyond the next beer can."

The hard edge to Kelly's voice softened. "Dad didn't fully have the guts to carry out his or Mom's dream of the land. Hell, maybe he even thought you'd appreciate owning the family farm and being a part of its rebirth. I'm not saying the old man was perfect or even a winner of a guy, just that he'd changed, and maybe it's time you stop letting who *he* was run *your* life."

Trey pulled the phone away from his ear and stared at it. There was a photo of his brother on the screen. Even in the thumbnail photo, behind Kelly's stupid face, Trey could see the farm. That goddamned farm that would never let him go, even after he'd sold the thing. It looked like a recent picture. This photo might have been taken by Sean, or even by Max.

The image he'd been fighting floated through his mind—all curly, red hair and freckles and hypnotic, green eyes. Strong and sure, brimming with vulnerability and fight. No matter how far he ran, he couldn't escape the images of Max his mind could conjure. And her presence was enough to overwhelm any audiobook he listened to.

And Dad had finally kept his promise. For Max.

Standing in Max's fields, Kelly stared back at him. Trey knew his brother couldn't actually see him, but the reality of life didn't matter. His field of vision narrowed until all he could see was the farm and Max's face and all he could hear was his father promising to quit drinking and then the *click* of another beer can opening.

Somewhere in the room a man called out, "Hello? Trey? Are you still there?" Trey swiped the screen and the voice disappeared. The phone clattered on the floor and the room was silent. The floor was no longer cool. The wall he leaned against was no longer cool. The entire room burned. He banged his head against the wall behind him. All that did was add to his headache.

Trey took off his shirt, balled it up into a damp, stinky wad and threw it across the room. It barely made any noise at all when it landed. Having not gotten any relief, he kicked at his phone. It sailed across the smooth floor before crashing against the tower of aerobic steps. He hoped the damn thing was broken. Then he lowered his head onto his knees and cried for a man he'd never known and would never know.

MAX WAS FIXING dinner when the phone rang. It was the house phone, so she couldn't check the caller ID. But she didn't have to check to know it wasn't

Trey. He wasn't calling her back. He wasn't going to email her back. He wasn't coming back. No matter what the deed said, in Trey's eyes, this would always be Hank's farm, and he could never come back to Hank's farm.

She kept looking at the handset, almost willing it to flash red like a superhero's phone. So she would know it was important. But all it did was ring. Finally, she picked it up. "Hello?"

"Max?" Kelly's voice was at the other end of the line. "You'll never guess what I found."

The key that would unlock Trey's anger? "No, I probably won't."

He sighed, but didn't make her continue to play the game. "The will. I found Dad's will."

"Oh." And did Hank disappoint her in the end, like he had done to both of his children? "Where was it?"

"Mom's Bible. I'd taken it home with me and didn't think to look there. Dad kept his promise to you."

"I didn't have to buy the farm."

She didn't realize that she'd spoken aloud until Kelly responded. "No, you didn't have to buy the farm. Trey may have said he would've sold the farm out from under you and paid the penalty, but I think he would have changed his mind."

"Oh." Max sat in a chair, not quite ready to process what Kelly was saying.

"I'm sorry you had to go through the hassle, but I'm glad the farm's in your hands. I think it's probably what Dad wanted to happen eventually. But I don't think he had the courage to do it while he was living."

He's not the only one who lacked courage. "It doesn't matter any longer. I own the farm. We can't really go back."

"No, but…" Kelly sounded disappointed. "I guess I thought both you and Trey would be happy. You know, that Dad eventually kept his promise."

"You told Trey?"

"I found out this weekend. He finally stopped ignoring my calls today. Neither of you seem as pleased about the will as you should be."

Between the bad summer season she'd had and the nearly empty bank account, Max wasn't sure why she should be pleased that one small, different decision by Kelly to look in a different box may have meant that she wouldn't have had to buy the property. She hadn't been ready to buy the farm. She'd wanted those three extra years.

But you don't want those three years any longer. Max leaned into the back of her chair. If Kelly had found the will, she wouldn't own Max's Vegetable Patch. Trey had been intent on selling. She'd have been so focused on holding him to the lease that she wouldn't have thought she could buy the farm. She wouldn't have the Kickstarter money going to fix up the second barn, nor would she have the new customers the Kickstarter had brought in—partially making up for the ones she knew would leave because of the bad CSA year.

"I'm glad you didn't find the will earlier, Kelly."

"It would have saved you all this hassle."

She shrugged. "It would have created new and different hassles. But I'm glad to know Hank kept his promise to me."

On the other end of the line, Kelly snorted. "Knowing he kept his promise to you helps me, too. If he was able to keep his promise to you, then maybe he was being honest to me."

"About?"

"About not caring that he had a gay son. About learning not to care that anyone had a gay son."

"I didn't realize..." Her words trailed off as the import of what Kelly was telling her sunk in. "You were just a good actor." All those years Max had watched Kelly and wondered how he could be so easy with his father, knowing Hank as she did. Kelly hadn't been easy with his father. Kelly had been acting with his father as if his father always acted properly toward him. Kelly had made that relationship work.

"Once Dad sobered up, I saw my chance. Not that Dad wasn't an intolerant bastard while sober—despite his many attempts not to be—but drunkenness made his prejudice angry. Under all that anger, I hoped I had a father."

Max took a deep breath and let Kelly's words soak in. "I'm really impressed. I guess that sounds condescending, but I can't imagine how hard that must have been for you. I don't think I could've stood Hank long enough to do that."

Hank had been a misogynist, but so long as he'd only ever saw Max doing farmwork and in farm clothes, he'd treated her as a farmer—his "lady farmer." She'd been careful not to let him see her as feminine because wrangling that respect back from him would have been too exhausting. And Kelly had done it.

"Dad wasn't a great guy." His chuckle was cynical and rough. "Even sober, he was an asshole. But he was my father and the only one I have. And, ya' know, given another thirty years, he might have even been ready to give me away when I got married."

Max was stunned silent for a moment, then burst out laughing. Kelly joined her. "If you had to wait for Hank's approval, you would have died an old maid."

When they finally stopped laughing, Kelly spoke. "I'm sorry I didn't find the will in time, Max."

"I'm not. I would have continued to be afraid to buy the farm. And I'm glad I did. Sink or swim, I'm glad I did."

"I hope Trey turns around. He's more malleable than Dad, but they have the same core."

The same stubborn, angry core. She took a deep breath, not willing to share Kelly's hope. He hadn't heard Trey's flat, unemotional no. Heard Trey list all the reasons—most of them dead and buried to everyone but Trey—that he couldn't move back here. It wasn't that she had no hope, just that her hope had grown smaller. It wasn't enough to hope Trey turned around about the farm. He had to forgive his father before he could consider being on the farm.

She hadn't realized that when she'd asked him to move, but she knew it now. And she was still glad she'd asked. Whether or not Trey forgave his father, she'd always know that she had asked for what she wanted. That she'd known she might be turned down and she'd taken the risk anyway. There was satisfaction in that knowledge that no empty farmhouse could take away.

"Don't be a stranger just because I own the farm and I'm not technically family."

"I won't be." They made plans to meet for dinner. "Do you want the will? So that you know?"

"No. I think you should keep it, so that you know."

His acknowledging grunt over the phone sounded so much like his brother's that Max's heart hurt. "Have a good night and a happy Thanksgiving, Max."

"You, too, Kelly."

When a dial tone sounded through the handset, Max stood and walked across the room to put the phone in its cradle. She looked around the kitchen that had been Hank's kitchen in the farmhouse that had been Hank's farmhouse on the farm that had been Hank's farm. It wasn't his anymore. The bones of the place still looked like his, but she was slowly changing the flesh, and soon it would even be unrecognizable to Hank as the same place.

Poor Hank. He'd died before he could be a good father to his sons, but he'd died trying, and that was probably all anyone could expect out of him.

The sky outside the kitchen windows had gone from twilight to night while she'd been on the phone. She called Ashes and fed him his supper. Then she opened her fridge and began making her own.

CHAPTER THIRTY-THREE

TREY STUMBLED THROUGH WORK. Not only was his heart not in the job, but his heart didn't want to be on the work, or even in D.C. His mind might want to be on his work, but his heart wanted to be on the farm. And his heart was winning.

Worse, he couldn't think of the farm without thinking of his father. *Have a little compassion for him,* Kelly had said about Sean. But when Trey had looked at Sean, he'd seen a younger version of his father and still didn't understand how Kelly managed to look at his boyfriend and see a man who had struggled, and was still struggling, with pain. Had Kelly also seen a man struggling when he'd looked at their father?

Trey stared at his computer screen. He was supposed to be drafting a rider on the budget. He had the research in front of him. He knew what it was supposed to say. The congressman's aide was expecting it in by Monday. And he could do the work in his sleep, so instead he opened a new tab in his browser and searched for information on alcoholism and Vietnam veterans. Nothing he read surprised him, but neither did it help him find compassion for his father. Alcoholism had been only one of his father's many bad qualities, though it had exacerbated all the others.

In the end, he'd kept a promise to Max. The reminder hurt, but it was also confusing. How did he understand who his father was if the man had died keeping a promise? And then there was the uncomfortable follow-up desire to discover that his father had kept a promise he'd made to Trey, especially when he knew no such treasure awaited him. *You're not a little boy who needs his father to read you a bedtime story like he said he would on the nights he was sober.*

How do you find compassion for someone who did nothing but disappoint you? Trey leaned back in his chair and replayed the conversations he'd had with Kelly about their father. Kelly had asked Trey to have compassion for Sean, but had only said that Trey should learn to accept their father for the man he had been.

Accepting didn't require him to like his father, or even to agree with him. And the man was dead, so accepting didn't even require Trey to defend his own views to his father. Acceptance didn't require Trey to *do* anything.

He rubbed his hand over his chin. Shaving was one more thing he'd let slide, and the stubble was starting to itch. A coworker would comment on the growth soon—or a congressman, God forbid. Looking the part was important and the ten-o'clock shadow he'd developed wasn't the part.

He shifted his chair forward again, going back to his computer. But he didn't go back to his work. Instead of staring down at a screen full of white and text, he was navigated away from a study on alcohol and veterans to the Carolina Farmers Association website. There was a bill in the local legislature regarding income taxes on businesses. Over a certain size, business income tax was being phased out. Under a certain size, business taxes were being raised. The bill rewarded employment. Hire lots of people, no income tax. Be a small operation, get taxed. Max's Vegetable Patch's taxes would go up because of this bill.

Her struggling and admirable existence was about to get harder.

The bill had been written by lobbyists. If Trey spent more time reading up on North Carolina politics, he would probably even be able to say which businesses have pooled their money for this. Since large hog and poultry farms were exempt from the people/tax ratio, he was certain agribusiness had some hand in the bill. Maybe at one time he would have been impressed at the craftsmanship evident in the bill.

Instead, he was just tired.

He minimized the screen and stared at the half-formed bit of pork that would add extra money to the kitty of his client. According to the aide, the congressman was drooling at the thought of this little add-on, due to Trey's encouragement. Trey had found the man at a couple Washington events, shared a few key facts with him and gotten enough constituents to call and email the congressman's office that this pork had to be cooked and served. It was going to be a major point in next year's primary election.

Or that was what the constituents had said.

The congressman was right where Trey wanted him. Right where Trey's client wanted him. Trey reviewed his emails and it exhausted him. He couldn't even say if the pork he was creating would have a net good, be neutral or damaging. He didn't care, couldn't remember the last time he'd cared.

A few clicks and Trey was back on the farming association website. As he read more about the bill, the anger that had become so familiar to him over the course of his life roared into new life. The sense of fighting injustice, caring about the little guy— all the reasons he'd decided to enter the world of government in the first place. He'd lost that anger somewhere along the line.

Not lost. He'd tossed it out into the world and the anger that had returned wasn't the same. This returning anger was no longer focused on him being right and the other guy being wrong, but that the world could be made to be better. This was a long-burning anger, one that provided warmth to a family. Heat to cook a dinner. Power to turn metal into tools. An anger to construct rather than an anger to destroy.

This anger left room for other feelings.

Trey navigated around the website a little longer, checking and rechecking a few resources until he found the information he was looking for. Then he opened up his personal email and crafted a letter. He read over his words, let their import sink into his bones, gave himself a chance to second-guess, then hit Send.

Rejuvenated, Trey turned back to the piece of legislation he was crafting and finished it. When he was done, he read over his words. They were as tightly written as he'd ever composed, with little room for interpretation by outside parties and enough presents to counter objectives of people who didn't stand to win or lose too much. It was some of his best work.

He had one more letter left to write. On the blank screen, Trey typed the date and his boss's name. Only a few sentences were required.

CHAPTER THIRTY-FOUR

MAX TOOK A slow breath in and paused, then pushed all the air out of her body. She'd read about this precise manner of breathing against stress in some magazine at a dentist's office. It helped with the stress, she supposed, but it also helped with her aim. Up until the moment she squeezed the trigger, her body was still. The breathing even helped with the recoil of the rifle against her shoulder.

Another slow breath in and she shifted—a smidge, not more—to the left for the next can. As she breathed out, the skin on the back of her neck tingled. She took her shot anyway and missed. Not only didn't the can fall over, but it didn't seem to have been dinged. The next breath that huffed in and out of her body was not at all relaxing. She turned to see the trunk of a familiar sedan in view from behind the farmhouse. Walking toward her, upright and stick straight, but with a relaxed slope to his shoulders she didn't remember, was Trey. His loosened manner wasn't the only thing different about him. Instead of a neat wool sweater and shiny loafers, Trey had on a drab, army-green zippered sweatshirt and work boots. By the weight of the clothing on his body, she could tell that his sweatshirt was thermal lined. His boots weren't scuffed, but they looked sturdy enough that he probably wouldn't begrudge them a scratch or two. If she didn't know better, and his haircut and jeans didn't look so expensive, she'd almost say he looked like a farmer. Almost.

His mouth was moving. She popped the earplugs out of her ears, letting them bounce against her own sweatshirt. "What are you doing here?"

He gave her a half smile, then gestured to the cans in the field. "Would you like help cleaning up?" His tone was polite, but his eyes were watchful. Cautious. He was on her land now. This was her farm.

She considered pointing out that fact, but instead asked, "Are you staying?"

"Long enough to answer your first question. After that—" he shrugged "—I suppose after that depends on you."

She didn't try to parse what *that* meant because she might only get her hopes up. From the barking leaking out from the farmhouse, Ashes didn't have the same worry, though her dog probably had the same hopes. "Yes. I'd like some help."

They picked up the cans in silence. She didn't know what to say. He, apparently, was waiting until they were inside to explain what he was doing here.

It didn't matter if they weren't talking or looking at each other; she knew he was here on her land because she could feel him next to her. Her entire body buzzed with awareness. She picked up the box this time, all too aware of the déjà vu from the first time she'd met him.

Passing his sedan on her way to her truck, she noticed suitcases piled in the backseat. "Visiting Kelly?" She nodded toward the suitcases.

"No. Why? Does he live here now?"

"No, but…" Her heart crawled and clawed its way up her throat, threatening to burst out into something resembling joy at the sight of Trey here on her farm. And wearing work boots. But she also remembered the stillness of waking up in a house where she had expected another person and found only Ashes. *That* memory kept her heart restrained, if not actually under control. Trey opened the tailgate of the truck and Max set the box of cans in the bed, closing the top of the box before pushing it closer to the cab. No matter what Trey had to say, she would be likely to forget about the cans the next time she drove the truck. Then she'd have whatever baggage Trey left her with *and* cans strewn over the road to clean up after.

But he had on that sweatshirt. And work boots.

Ashes's barks were sharp and insistent. He was an old dog now and expected to have his whims catered to more than he desired to prove his worth.

At least that was her understanding of why he kept moving his bed to sit in front of the heating vent—and in the middle of a walkway—no matter where she put it. She sighed and opened the door so her dog could greet Trey.

Ashes eased and stretched his way out of the house before he limbered up enough to bound up to Trey. Still a good dog, even if a good old dog, Ashes didn't even try to jump on Trey's jeans, but sat and waited for his ears to be scratched. When Trey sat on the steps, Ashes leaned up against him, a big doggy smile on his face.

For several seconds, the birds singing and Ashes panting were the only sounds she could hear. Trey had always played his cards close to his chest. She couldn't even hear him thinking.

"I quit my job."

"Oh?" She kept her tone light, still afraid of anything that felt like hope. She had to raise her hand to block the glare of the sun off the shine of his car, but she couldn't stop looking at the suitcases she saw through the window.

"I'm not unemployed—or at least I don't think I will be. I've got a pretty good hook into another job. It's similar to what I was doing, but I think I'll like it better."

"Oh?" Why was he here? She wanted to ask, but having asked the big question once, the smaller questions seemed out of her reach.

Still, the winter sky seemed a bit bluer today.

He smiled at her, a soft smile, full of promise and warmth that matched the relaxed set of his shoulders. "I think you'd approve of the job. I'd be working for the Carolina Farmers Association, running their grassroots campaigns." He shrugged. "Lobbying when they need it."

"So you're moving to North Carolina?" She nodded again to the suitcases, the movement keeping a check on her rising hopes. *He left without even a note.* Somehow that didn't seem as important right now, with him sitting on the porch steps. He was here now.

"Yes."

"But you don't yet have the job?"

This new smile was sheepish. Like he'd overstepped some boundary, or was unsure of his footing. "I've got enough money to keep me fed for a while. And keep a roof over my head, even if I don't get the job. I'm pretty employable, though I'd like to be able to pick my job, rather than be forced to take one."

"And why are you here? On *my* farm?" Listening to him dance around his point was getting irritating. He had a point somewhere. A point that involved the farm.

His sigh was deep enough for even the dog to look up at him. "I originally started working for government because I believed I could do some good. It didn't have to be big, just good. Provide one returning vet with better mental health services so alcohol doesn't become a way to self-medicate. Or give one young mother the ability to finish college so she can work forty hours for the same amount of money it was taking her eighty hours to earn without an education."

She didn't interrupt him. So many words were bubbling up inside her, but she felt that his needed to come out more.

"Somewhere along the way I stopped caring—in any sense of the positives of the word. Someone paid me money and I convinced someone with a vote where it counts to care. I was just the go-between."

He rested his elbows on his knees and chin in his hands, looking out over her land. "Maybe that wouldn't have been so bad, but I was still angry and it wasn't going anywhere good. I wasn't helping anyone with my anger. And anger is great. I've motivated a lot of people by making them really, really angry. So angry they couldn't see straight. When you're angry, you're convinced you're right and the rest of the world is wrong. About everything. It's satisfying not to ever be wrong. God, it's like a drug." He rubbed at his cheeks and the bridge of his nose with his fingers.

"But anger is a hard beast to maintain. You have to feed it. Take it out every hour or so and examine it. If you leave it alone, it dies. And if it's all that's sustaining you, having your anger die is frightening because you don't have anything else. But it's also exhausting. Anger leaves no room in your life for any other emotions. It takes everything you've got and leaves you with nothing. Just ashes—" her dog raised his head and wagged his tail at his name "—that a puff of wind could blow away. Not even any warmth."

Trey clicked his tongue. Ashes lowered his head back to Trey's knee. The dog looked blissful as his ears were scratched. Max could sympathize. Trey had great fingers.

Ashes's eyes nearly rolled back into his head when Trey hit a good spot. Trey's smile was soft as he looked down at the dog. "There's warmth here. My anger kept me from fully understanding it, but I felt it. It's why I couldn't stay away. It's why I didn't counter your invitation for me to move here with an invitation for you to move to D.C." He shrugged. "I don't want to be in D.C. any longer. I want to be with you, here. I'm so stupid. I didn't realize it earlier, but I love you. And I want to be a part of the warmth and life of this farm."

Max opened her mouth to argue with him. To tell him that if he really loved her, he'd be happy with her in D.C.—he'd be happy with her anywhere. The words wouldn't come. She couldn't separate herself from this farm. He knew that as well as she did and he'd quit his job, packed his bags and come down here anyway.

"Can you be happy here?"

"I don't want to be happy anywhere else." Her face must have given away dissatisfaction with his answer, because he continued, "I left Durham and this farm originally because I was running away. Away from Dad, away from a future I didn't want, away from being trapped. I had all sorts of negative reasons for action. This farm is now a positive reason for action. *You* are a positive reason for action. Working for an organization struggling to make their voice heard is a positive reason for action."

He sighed and went back to scratching Ashes's ears.

Trey looked tired. Normally he stepped out of his car after his five-hour drive as crisp as a freshly picked cucumber. Today his jeans were rumpled. He had lines at the corners of his eyes that puffiness couldn't quite get rid of. She closed her eyes. When she reopened them, Trey looked different. Still tired, but the lines at the corners of his eyes could be laugh lines. The wrinkles in his jeans could be the sign of a man who was finally ready to relax. Between helping her with the cans and sitting on the front steps, he'd acquired a smear of red clay on his boots.

"What's with the sweatshirt?"

When he looked down at his sweatshirt and then

back up at her with a smile in his eyes, his laugh lines had deepened. "Do you like it? I wasn't sure how to arrive and communicate 'I'm serious,' so I drove west from D.C. until I found a hunting-and-fishing store. They also helped with the boots." He held out a booted foot for her to admire. "But my regular clothes are packed in those suitcases."

Suddenly, his vulnerability made her angry. "Am I supposed to open the door and let you in? Just like that?"

"Supposed to?" His eyes were serious again, but the laugh lines were still present. "No. I've got a reservation at a hotel in town. I'm hoping to cancel it, but I'm moving down here whether or not you let me in today." When she sat on the steps next to him, he looked sideways at her, full of mischief and hope. "Though if you send me packing, I'll call you up and ask you out on a date."

A date. Imagining him showing up at her house in his nice clothes with a bouquet of flowers in hand was a nice thought. Being taken out to dinner was better. Maybe a movie or to Chapel Hill for a play.

"You wouldn't take me out for a date anyway?" Just because she was the farmer didn't mean Trey didn't have to work for the cows, or the milk.

"I'm a new man. Maybe I'd expect you to take me."

He'd finally made her laugh and she gave him a

shove. When his body returned to upright, she rested her head on his shoulder. "We can trade dates."

"Does this mean you're letting me in the house?"

A brief flurry of panic rose in Max's breast as she considered all the ways taking a chance on Trey and love could go wrong. Before the panic could rise any higher, she stopped herself by thinking of all the ways this could go right.

Max stood and offered Trey her hand. She had to brace herself to help him up off the porch steps, and Ashes gave her a dirty look for interrupting his petting session, but once the man she loved was standing, Max turned to her house, opened the door and walked in. When she heard heavy footsteps on the stairs and then the door shut, she smiled.

Trey was home.

* * * * *

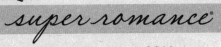

Cop by Her Side

By **Janice Kay Johnson**

When Lieutenant Jane Vahalik met
Seargent Clay Renner she thought she'd
finally found the one man who could accept that
she was a cop. Too bad he proved that wrong.
So why does she get a thrill when he calls out
of the blue? Read on for an exciting excerpt of
the upcoming book **COP BY HER SIDE**
by Janice Kay Johnson, the latest in
The Mysteries of Angel Butte series.

Jane felt a weird twist in her chest when she saw the displayed
name on her cell phone. Clay Renner. Somehow, despite the
disastrous end to their brief relationship, she'd never deleted
his phone number from her address book. Why would *he* be
calling in the middle of the afternoon?

"Vahalik."

"Jane, Clay Renner here."

As always, she reacted to his voice in a way that aggravated
her. It was so blasted *male*.

"Sergeant," she said stiffly.

"This is about your sister." He hesitated. "We've found
Melissa's vehicle located in a ditch. She suffered a head injury,
Jane. She's in ICU. But I'm focusing on another problem.

The girl, Brianna, is missing."

Of all the things she'd expected him to say, this didn't even come close.

"*What?*" she whispered. "Did anyone see the accident?"

"Unfortunately, no. Some hikers came along afterward."

"If another car caused the accident and the driver freaked…?" Even in shock, she knew that was stupid.

"A logical assumption, except that we've been unable to locate Brianna. We still haven't given up hope that your sister dropped her off somewhere, but at this point—"

"You have no idea where she is." Ouch. She sounded so harsh. "Thanks for the vote of confidence, Lieutenant."

She closed her eyes. As angry as she still was at him, she knew he was a smart cop and a strong man. He didn't need her attitude. "I'm sorry. I didn't mean…"

"We're organizing a search."

She swallowed, trying to think past her panic. "I'll come help search."

"All right," Clay said. He told her where the SUV had gone off the road. "You okay to drive?"

"Of course I am!"

"Then I'll look for you."

Those were the most reassuring words he'd said during the entire conversation. And as Jane disconnected, she didn't want to think about how much she wanted *his* reassurance.

**Will this case bring Clay and Jane together?
Find out what happens in COP BY HER SIDE
by Janice Kay Johnson, available July 2014 from
Harlequin® Superromance®.
And look for the other books in
The Mysteries of Angel Butte series.**

LARGER-PRINT BOOKS!
GET 2 FREE LARGER-PRINT NOVELS PLUS
2 FREE GIFTS!

HARLEQUIN

super romance

More Story...More Romance

YES! Please send me 2 FREE LARGER-PRINT Harlequin® Superromance® novels and my 2 FREE gifts (gifts are worth about $10). After receiving them, if I don't wish to receive any more books, I can return the shipping statement marked "cancel." If I don't cancel, I will receive 6 brand-new novels every month and be billed just $5.69 per book in the U.S. or $5.99 per book in Canada. That's a savings of at least 16% off the cover price! It's quite a bargain! Shipping and handling is just 50¢ per book in the U.S. or 75¢ per book in Canada.* I understand that accepting the 2 free books and gifts places me under no obligation to buy anything. I can always return a shipment and cancel at any time. Even if I never buy another book, the two free books and gifts are mine to keep forever.

139/339 HDN F46Y

Name	(PLEASE PRINT)	
Address		Apt. #
City	State/Prov.	Zip/Postal Code

Signature (if under 18, a parent or guardian must sign)

Mail to the **Harlequin® Reader Service:**
IN U.S.A.: P.O. Box 1867, Buffalo, NY 14240-1867
IN CANADA: P.O. Box 609, Fort Erie, Ontario L2A 5X3

**Are you a current subscriber to Harlequin Superromance books
and want to receive the larger-print edition?
Call 1-800-873-8635 today or visit www.ReaderService.com.**

* Terms and prices subject to change without notice. Prices do not include applicable taxes. Sales tax applicable in N.Y. Canadian residents will be charged applicable taxes. Offer not valid in Quebec. This offer is limited to one order per household. Not valid for current subscribers to Harlequin Superromance Larger-Print books. All orders subject to credit approval. Credit or debit balances in a customer's account(s) may be offset by any other outstanding balance owed by or to the customer. Please allow 4 to 6 weeks for delivery. Offer available while quantities last.

Your Privacy—The Harlequin® Reader Service is committed to protecting your privacy. Our Privacy Policy is available online at www.ReaderService.com or upon request from the Harlequin Reader Service.

We make a portion of our mailing list available to reputable third parties that offer products we believe may interest you. If you prefer that we not exchange your name with third parties, or if you wish to clarify or modify your communication preferences, please visit us at www.ReaderService.com/consumerschoice or write to us at Harlequin Reader Service Preference Service, P.O. Box 9062, Buffalo, NY 14269. Include your complete name and address.